Jason Love and his creator James Leasor share an affection for the Cord car and a love of sunny countries. Both were at Oriel College, Oxford, but while Love read medicine, Leasor read English. Love is a bachelor; Leasor is married with three sons. *Love Down Under* is the ninth of Dr Jason Love's Case Histories of Suspense.

Praise for James Leasor and Jason Love:

'Modern thriller writing at its best.'   *Sunday Express*

'The pace is fast, the writing solid and the suspense sufficient to tie the most indifferent reader into knots – an excellent thriller.'   *National Observer*

'Beautifully detailed and documented.'   *Saturday Review*

'A classic of its kind.'   *Scotsman*

'Splendid sit-up-all-night-to-finish fun.'   *Sunday Telegraph*

'Action driven along with terrific vigour.'   *Sunday Times*

'An expert thriller full of perils.'   *Spectator*

D0496198

LOVE
DOWN UNDER

James Leasor

Grafton
An Imprint of HarperCollinsPublishers

Grafton
An Imprint of HarperCollins*Publishers*,
77–85 Fulham Palace Road,
Hammersmith, London W6 8JB

Published by Grafton 1993
1 3 5 7 9 8 6 4 2

First published in Great Britain by
HarperCollins*Publishers* 1992

The Author asserts the moral right to
be identifed as the author of this work

ISBN 0 586 21116 0

Set in Janson

Printed in Great Britain by
HarperCollinsManufacturing Glasgow

CHAPTER ONE

THE PAST: BOMBAY, INDIA, 1980

All that week, sombre April clouds hung like a leaden shroud above the sea off Bombay. This frequently happened just before the monsoon broke, when contrary currents stirred sand on the harbour floor, and briefly transformed murky amber water into a lake of liquid gold.

Andrew McTavish, the Docks Superintendent, knew these signs too well for them to bring any joy to his heart. For him, they marked the passing of another year, no more, no less. He was one of the old hands, possibly the only European left in Bombay in such a senior position. He had already worked there through forty monsoons, and had it not been for the fact his wife was dead, he would probably have retired years ago, to the house he had bought in Carnoustie, near the Links.

But now that he was a widower, he hung on here, doing a job that had become routine. In such familiar work with ships – loading, unloading, reloading – he felt among friends. He was not lonely, on his own, as he might be in Scotland, which he had not visited for years. He liked India and the Indians; this was his life. Beyond his work, his future seemed too bleak to contemplate.

The approach of the monsoon made everyone irritable. Electric fans in homes and offices, punkahs in restaurants, even air conditioning, could do little to dispel the heavy oppressive heat. And the questions the two men sitting in his office were now asking him only increased McTavish's irritation.

The younger man, John Winters, was English. He had something to do with the Oriental–Occidental Bank, but being some*thing* in a bank was not the same as being some*one* in a bank. And while McTavish had nothing personally against this young fellow, he could not help contrasting him with his own only son, killed years ago as a corporal in Malaya, now changed, like so much else, into Malaysia. This fellow would die in his bed; or, more likely, he thought sourly, in someone else's.

Frankly, Winters was a bit of a shit, so he had heard in the club. He'd let down a girl McTavish rather liked. She worked for a colleague; very pretty and no fool, name of Victoria da Souza.

When McTavish first came to Bombay, there had been many half caste Eurasian girls like Victoria. Now, there seemed very few. Most had emigrated to Canada or Australia, to start afresh in countries that did not know or even care about the strange inbetween lives so many Eurasians had led in India.

Half Indian, half British, they had not really fitted in with either race. He wondered why Victoria hadn't gone, too; but then, that was none of his business. They favoured Portuguese surnames, so they could claim to come from Goa and thus avoid what had once been the social stigma of having to admit to one white parent and one dark.

Winters had definitely promised to marry her, so it was widely rumoured. The poor kid had even bought her wedding dress. McTavish's Indian secretary had told him how Victoria brought this into the office for the other girls to see and admire. Then – bang! – he'd dropped her. Cut her dead.

She'd taken that very badly. Been off sick for the past few days. Apparently she couldn't bear to come in and face her colleagues and admit she'd been let down, so McTavish believed. Matter of pride. And if this young fellow Winters had the brains of a louse he'd know Victoria was far cleverer than he would ever be. More, she wouldn't forget how he had treated her, and if ever she had the chance, she'd pay him back in full. And bloody good luck to her.

Mr Lee, the other man in McTavish's office, was older. He had arrived in Bombay only that morning from Karachi. Now that McTavish was thinking about Victoria's background, he wondered who exactly Mr Lee could be. He was not English. Equally, although he said he was working for a Chinese firm, he was not Chinese. Perhaps he was half-and-half? Or he could even be middle-European, one of the unnumbered dispossessed who roamed the world on odd sets of identity papers, finding what jobs they could. Why, only the previous week McTavish had interviewed a man who had once been a lecturer in pathology at Leningrad University. Somehow, he had come over the wall. His qualifications were not recognised in the West, and he said, desperately, that *any* job would suit him. But what use could a former university lecturer be on Bombay docks?

This man Lee had some kind of advisory post with a Chinese import and export firm in Pakistan – which made him almost unacceptable in India. Didn't he know India and China had been on the verge of war for year after year? No doubt he wanted a favour of some kind, thought McTavish sourly – or else why was he here?

Lee kept glancing out of the window at the masts and superstructures of cargo vessels level with their first floor office. He is nervous about something, thought McTavish. I wonder what the hell it is? I don't trust this fellow entirely.

McTavish felt his stomach rumble with the acidity of irritation at having to bear with two such dissimilar visitors. He should not have downed those two *burra* whiskies before that prawn curry lunch. The fact was, he often admitted to himself, he had probably been in India for too long. He felt isolated, like some sea-beast left stranded on the sand when the tide had gone out – and would never be coming in again.

To be in Bombay as a European office wallah was all right

years ago when the *raj* ran the country; or even now, if you were successful and had an air-conditioned office, and minions on whom you could rely to do the boring work. But not when you were past retiring age and only relatively successful. If he was really successful, he wouldn't still be here, widowed or not. He opened the side drawer of his old-fashioned wooden desk, took a digestive mint from a packet he kept there, sucked it noisily.

John Winters was speaking.

'It is good of you to see us without an appointment, Mr McTavish,' he said unctuously. 'I thought I'd better come to you direct. Mr Lee here is concerned about a consignment of urgent medical supplies for relief in the earthquake in Chungking. They should have been off-loaded in Karachi, when the ship docked there, but through some bureaucratic oversight they were missed. He's rather concerned, because you know that relations between India and China are rather difficult at the moment. Whereas, in Pakistan, there would have been no problem.'

'There shouldn't be any problem here, either,' McTavish assured him. 'He's no need to be concerned.'

McTavish hadn't heard there had been any earthquake in Chungking; but then, why should he? Catastrophes in far-away foreign cities made little impact on him in Bombay.

'As soon as they are unloaded,' Winters went on, 'they can be flown from Santa Cruz airport here to Calcutta, and then over the hills to Chungking. The ship, the *Kansas Rose*, was apparently due here last week, so he understands, but he has not heard anything about it. Has anything happened to it?'

'Nothing has happened to *her*,' McTavish replied shortly, deliberately correcting Winters' use of the neuter pronoun. Didn't this cocky young sod know that a ship was always feminine?

'She's right here, in Victoria Dock. Unloading is due to start tonight or early tomorrow.'

It was a curious fact, which McTavish could vouch had happened many times in his experience, that cargo destined

8

for the most contrary or litigious customer was invariably the one lost or damaged or broken into on the voyage. He ruffled some papers on his desk, read from them.

'She's had a rough passage from the States, the *Kansas Rose*. Called at Gibraltar. Took on oil at Alexandria. Next port of call, Karachi. There she offloaded a number of aircraft supplies, all completely knocked down and packed in crates, and she came on here with one of the oddest mixtures of cargoes I've ever heard of.

'Fourteen hundred tons of shells, torpedoes, mines, incendiary bombs, magnesium flares, signal rockets, what have you. Nine thousand bales of raw cotton. A mountain of scrap iron and copper, timber, sacks of rice and seven hundred and fifty-nine drums of turpentine. And if that is not enough, any spare space is given over to fifty drums of lubricating oil and wooden and metal crates, filled with goodness knows what, just marked on the manifest as sundries.'

McTavish paused, waiting for any comments, any expression of surprise. Neither of his visitors spoke. They knew as well as he did that India's arms had to come from overseas, since they did not manufacture enough themselves. So, of course, did arms and ammunition, shells and bombs and rockets required for other usually undeclared destinations. Ships on all the seven seas were packed with weapons of war, sometimes for both sides in a conflict. During one of the endless outbreaks of fighting in the Middle East, the hold of one ship was filled with canisters of poison gas for each side – and the ship in the next berth was heavy with a cargo of broken-down coffins for both.

And while manifests might disguise tanks as tractors and shells and cartridges as special explosives for use in mining, McTavish saw no reason to conceal realities from his two visitors. It was best that they knew the truth. Then perhaps they could appreciate that Mr Lee's boxes might not have the priority for which he hoped, humanitarian as their purpose was claimed to be.

'What are you unloading first?' Lee asked him.

McTavish did not reply. Instead, he stood up behind his desk, opened the window. On the far side of the concrete quayside, several cargo ships were moored fore and aft to huge bollards. Great scabs of rust, daubed here and there with reddish paint, scored shabby black hulls. Kite hawks and other carrion birds dived and swooped greedily around open hatches. McTavish ostentatiously took a deep breath. A stench of rotting fish had suddenly filled the room.

'*That's* coming off first,' he said shortly. 'Something I didn't mention before. Fish manure. Tons of the bloody stuff. Stinks to high heaven. After that's out, the air should be a bit fresher. Then it simply depends what is next in the hold. What does your stuff look like?'

'Wooden boxes – perhaps the ones you mentioned. Each crate is stencilled with a red cross.'

'Many of them?' McTavish asked him.

'Thirty-one. Each, six feet by six by one. And two metal crates, four by three.'

McTavish's stomach ache was fading. Those tablets were marvellous. Perhaps he had been too critical of these fellows? After all, they had a job to do, just like him.

'Well, we should see those easily enough. I'll do my best for you. We've all got to help each other as much as we can.'

'Any chance of showing Mr Lee where these might be aboard the ship?' Winters asked nervously.

'We can't move anything out until tonight or tomorrow, as I said, no matter where they are,' McTavish replied, suddenly irritable again. Pain prodded his stomach, reminding him it had not gone away; it had just been asleep. 'What good can we do, just looking at them?'

'It would put his mind at rest to know they're actually there, sir. They are very important.'

McTavish grunted, then changed the grunt into a cough. No good being uncivil to these visitors. He might want a favour from them some time, although quite what it would be he could not possibly imagine – except to get the hell out of his office and stay out.

'All right,' he said. 'I'll take you aboard now. You should have passes, but as you're with me it will be all right. I know the guards. But unless these crates are right on top of other cargo, you're not even going to see them. These holds go right down inside the ship, and there are four of them. But if it sets Mr Lee's mind at rest . . .'

His voice trailed away. He stood up, put a lightweight hat on his head, nodded to them to follow him.

They walked into the steamy afternoon, down a flight of stone stairs, along the concrete quay, streaked with oil. Huge cranes towered above the docks. Stepping over railway lines, half sunk into the concrete, they reached the gangway of the *Kansas Rose*.

'She's an old tub,' McTavish said conversationally. 'Like an oven in this weather.'

He paused.

'Do you know what today is the anniversary of, by the way?'

His companions looked at him blankly, shaking their heads.

'I'll tell you. Sixty-eight years ago *exactly* the *Titanic* hit an iceberg. We could do with a bit of that chill here, couldn't we, eh, gentlemen?'

McTavish smiled. He had made a joke. The others grinned weakly to show they realised this. They climbed up the gangway. A Lascar seaman crossed the rust-streaked deck towards them, smoking. Next to him stood three men discussing something earnestly. They paid no attention to McTavish and his companions. He wondered who they were; he had never seen them before. But so many odd characters were walking about the docks now – sailors, officials of one sort or another, businessmen. It wasn't like the old days, difficult to get on the docks. Now anyone could come in.

'Perhaps they're looking for some stuff, too,' Winters suggested. 'Was there much missed at Karachi?'

McTavish shrugged. What did it matter now what had

been missed there? They were in Bombay. Everything would come off in the morning.

'I don't know,' he said shortly. 'It hasn't been checked out yet.'

The seaman stubbed out his cigarette amid a litter of oily ropes and cables, looked at them enquiringly. McTavish showed him his docks pass. The man waved them on, lit another cigarette.

'Why these people are allowed to smoke is beyond me,' said McTavish peevishly. 'It's against all orders – and common sense with such an inflammable cargo. Probably no officers left aboard to stop them.'

'Someone's still in the engine room,' said Winters.

'What d'you mean?'

Winters pointed at one of the ventilators towards the bows. Wisps of black smoke curled lazily from its mouth.

'Maybe they're electing a new Pope,' said McTavish, again trying to be humorous. 'The engine room's not below that, anyhow. Matter of fact, I don't know what the hell *is* under it. I rather fancy, a hold. But maybe I'm wrong. Perhaps the smoke's coming from an auxiliary engine powering a standby dynamo. Anyhow, forget it. It's nothing important. Now, here's the hold where Mr Lee's boxes *should* be.'

They came to the edge of a vast square opening, and stood peering down into the deep darkness of the hold. The cavernous hole had been roped off to prevent anyone falling down it in the dark. In the dimness far below they could see a clumsy pyramid of wooden crates, each one bound with thin metal strips, stamped with coded numbers. Huge whitish bales shrouded in canvas were stacked next to them.

'There's the cotton,' McTavish explained. 'That's the only thing I'm certain of. Those crates could contain anything. Anyway, that's the only hold that's open. They'll open the others when this one's been emptied. Not much help to you, I expect, Mr Lee, but there it is. I did my best.'

Mr Lee peered down into the heart of the ship, frowned.

'So,' he said. 'I will have to wait in my hotel until tomorrow, yes?'

'Afraid so. Be in my office by ten. We should have all the stuff off by then. So even if yours is the last lot to come out, it will be waiting for you. Anyhow, you've had a look. Sorry there wasn't anything much for you to see. But even if there was, as I said, we couldn't move it now.'

They went down the gangway, back along the quay towards the administrative buildings. Winters suddenly stopped, turned his head into the wind, sniffed the air.

'Someone's burning paint,' he said, puzzled. 'I can smell it.'

'Maybe they're dealing with the rust,' McTavish replied. 'They often burn the worst of it off and then slap on that red paint. Not a *pukka* job, I agree, but that's how things are nowadays. Near enough is good enough.'

'I can't see anyone doing anything from where I stand,' Winters went on slowly, looking up at the hull. 'Yet the burning's somewhere near.'

They were barely a yard from the ship's side. As they stared at metal plates lined with dome-headed rivets, the black paint suddenly began to bubble and blister. McTavish put a hand towards one plate, then drew it back smartly. The heat was already too great for him to touch.

'What the hell?' he asked in astonishment. As he spoke, the patch of bubbling spread rapidly. Blisters swelled, cracked, burst, smoked. New ones appeared at different points along the hull. And all the while the smell of burning grew stronger. The air around them suddenly felt hot and dry and acrid.

'The ship's on fire,' said McTavish suddenly. In all his long career on the docks, he had never experienced such a situation.

'What d'you mean, on fire?' Winters asked him nervously.

'Something's burning inside the hull. Cargo, most like. Spontaneous combustion, maybe. All that bloody cotton and turps and oil. In this heat, it's madness to stack 'em all

13

together – and *then* let the crew smoke cigarettes! Follow me
– *now*!'

He ran across the quay to a red wooden box fixed to a wall,
pulled open the door. Inside was an emergency telephone. He
lifted the receiver, cranked the energising handle furiously.

'Fire brigade control room!' he shouted to the operator.
'Hurry! Emergency!'

Winters and Lee stood awkwardly, looking now at him,
now back at the ship. This was something altogether outside
their experience, even their imagination. Could it really be as
urgent as McTavish's attitude suggested? Or was he simply
being an alarmist, perhaps even enjoying his moment of
importance?

Smoke now began to billow out of portholes and ventilators in thick black clouds, hot, pungent, deadly. It caught in
their throats, made them cough and their eyes water.

McTavish shouted down the receiver as the operator connected him.

'McTavish here! Superintendent, Victoria Dock. A ship's
on fire. Red Alert! The *Kansas Rose*, waiting to unload. Get
as many engines out here as you can – *at once*! She's packed
with cotton bales and high explosives.'

He slammed down the receiver, picked it up again, asked
the operator for the police emergency room.

'Ship on fire, Victoria Dock,' he told the duty officer more
calmly. 'I've alerted the fire brigade.'

'We've had a report about that already,' came the reply. 'An
American cargo ship. That's all in hand. Being dealt with by
the crew, we understand. Thanks for reporting it, but it's not
really our affair.'

'Well, make it your bloody affair! There's only a skeleton
crew aboard, a handful of men. They can't possibly cope with
this. The cargo contains tons of high explosives. The whole of
Bombay docks could go up if they're set off. Clear the dock
area in case that happens!'

As he slammed down the receiver, eight fire engines raced
in through the main gates, warning bells ringing. The brigade

hadn't wasted any time, he thought approvingly. Firemen jumped down as the engines swung round in line by the edge of the quay. With the speed of long practice the men began to unreel canvas hoses, connect them to hydrants.

Other firemen threw the ends of other hoses, protected by wicker filters like huge lobster pots, into the filthy water of the dock. Pumps started with a great roar of engines. Jets spouted arcs of yellowish sea water on the blistered hull, so hot now that as the water struck the metal it turned instantly into huge clouds of foul-smelling steam.

Firemen climbed ladders to direct hoses on the decks and down into open hatches. Tally clerks, stevedores and the few seamen left aboard now came running down the companionways. Some carried a few belongings under their arms, or crammed into a carpet bag, a cheap cardboard suitcase. Several, roused from their bunks by the clanging of the fire bells, were barefoot and still in their underpants.

A black Land-Rover swept in through the main gates. The general manager of the docks jumped out as the vehicle stopped. McTavish explained the situation.

'Slip her moorings, and tow her out to sea if she can't travel under her own power,' said the manager at once. 'Then if she goes up she won't take all the docks with her.'

The ship's captain came up to them at a run. He had been aboard ship in his cabin when he heard the alarm. He could not accept the manager's advice.

'If she blows up out at sea with any crew aboard, none of them will stand a chance,' he told him.

'Nor will many more people if she explodes where she is,' retorted the manager. 'I have responsibility for the entire docks, not just one ship. If that cargo explodes, the death toll could run into thousands. The docks are in one of Bombay's most crowded areas.'

'We can contain the fire with the appliances we have,' the fire brigade commander assured him. 'It's not getting any worse.'

'But how do you *know*?' asked McTavish. 'It looks and smells bloody awful to me. What are conditions like aboard?'

'Terrible,' the captain admitted. 'I had a look in Number Two hold. Cotton bales, turpentine, fish manure – all blazing. The drums of oil haven't gone yet, but when the solder on their seals melts, they'll catch fire. The smoke is already so thick it's difficult to see into the other holds at all. And with all these odd items blazing, the fumes are lethal.'

'Have the crew got gas masks?'

'No.'

'If anyone's left aboard, get them off the ship – now! If the firemen can cope, they'll be safer here.'

The captain ran back up the gangway to give the order, 'Abandon ship'. Most of the seamen had already gone, but holding a handkerchief to his face to try and filter the choking, sulphurous smoke, he went through their quarters, checking no-one was still left on board.

Other ships moored alongside were casting off, moving slowly out to sea. Tugs thrashed the water frantically into a scummy, oily foam as they towed them from the quay. McTavish counted sixteen heading towards the ocean. Several were still tied up. Their crews were either all in Bombay, or they had fled when they saw the extent of the fire.

'Can you get any more pumps and hoses here?' the docks manager asked the fire brigade chief.

He shook his head.

'No. Everything we have is here. We've sent a call for reinforcements – men and pumps – from outlying stations. But it'll be at least another fifteen minutes before they get here.'

'You still optimistic?' McTavish asked him. The officer shrugged.

'In my business you have to be,' he replied quietly.

A huge dark cloud of smoke now hung over the docks, pungent, evil smelling. Fragments of burning, charred cotton waste soared up, feather-light, into the air and then disintegrated, dropping like a black snowstorm. The ship began to list slightly under the immense weight of water already pumped into her blazing hull. Flames roared and crackled. Ropes parted with reports like gunshots.

'Can't you scuttle her now?' the general manager asked the captain. 'Let the sea put the fire out.'

'I don't want to do that – yet,' the captain replied cautiously. 'We're carrying a very valuable cargo. If we scuttle her now, everything will be lost, the whole voyage wasted.'

Then, before anyone could reply, the ship exploded.

Winters saw, as though in some horrific slow motion film, giant plates on the hull buckle and burst. Out of huge jagged-edged holes in metal an inch thick, poured a cataract of burning bales of cotton, a cascade of blazing oil and turpentine. He watched, mesmerised, as metal spars, doors, pieces of decking shot up into the smoke-filled air and then rained down on the docks in a deadly hail.

He heard a sudden choking cry of pain and surprise. McTavish dropped on the ground in a pool of blood. His head had been severed by a jagged piece of red hot metal. Blood spouted from his trunk. Winters ran for cover – but there was none to find. Dock buildings were collapsing under the force of the explosion. Bricks, doors, windows showered around him.

The fire brigade chief staggered to one side, hit by a falling door. His Land-Rover suddenly surged forward, and raced head-on into a crumbled wall. His driver sprawled inelegantly across the steering wheel, right foot jammed down on the accelerator. Through a hole in the vehicle's roof a long strip of metal stuck out like a thrown spear. The other end had pierced the driver's back.

The ship's captain had simply disappeared, apparently vaporised or blown to pieces by the blast. Yet, through the heat and roar of the incandescent inferno, Winters could see firemen still high up on ladders, still spraying decks now red with heat from the fury of the fire beneath them.

The water from their hoses changed instantly into a caustic, poisonous fog. A cloud of black, oily smoke a mile high surged up in the air, darkening the afternoon sun. Thousands of sea birds, terrified by the noise, the smoke, the fearful stench of burning, hovered above this cloud, fluttering their wings.

The explosion momentarily created a giant vacuum, and the sea rose to fill it like a tidal wave. Water surged up from the harbour and across the dock, swamping everyone, everything in its path. This huge, spuming flood lifted several other smaller ships like toys and deposited them on the quay, ramming their bows or sterns into godowns that instantly collapsed in a shower of bricks and tiles and beams.

Buildings half a mile away buckled and fell beneath the weight of millions of tons of sea water. The flood swept dead and mangled bodies from the quayside, over the floors of ruined offices. By some freak of fire and the wind it created, many of the dead were stripped of their clothes. They lay naked in twisted, tortured positions, flesh blackened or calcined. Others still writhed on the streaming quay, as the sea receded. Dead, charred flesh fell in folds from their fearfully disfigured faces.

And then, as Winters stood, unable to move, or even comprehend the magnitude of the disaster, there came a second explosion.

This was much stronger than the first because it involved the explosives in the holds. But instead of blowing outwards, the erupting shells and rockets tore upwards through the blazing deck. Flames soared hundreds of feet into the darkened sky. Blazing bales of cotton, shell cases, torpedoes rose, seemingly without weight, then dropped across the docks, some red-hot, others still erupting in flames.

Hundreds of people who had heard the noise of the first explosion and came racing to the docks to see what was causing it, now died instantly and terribly. The quay was littered with bodies, some blazing like human torches.

Winters heard whistles blowing, sirens sounding, and above them the terrible, unforgettable cries of the injured and the dying. The propellers of tugs and cargo ships, desperate to escape the holocaust, and fearful in case of a third explosion, churned the harbour water into a filthy, oily froth. But miraculously, almost unbelievably, he was still alive, still standing, still unhurt. In the midst of violent death on a prodigal scale, somehow he had survived.

He was not sure what had happened to Mr Lee. One moment he had been standing next to him, and the next he had gone. Had he simply vanished like the ship's captain, been vaporised, blown to pieces, sucked into the sea by the great vacuum after the blast? Or had he survived somewhere?

Shakily, Winters put up one hand to his head, as though somehow he could blot out what he had seen, what he had endured. Then his face wrinkled with horror. All his hair had been blown from his scalp. He was bald as an egg. His hand came away, thick with oily grime and strips of flesh. He looked down and saw that his jacket had been torn from his body. He had no recollection of this, but then, he had no clear recollection of anything, save that he remembered McTavish telephoning the fire brigade, and then seeing the metal plates burst half way up the hull.

Slowly, with the faltering steps of a very old man, Winters began to walk across the quay. He tripped over lumps of concrete and fallen cables and bodies he had not seen, or if he saw did not comprehend they were in his path. He walked, almost unseeing, without aim or purpose, like a character in a nightmare.

The administrative building, where only moments before he and Mr Lee had met McTavish, had totally disappeared. Dazed and bewildered, Winters still could not understand what was happening. Was he alive – or was he dead, in some unspeakable limbo of the damned?

He saw a ruined typewriter on an upturned table. Files of paper, soaked by fire hoses or blackened by soot, fluttered in the hot foetid air like oversized confetti. He picked out a piece of paper from the machine and read, uncomprehendingly, the fragment of a letter, to whom, from whom, he had no idea: 'Dear Sir, Yours of the seventh inst to hand. I beg to state that the undermentioned goods, recently arrived from Durban, are . . .' The rest of the letter was indecipherable.

Locomotives lay on their sides, steam roaring from broken safety valves. Trucks had voided loads of bricks and timber beams across the rails into the sea. The entire docks, acres of ancillary buildings, warehouses, godowns, sheds, had vanished. In their place hung a reddish pall of brick-dust. The sun was darkened as by some unusual eclipse.

Winters did not know who he was or now even where he was. He could be the last man left alive in a world destroyed by fire and heat. He took another shaky step forward – and the whole world turned upside down.

Winters fell and lay where he fell, among the dust and the debris, the dying and the dead.

CHAPTER TWO

THE PAST: BOMBAY, INDIA, 1980

Victoria da Souza was washing her long dark hair when all the window panes rattled in the room she rented in the house of a distant relation. One window splintered and jagged spikes of glass fell into the wash-basin. She stood up, wrapped a towel around her head, peered out through the broken window.

A great black pall of smoke and debris hung like a nimbus over the docks. Sabotage, she thought instantly. There was so much of it. Warring factions around the world used India as a base to carry on their fight. Sometimes they suspected that weapons had been supplied to allies by their enemies, and they were probably right. But it did not help by blowing up trains, bridges, hiding bombs in cars. And now – the docks? Life was so violent; quite different from times she read about in women's magazine stories of the past, when every family seemed to employ servants and have fine cars, and there was gentleness and graciousness and, above all, money. There was never any scrimping and saving in those stories: no pretence that the cheapest was as good as the best, when you knew it wasn't.

She was nearly twenty-five now, untrained for any career, and still unmarried; old in India to find a husband. She had already had many jobs – Delhi, Calcutta and here. How could she possibly meet any European except through her work? If she had a job in a smart club, or perhaps in a casino, or a hotel where rich Westerners came to stay, she might meet someone who would take her away from this drudgery – but not in the docks.

She rather liked old McTavish and the other Englishman who worked with him, but they were both very near retiring age – in fact McTavish was probably years past it. When they went, their places would be taken by Indians; and not belonging totally either to a white or a coloured world, she somehow resented working for Indians.

This was ridiculous, of course, just as it was ridiculous for Europeans to have looked down on her and her family over the years. Things were better now, but there was still a long way to go, and she felt that by the time people like her were genuinely and fully accepted, fully integrated, she could be too old to care.

Winters was her best bet; indeed, now probably her only one. She must persuade him to marry her. They had been to bed often enough. He had said he loved her, he had proposed, she had accepted, he'd bought her a ring and she had bought a wedding dress. So what else could she do? She did not know. But she realised she had made a fool of herself over the dress. She should never have taken it into the office to show to the other girls. And now John was always busy, always elusive, when only weeks ago he had been so anxious to take her out, or back to his own apartment. Now he had no time: he had to see an important client, to fly unexpectedly on business to Delhi or Calcutta; he couldn't say when he would be back. He would ring her. But somehow he didn't.

What the devil could have happened at the docks? On an impulse, Victoria crossed to the telephone, dialled the number. It was unobtainable. She rang the exchange, asked the reason why.

'I'm sorry, caller,' the girl operator explained. 'But there has been an accident. All lines to the docks are affected. They will be repaired as soon as possible.'

Victoria wondered whether Winters had been there. She knew he was seeing someone about a cargo that had gone adrift or should have been off-loaded at Karachi, so it was

22

quite likely he was. She caught sight of her face in the mirror. She thought she looked as she would look in ten years' time, tired, drawn, defeated – unless she could escape from her dull routine life, from this country with its delight in procrastination and bureaucracy. But short of a miracle, there was no hope of that, no chance whatever.

Of course, there might be a miracle. At church every Sunday, when she prayed for a way out of her monotonous life, she listened to readings about miracles, how people were raised from the dead, crowds fed with a few loaves and fishes, the Children of Israel escaping from the Egyptians through the Red Sea.

There had been miracles once. Perhaps there would be miracles again? Victoria told herself that this must be possible, but somehow she never quite convinced herself.

An emergency hospital had been set up in one of the large Edwardian houses on Malabar Hill, overlooking the sea.

It was cool up here, overlooking Back Bay and Chowpatty Beach towards the town. On this beach, men hoping for a few annas baksheesh had built sandcastles in the shape of people, animals, birds. Professional contortionists were escaping from their chains and bindings or doubling their bodies backwards and sideways. Families walked past them, between wooden kiosks selling ice cream.

Up in the house the injured paid no attention to such everyday activities. They lay on beds under sun blinds and canvas awnings on a terrace facing the sea. What had happened, how they had escaped alive was the main topic of everyone's conversation.

Fourteen acres of docks had been destroyed; thousands of people were thrown out of work. Thousands more, mostly Indian labourers, living near the docks, had lost all their possessions – except the clothes they were wearing – and, worst of all, two thousand had lost their lives.

The Indian manager of the Oriental–Occidental Bank sat awkwardly by the side of John Winters' bed while he related these melancholy statistics. As he did so he tried not to look at Winters' face; he found the sight immensely disturbing. The doctors had not allowed Winters the use of a mirror, explaining, almost facetiously, that he had no need of one – he was handsome enough as he was.

This was to keep him from discovering that his face was deeply pitted and scarred, in addition to losing his hair, his eyebrows, his eyelashes. It was hoped that all would eventually grow again. But when, no-one could say.

'You are very lucky, John,' the manager assured him earnestly. 'You have a lucky life.'

He *was* lucky, of course – or perhaps crafty would be a better word. Privately, like McTavish, the manager regarded Winters as a cad, a bounder, in his rather dated vocabulary of English slang. He'd had a number of affairs, so several fathers of the girls involved had told him, and to his own knowledge he'd let three girls down badly. He had promised to marry each of them and then ducked out on some pretext.

He'd behaved abominably too, to that girl Victoria da Souza in the docks office. He had led her on almost to the altar and then suddenly dropped her. She had taken it very badly, so he'd heard. However, perhaps Winters' experience now would make him change. The manager, a strict Hindu, believed that this could be in the nature of a divine warning.

Earlier, the ward sister had told him that a Miss Victoria da Souza had telephoned every day, enquiring about Mr Winters' condition, but asking her not to mention her calls to him. The manager sighed enviously. Winters must have a very strong attraction for women, he thought. He couldn't imagine any woman enquiring after him if he were in hospital – even one of those phenomenally rich old Parsee biddies who continually complained to him about the size of bank charges.

He banished such uncharitable thoughts from his mind as he went on talking.

'I'm telling you, this was the worst disaster ever to hit Bombay.'

'Sabotage?' asked Winters weakly.

'I don't think so. The police have rounded up a few hotheads, but that's really just to make people think they're doing something. General view is that it was just a combination of many follies.

'When the ship off-loaded at Karachi, it seemed a good opportunity to use the space for a mass of goods that had been waiting on the docks there for weeks. Cotton, oil, sulphur, rice, fish manure, turpentine, I don't know what else. All these were crammed in higgledy-piggledy and battened down at the hottest time of the year.'

'No word of Mr Lee?'

The manager shook his head.

'None, I'm sorry to say. Nor of sixty-five firemen. All burned to death – or just vanished in the blast. The government is doing all it can to help, but we can't bring back the dead. And even the most generous help never covers everything that has been lost. Mind you, there is a lighter side to it all.'

'How?'

'Well, the ship was apparently carrying a consignment of gold bars packed in crates. They were blown up like everything else. Beggars sitting outside the Taj and Green's Hotel here, hoping to collect a few annas from foreign tourists, suddenly found bars of gold landing on the pavement right in front of them. You should have seen the lame run – led by the blind!'

'Where did the gold come from?'

'The States. Apparently for the Bank of India.'

'Any of it been found?'

'Oh, yes. Quite a lot. People are honest by and large. Or else they just didn't know how to get rid of it. Best give it up and claim a reward.'

Winters closed his eyes and pretended to sleep. He wished some of the gold bars had fallen near him; he'd have known what to do with them. The manager helped himself to a handful of grapes from Winters' bedside table, nodded to a man he knew vaguely in the next bed.

'The insurance claims will be very large,' he said, dredging to make conversation. He was not at his best by a sickbed. 'I don't know about Mr Lee's medical supplies. I have not seen the cargo manifest yet.'

He watched Winters as he spoke, trying to ignore the man's injuries, hoping he might reply. But when Winters did not even open his eyes, the manager stood up, tiptoed out of the ward.

On the steps of the hospital, he met Victoria da Souza coming in. He paused, feeling sorry for the girl.

'I've just been to see John,' he explained. 'I think he is now asleep.'

'You don't think I should go in, then?'

'Well, that's up to you. Have a word with the ward sister. But he's been pretty badly shocked. All his hair's been blown off, and his face is scarred.'

'But you think he'll be all right, don't you?'

'Oh, he'll be all right. And having a pretty girl ask after him is bound to make him feel just that much better.'

Victoria smiled, paused for a moment as though still undecided whether to go in or not. Then she came to a decision. She would not go in and see him now. She would wait until he was better. Then she must see him. She had to.

When Winters came out of hospital, the doctors told him he should have at least one week's leave before returning to the bank. On the first day, he took a short walk along Marine Drive. He liked the feel of sun on his face and the smell of the sea. He thought of having a drink at the Taj bar. He stopped, glanced each way before crossing the road: there were so many careless drivers. Then he saw someone who seemed vaguely familiar.

A European had stopped on the other side of the road,

looking at the door of one of the buildings as though searching for an address. Where had he seen him before? Then Winters remembered – he was one of the group on the deck of the *Kansas Rose*. He must have had a very lucky escape. He wondered if the men who had been with him had escaped, too. He crossed the road to find out.

'Excuse me,' he said. 'But didn't I see you in the docks on that ship that blew up the other day?'

The man shook his head, looked at him, puzzled.

'I don't know what you're talking about,' he said. 'I've just arrived.'

'How odd. I could have sworn I saw you. I was lucky to escape with my life there. I wanted to congratulate you on doing the same.'

'I think you've made a mistake, sir,' said the man stiffly. 'I'm sorry. Good-day.'

He walked on. So did Winters, but somehow he felt uneasy. Why should this man deny being there when he *knew* he had? He must have a reason; a simple one, no doubt. Anyhow, what did it matter? He was alive and the sun was warm. His face would get better – it must do. He went into the Taj and sat in the bar drinking an iced beer, thankful to be alive when so many others had died.

He glanced out of the window, saw that the man had stopped, bent down, fumbled with his shoelace. This took him a moment because he had to undo it before he could tie it up. He checked that Winters had definitely gone into the hotel. No-one else was across the road walking parallel with him, on the opposite pavement, the usual way to follow someone discreetly. No-one was on his side of the road, either.

He stood up, lit a cigarette, walked back slowly, turned into a side street. A beige-coloured, Indian-built Hindusthan Ambassador car, based on the Morris of the 1950s, was waiting by the kerb. He climbed in behind the wheel. Two men were sitting in the back.

'Well?' asked the one nearest to him. 'Where did he go?'

'The Taj hotel. He recognised me.'

'How?'

'He had seen me on the deck.'

'What did you say?'

'I denied it, of course.'

'Did he believe that?'

'I hope so. He certainly didn't query it. It's easy to make a mistake.'

'Was he injured?'

'His face was badly cut about. He had a hat, but there was no hair above his ears. I'd say he lost that.'

'When he comes out, follow him and find out where he lives. Put on a dark wig and glasses, a different suit,' he told the man behind the wheel.

He nodded, turned the ignition key to start the engine.

On Winters' second day out of hospital, he felt strong enough to take a taxi to Victoria Docks to see for himself what had happened. He told the driver to wait for him; he knew it might be difficult to hire another taxi from that part of Bombay.

He was astonished at the immensity of desolation that faced him: blackened buildings, charred rafters, a whole area totally flattened. The enormous force of the explosion had blown several ships right out of the water, up on the quayside. They lay like huge bathtub toys abandoned by a giant. Superstructures of other vessels sunk in the harbour stuck out of the muddy water. Sea birds perched insolently on funnels, bridges, masts, calling noisily to each other.

The quay was littered with scorched crates, some split open, and sodden cardboard boxes, coated with a thick oily film of black ash. Across the dockyard, groups of Indian soldiers were working with bulldozers and shovels. Hundreds of coolies had been brought in to clear up the debris, a task that would take weeks.

No-one stopped Winters or asked him what he was doing there. He saw other civilians, European and Indian, also poking about in the rubble, peering into opened boxes, searching for goods their firms had ordered, trying to find whether anything was salvageable.

Farther along the docks he saw the man he had seen the previous day in Marine Drive, and before that on the deck of the *Kansas Rose*. But he did not want to accost him a second time. The man could turn nasty, and the last thing Winters wanted now was any commotion, any trouble. The fellow probably had some perfectly legitimate excuse for being here, or at least nothing more dubious than Winters' own explanation – if anyone asked – that he was looking for crates addressed to the bank. Suddenly, he drew back behind a truck. He had seen Victoria da Souza only fifty yards away, examining a charred manifest she had picked up. She threw it away, wiped her hands clean with a tissue, went on looking through the debris – for what?

Before he had ended their affair, he would have called out to her. They would then have gone back to his flat and to bed. But not now. He could not bear to talk to her. He did not feel embarrassed; he had treated other girls badly and never suffered a moment's regret. But he had abandoned Victoria not so much because he had grown tired of her, but because she had begun to frighten him. She had a strong character and he did not.

Many boots had trodden hundreds of individual letters, ledgers, folders into a sodden mass. Some had dried out, and were hard and stiff, like boards. Winters bent down, picked up a folder, opened it. Water from firemen's hoses had blurred the ink and typing on the pages it contained into unreadable black streaks. He picked up other ledgers idly, pieces of paper, threw them away; they meant nothing to him.

He walked along the quay away from Victoria, keeping his back to her, carefully stepping over ropes and cables and lengths of thick canvas hose. Against the side of one of the small ships blown out of the harbour someone had lashed a fire-ladder. Winters climbed this and stood on the sloping deck, looking down at the damage that stretched in every direction.

The hold was open, and clearly no salvaging had begun here. The ship was small, not much larger than a coaster, so would not have been carrying a valuable cargo. Quite possibly, she could simply have been at anchor, empty. To examine such a humble vessel would not be a very high priority.

The deck was covered with sheets of paper and files that had burst open, carried there by the force of the explosion. Most were stuck together by sea-water or water from firemen's hoses, and then had dried against the metal deck under the sun. Winters bent down, peeled one away from the rest, glanced incuriously at any typing which was still legible.

He saw half a sheet where the typing was still clear. This paper had been partly preserved under the cardboard cover of another folder, and was headed '*Kansas Rose*. No.3 HOLD. TWO SEALED STEEL CONTAINERS. RED CROSS SUPPLIES. KARACHI AGENT TO COLLECT. CHINA IMPORTS/EXPORT GUARANTEE COMPANY.' What agent? he wondered idly.

The folder had obviously been blown here from the *Kansas Rose*. Was it possible that the explosion had also lifted the containers to which it referred? These could well be the two metal containers of medical supplies that Mr Lee had wanted so urgently, with the other wooden crates. Winters put the paper in his pocket, and having nothing else to do, decided to find out.

He crossed the deck and peered down into an open hatchway. It yawned like a black cavern, with a metal ladder bolted to one side. He climbed down this carefully. Several feet of filthy water covered the bottom of the hold, with a scum of oil and charred wood and pieces of paper floating on it. He paused. A sour stench came up from part of the hold he could not see. He did not want to go down any further; there might be dead bodies in there, and he did not wish to see any more mutilated corpses.

Also, he would never get the oily muck off his clothes and shoes.

He was about to climb up again when he saw the corner of a black metal box, like a tin trunk, sticking out of the water. Holding on to the ladder with one hand, he bent down and tried to move this with the other, but it had stuck fast.

This could well be one of the boxes referred to in the note. Curiosity consumed him. He must discover whether it was or not.

Winters climbed back on to the deck. An Indian corporal, a *naik*, was marching a squad of Pioneers across the quay. All carried shovels. He called out to him. The corporal understood English, halted the squad. He looked up at Winters enquiringly.

'Forgive me, corporal,' said Winters, almost unconsciously adopting a deeper, more authoritative voice. 'I am looking for some medical supplies shipped in two crates for the Government. I think that I have found one of them. Do you think you could get your men to shift it out, and then I can see if the other is also there?'

Put like this, the request did not sound like an order; but it did sound official. The corporal regarded Winters warily, taking in his well-cut lightweight suit, his air of authority. There was no saying who this European fellow might be, but he could conceivably have the power to make life hard for him if he ignored his request for help. The corporal made up his mind quickly where his own interests lay.

'Very good, sir,' he said smartly. 'We are just now coming.'

He ordered the squad up the ladder and down into the hold. They brought ropes and tackle with them and pulled out two metal boxes in a matter of minutes.

'We have a truck here, sir,' said the corporal. 'Do you want them taking anywhere?'

Just for a moment, Winters paused.

'No, thank you. I have a taxi waiting. If your people will put them in the boot for me?'

He did not want the corporal to know he was taking them to his apartment in a house on the road to Juhu Beach. They were far heavier than he had imagined, but when they reached the house the taxi driver and he managed to manoeuvre them into the garage of the house.

When the driver had gone, satisfied with a generous ten rupee tip, Winters came out on the pavement for a moment, stood in the sunshine getting back his breath. Several cars were parked along the road. Twenty yards away, a beige Hindusthan Ambassador had its bonnet open and a man was looking at the engine in a rather disconsolate sort of way. Someone else was sitting in the car behind the wheel.

Winters heard the starter motor chug slowly, wearily. The man outside shook his head, raised both hands in despair.

On any other day, Winters would have asked him if he could help him. There weren't too many Europeans around here now; he felt they had to stick together. But today he had more pressing business to do on his own. He might get talking to these fellows, they might ask him in for a drink, or he might have to ask them back to wash their hands if they were covered with oil, and who knows then when he would be rid of them?

He went into his garage, locked the front door from the inside. Then he examined the boxes closely. They were made of some light galvanised metal. Where this had been manhandled, the metal shone brightly through black paint and a thick coating of soot and oil. Winters poured some petrol from a can on to a rag, wiped clean the top of the nearest box. It bore no name, no address, no number. These details, presumably on an invoice pasted on the metal, must have become detached.

There was only one way to find out what was inside. He picked up a chisel and hammer from the bench, tapped a small hole and then cut along three edges of this side. Gripping the metal carefully with pliers in case he cut his hands, he pulled back a corner like the lid of a giant sardine can.

Inside he saw an opaque waterproof cover, concealing

32

whatever the box contained and sealed by hardened adhesive. He cut out a section of this with his penknife. Then, squatting on his haunches on the concrete floor, Winters almost fell on his back in amazement.

He was looking at piles of one thousand United States dollar bills, all neatly bound in strips of brown paper, thousands and thousands of them – a fortune beyond all imagination.

He had often handled huge sums of cash in the bank, but as every bank clerk knew, that always seemed like stage money, paper money. Somehow, it wasn't real money. This was. And it was not in someone else's account, impersonal and inviolable. It was right here, in his hands.

A tiny sound made him look up. A door at the back of the garage, that led into the house, had opened.

A man was standing in the doorway, looking at him. With a start, sharp as a blow to his heart, Winters recognised the man he had seen on the *Kansas Rose*, then on Marine Drive and on the docks barely an hour earlier.

'Who the devil *are* you?' he asked.

The man did not reply.

'You *were* on the ship, weren't you?'

The man nodded.

'Yes.'

'Then what do you want here? Why did you say you weren't when I asked you yesterday?'

The man came into the garage now. He walked slowly, quietly, as though he owned the place.

'What the devil do you want?'

Winters felt hairs on the back of his neck prickle with dislike, a warning of danger.

Now a second man came into the garage. He was older and tougher. He wore a linen safari jacket, linen trousers, and he had about him an air of authority, of immense power. He wasn't the sort of person you argued with. Winters recognised him; he had also been on the deck of the *Kansas Rose*, and he felt afraid. These two men were not paying a social call: they exuded an aura of violence.

Winters glanced round the garage for a weapon, but there was nothing near. A crank-handle on the bench, a large open-ended spanner hanging on two nails from the wall, were too far away. Anyhow, it would be two against one and he had just been in hospital. And even if he hadn't, he sensed, as an animal senses, he was facing deadly enemies. These men could overpower him before he could get in a single blow.

'What do you want?' he asked with all the outrage he could command. 'This is private property. My garage.'

They came towards him. Obliquely, he noticed they walked in step. Were they policemen? There was some sort of military bearing about them. Instinctively, he took a step back to avoid them. The calf of his left leg touched the edge of the metal box. He had forgotten it was so close. He nearly lost his balance, over-reacted, threw out both hands and arms to save himself from falling.

The first man thought Winters was coming at him in a crude attack. He hit him twice so quickly that the blows, a left and a right to the jaw, landed in exactly the same place. Winters stood for a moment. Then his eyes glazed, his legs buckled and sagged under him like the legs of a rubber man.

He fell backwards across the box. His body pivoted on it. His skull hit the hard concrete floor with all the force of a heavy hammer blow. He lay where he fell without moving.

'You bloody fool,' said the second man in English. 'You've hurt him.'

'He was coming for me,' said the first man sullenly. 'It was him or me.'

'Rubbish. You have to control your reactions. Last thing we want is him dead.'

'Who says he's dead?'

They bent down, one each side. The second man placed the back of his hand against his temple, feeling for a pulse.

'I do. His heart's not beating,' he said.

'It *must* be,' said his companion.

He took Winters' wrist. There was no pulse. They shook him. Winters' head lolled like the head of a sawdust doll. His eyes had opened now and stared up at the ceiling of the garage, seeing nothing. The second man moved one hand quickly to and fro in front of Winters' gaze. The eyes did not flicker. Both men knew Winters would never see anything again.

'You've killed him,' said the second man. 'And he's our only link.'

The first man stood up, head bowed. He knew he had over-reacted. Worse, he had failed, and failure inevitably brought harsh punishment. He glanced at his companion, waiting for orders, anxious to expiate his error. But the man wasn't looking at him, he was looking past him, past the corpse of the Englishman, down to the box over which he had fallen.

'Look,' he said hoarsely. 'It's there. The money.'

The other man stared, astonished at the sight of so many notes packed tightly, neatly, each wrapped in its paper band, each note worth a thousand United States dollars. A fortune lay at their feet.

Separately, or together, if they lived ten lives, maybe a hundred lives, they would never see so much money in one place. And it was theirs for the taking.

The man who had killed Winters tugged at one of the bundles of notes. But they were so tightly packed, so close together, he could not get a grip on them. He would have to pull back the lid.

'Leave it,' said his companion. 'We'll take them off in the box.'

'Very good, sir. But I'll just check how many bundles there are, how many in each bundle. Then we'll know how much it's worth.'

He put one foot on the end of the box, wrapped his handkerchief around his hand to save it from the jagged edge of the metal, and pulled with all his strength.

The explosion blew the front of his face away and tore the fingers from both his hands.

The man screamed in his ultimate, unbearable agony, and the sudden shock of blindness. Blood and thick black liquid oozed and streamed grotesquely down his face. Through the fog of cement dust and plaster that the explosion had raised, his companion could see him press the jagged pumping stumps of his hands against his eyes, as though somehow he could force away the pain.

He crouched in a foetal position. His companion watched him impassively; he had acted impulsively, without forethought. He felt neither pity nor grief, only concern about what he should do now.

There must have been a charge hidden in the box to deter any thieves. They'd both been fools not to think of that. It was the sort of thing they'd have arranged themselves. He didn't imagine these foreigners would be so crafty, or so clever.

The man on the ground sank lower and then suddenly slithered to one side and lay on his back amid the debris. His companion bent down, felt his pulse. In the blood and slime and filth of the explosion, through the thick abrasive dust that covered everything, he could not feel a beat. He was alone in the garage with a fortune and two dead men – and he would be held to blame.

He stood up, his mind working in its trained, analytical pattern; no panic, no quick decisions. Think it out twice, three times. Then do it.

He heard a sudden click outside the garage. A car door shut. Someone was stopping. They could come in. If they found him here, he would have to kill them. His situation was as serious as that. He must escape.

He felt along the wall behind him. The dust was still so thick it was difficult to see anything clearly. His hands touched a door handle. He turned it, pushed. The door opened into a small room that smelled strongly of petrol and oil. He could see an electric drill on a bench, a small lathe; he was in some kind of workshop. He went in, closed the door gently behind him, and stood to one side, flattened against the wall, listening. Through a window he saw a woman lock her car door, run up the steps of the house. He made a note of the car's number.

Victoria pressed the front door bell. She must see John. It was useless, looking for him at the docks, being told at the bank he was at home; then going to his house, to find he wasn't there. He must be back now, she thought. She heard the bell peal urgently through the hall. There was no answer. She banged on the door with her fist; still no answer.

She looked at the garage. Dust was blowing out from under the door and on top of it. What was happening in there? Perhaps he was working? He was very good at do-it-yourself things. She would see.

Victoria ran down the steps, round the garage to the side door. The dust was so thick and unexpected inside that it made her choke. What had happened? She saw two men lying on the ground. One lay crouched in a foetal position on his back, his face a mass of raw bloodied flesh. He seemed to have no hands, just stumps. She retched and vomited.

The other man was her fiancé, John. She knelt by his side, slapped his face hard. The flesh felt cold and clammy. He was dead. Debris lay all around them. They had been killed in an explosion – but what had caused it?

Victoria stood up, trying to comprehend what could have happened. Was this something to do with the business at the docks? Then Victoria saw the metal box.

She bent down again, slowly now. The explosion had ripped away the lid. She picked out a wad of notes, flicked them between her fingers. She had never seen so much money, never even imagined it. Instinctively, she made the sign of the cross. This was an answer to her prayers, this was the miracle she had sought and never expected to see. This was her passport to freedom, to a different life, a totally different world; goodbye to everything she hated.

But first she had to move the money. She tried to lift the box. It felt very heavy, as if it was weighted. She could never move this on her own. And she had to get out before someone else came in. She looked on the bench; nothing. Under it, she saw a plastic sack. She picked this up, and holding it open, like the sack Santa Claus used to hold in the big shops at Christmas time when she was a girl, she held the mouth of the sack wide and dropped the wads of notes into it. Then she put the sack on her back.

As she passed the window of the workshop, she was astonished to see a man looking out at her. His face was framed in the window: tense, pale, totally without expression – and therefore, to her mind, all the more terrifying.

Victoria did not know who he was, why he was there. But every nerve in her body warned her, she had to escape now, before he came through the door after her.

It was unlikely he knew who she was, any more than she knew his identity. But she could never forget this disembodied face at a dusty window in a house of death.

She ran out into the street, threw the sack into her car, and drove away without a backward glance.

Down the street, the third man in the Hindusthan Ambassador made a note of her car's number. His orders were to stay in this vehicle; not to move on any pretext. He always obeyed his orders. The man who gave them did not give them a second time.

Back in the little workshop, this man now came out. He had seen the woman close to: he would remember her face, although he did not know her name. She had taken the money from one box, but the second remained. Also, his colleague was still waiting in their car. He could not involve him; that would be far too risky. He wanted for himself all the money the second box must contain. He'd carry it out through the back entrance of the garage, behind the house, down the labyrinth of alleys he had already investigated. Then he'd hire a taxi. But he had no intention of returning to the safe house on the outskirts of Bombay where the three of them had been living. He was going elsewhere, going away altogether.

That would be dangerous, of course, deadly dangerous. But only the man left in their car could say he had gone into the garage, and he had not seen him come out. There would be trouble for him afterwards, bad trouble. He would be rigorously dealt with. But in this world – and maybe in the next – the rule of survival was everyone for himself. If you didn't kill your enemy, he would kill you. And the only rule for advancement was equally blunt: if you did not seize your chance, someone else would.

He picked up the box, carried it out into the hot, bright sunlight. Like Victoria, he did not look back.

CHAPTER THREE

THE PRESENT: BISHOP'S COMBE, WILTSHIRE, ENGLAND

It was that special, so swiftly fleeting hour of evening, when day trembles elusively on the hinge of darkness, and a man can be alone with his thoughts, the hour Dr Jason Love savoured above all others.

He had just seen his final patient in his surgery. Now, on the eve of leaving for his first visit to Australia, he stood, off duty at last, watching the sun slide slowly down behind the Edwardian motor house of his Wiltshire home.

Like a trailer for approaching autumn, Love could feel a first faint hint of coolness in the air; evenings in late summer often seemed symbolic of all human life and expectation. No matter how warm the morning sun had been, or how bright afternoon laughter on the lawns, shadows and the dark were moving closer all the time.

Moments like these made Love appreciate the rather melancholic philosophy of the seventeenth-century Norwich physician Sir Thomas Browne, whose droll assessments of the human condition appealed to him. 'Life itself is but the shadow of death, and souls departed but the shadows of the living,' Browne had sonorously declared. 'Light is but the shadow of God.'

Through the generosity of a patient who also accepted Browne's belief, ''Tis opportune to look back upon old times,' Love was now packed and ready to fly Down Under. This patient, Colonel Sam Wargrave, a tough old bachelor, had spent much of his early life out in Australia. Love first met him when, as a relatively recent arrival in Bishop's Combe, he was called out to stitch up a deep cut in the colonel's leg. Wargrave drank at least a bottle of whisky a day – more on Sundays – and by evening was frequently unsteady on his feet. On this occasion, he had fallen in his workshop and cut himself badly.

When Love finished, the colonel remarked: 'Now I look like Cowboy Collins. Glad I wasn't hurt as badly as he was – or in the same place – the family jewels.'

'Who was Cowboy Collins?' Love asked him.

'Great fellow. A butcher, who lived in Katherine, in the Northern Territory in Australia. Years ago, out in the Never-Never, where he had some cattle, a bull charged him. Cowboy jumped for a tree, and reached a branch – but it snapped under his weight – which was considerable, Doctor.

'Cowboy fell to the ground and the bull gored him badly. One of his balls was nearly torn off. He was in frightful agony. Fortunately an Abo – Aborigine to you, Doctor – with him drove off the bull. Then Cowboy realised he couldn't walk a step in his state, let alone get on a horse. So he had to patch himself up.

'He got the Abo to pull a hair from the tail of his horse and find a needle in his swag, and boil them together in a can. This took ten minutes or so. Then Cowboy sewed up his wounds himself. He had to, or die out there in the Outback. And it wouldn't take too long to do that, either.

'On the ride back, his wound burst and he restitched it. And when he got home the doctor saw him and said, "Paddy, I couldn't have done a better job myself."'

'You liked it out there in Australia?' Love asked.

'Who wouldn't? You see, like Cowboy, everyone relies on themselves in the Outback. A hundred miles is like going next door here. There's no soft welfare. Your welfare is in your own right arm, and your own right hand. You want to get out there, Doctor. A great country. To my thinking, the greatest in the world.'

'Then why didn't you stay there?'

'Because I'm getting old and on my own. It's fine being a bachelor when you're young like you, Doctor. But it can get kind of lonely when you're old, like me. I've a sister here, married, with sons and daughters. I'd rather be near them. A man's like an animal – he *is* an animal. When his time is running out, he likes to be where he was born, with his own folk. But *you* want to get out there, Doctor.'

And whenever Love called on the colonel, Sam Wargrave repeated this. Then the colonel died and left five thousand pounds to Love – on condition he spent it all on a trip to Australia.

'There's so much to see,' the colonel wrote to him in a covering letter. 'A lifetime is barely long enough. I would suggest you visit Ayers Rock first in the Red Centre of Australia. The rock is named after Henry Ayers, who was Prime Minister of South Australia when settlers discovered the Rock in the late nineteenth century. It must be the world's biggest memorial stone to any man anywhere, and, mind you, the Abos had discovered it thousands of years before.

'Ayers Rock is nine kilometres round its base, three hundred and forty-eight metres high and at least another six hundred metres of it goes down into the earth.

'It's been a sacred site to Aborigines for around forty thousand years, which makes places holy to other religions look pretty modern. But see it and judge for yourself why it has this hold over people.

'Then go north up to Cairns, to what they now call the Marlin Coast. The biggest marlin in the world are fished there, which is only right and proper, because Australia is the world's biggest island. This way, you will see something of the land, something of the sea. I wish I were going with you. I am putting my money, Doctor, where my mouth is. You put your legs where my money is. And as they say Down Under: Good on you, sport, you'll be right.'

There was another reason why Love was going to Australia, had indeed decided on a visit months before the colonel's death. This was connected with the car Love kept in his motor house – somehow the word garage did not seem a suitable description for such a splendid building with a floor of blue-patterned Portuguese tiles, and its own antique, coke-fired central heating boiler.

This car was as unlike other more modern mundane cars as Love's motor house was unlike lesser garages. This car was a Cord, a car built by an American entrepreneur in the 1930s, and looking like no other vehicle made then or since.

Some people find a painting, or even a person, so attractive they can (and sometimes do) spend hours lost in admiration, and contemplation, drawing pleasure from the sight or the company of whatever or whoever has this astonishing effect upon them. So far as Love was concerned, the Cord held this attraction for him. To contemplate it gave him more pleasure than any mistress, any wife, and, as he had to admit to himself, the Cord was probably more expensive than either.

Long, low and white, with two stainless steel exhaust pipes curving from each side of its blunt coffin-nosed bonnet, this car's real home was the open road. Just looking at it always gave Love a totally absurd thrill of pleasure. The Cord was never intended simply as a means of transportation, to be left in supermarket parking slots, or outside suburban railway stations; it was the fulfilment of a dream.

Mr Errett Lobban Cord had started life as a salesman, painting Model T Fords in brighter colours than Henry Ford allowed – and consequently selling huge numbers of them. Banks at that time were losing money on a motor manufacturing company in Auburn, Indiana, and suggested to Cord that he might be able to reverse this situation. Cord agreed – on condition he was given a huge parcel of the company's virtually worthless shares. The banks complied: any proposition seemed more attractive than to continue losing money. Cord revitalised the company – and never looked back.

The car that bore his name failed commercially because it appeared when the United States was still suffering from the effects of the slump. But this in no way detracted from the beauty of the result, or the braveness of his attempt. Rather did it increase the attraction in Love's mind.

Designers and engineers had worked against the clock, desperate to produce a car in time to be exhibited at the New York Motor Show. If they could complete so many cars, they had a chance of large-scale production and survival.

They built the cars, but the complexities of the transmission system, with the gear change worked through a tiny electric switch on the steering column, produced many problems. Motorists are basically conservative. They loved the look of the car, but distrusted such radical innovations. Although the problems were soon overcome, this came too late and production ceased.

When mechanics unfamiliar with its peculiarities raised its alligator mouth bonnet and saw for the first time the Cord's huge eight-cylinder engine, turned back to front, with its inordinately complicated combination of vacuum servos and electric solenoids to change gears, they would crudely paraphrase the words of Ozymandias: 'Look on my works, ye Mighty, and despair!'

Yet the cars appealed in spite of their mechanical complexities – or maybe because of them. In Love's opinion, a great car, like a ship, was always feminine. And from a beautiful, if wayward, creature men might stoically endure – even condone – all manner of irritations and infidelities, but not from any woman (or car) lacking in looks or charm or charisma.

A club for such aficionados, with the motto, 'For those who have never relished the commonplace', thrived in the United States, with members in many other countries. This club published a regular newsletter, and one member in Australia, in the seaside resort of Cairns in North Queensland, had been corresponding with Love for some time.

It seemed unlikely he and Charles Robinson would ever meet. But, earlier that year Robinson wrote to Love, inviting him to call should he ever be in Cairns. The envelope bore the familiar Cord crest of three arrows and three hearts, originally part of the arms of the Scottish M'Cord family, so Love knew before he even opened it that a fellow enthusiast was writing.

Some said unkindly that Errett Lobban Cord had little right to this crest. But then men with no more right to authority had seized the thrones of kings, and ousted the presidents of countries.

'I hope you have not forgotten my invitation of hospitality should you ever be in this country,' Robinson wrote. 'I would very much like to meet you, and discuss the Cord, which we both hold in such esteem. I would also greatly value your advice on another matter which has arisen since we last corresponded. Please don't postpone your visit too long.'

Now Love had cabled to Robinson explaining he was going first to Ayers Rock, and would then fly up to Cairns to see him. He did not know how old Robinson was, or what his profession might be, although he had hinted at interests in garage and scrap metal reclamation; even what he looked like, whether he was married or single. But to find out these facts would be part of his journey of discovery.

Equally, Love had no idea about the matter to which Robinson referred so carefully. But, as one interested in problems of the human mind as much as ailments of the human body, Love suspected that it might probably be some medical condition on which he sought an outside opinion.

Sometimes people, advised by their own doctor that they were suffering from an ailment that caused them concern, would seek the view of a total stranger, often a doctor picked at random from a name on a brass plate on a Harley Street front door. They felt that the diagnosis of such a person would be impersonal – and so hopefully more encouraging.

For this reason, many doctors did not enjoy cocktail parties. They wished to avoid being accosted by strangers who sought a free conversational consultation for some complex medical condition between drinks. Could this be why Robinson wished to see him? Love knew he would never discover if he declined Robinson's invitation – and people's motives for apparently simple actions were often so devious, and so fascinating, that in their complexity they reminded Love of the Cord.

As Love brooded on this strange relationship between man, medicine and motor, surely an extended twentieth-century love affair, the mobile telephone in his pocket began to ring.

He was off duty now, but like all doctors, he felt an imperative urge to answer any ringing telephone. Not to respond to its urgent summons might mean for someone the closure of the narrow divide between life and death. As with Pavlov's dogs, action brought reaction. Love took the instrument from his pocket, pressed the button. A woman's voice spoke nervously in his ear.

'Dr Love?'

'Yes.'

'You don't know me – Miss Dukes. I am not a patient. I am speaking for Mrs Green at The Hall.'

She paused. Love had heard of Mrs Green, of course, but strangely, in such a small village, he had never met her. So far as he was aware, he had never even seen her. He knew that she was mysteriously elusive, a recluse, apparently a widow of indefinite age and great wealth, who for the past few years had lived her life almost entirely behind the high brick walls that surrounded The Hall. Was she old, young, middle-aged? No-one seemed to know for certain.

Groceries were delivered to her house; she had never been seen to shop locally. Her companion, Miss Dukes, shopped for her, and what could not be supplied from nearby towns came down from London. In the local phrase, she kept herself to herself, but in this she was not alone. Every village had its eccentrics, and so, of course, did every town and city. But in a village, people's idiosyncrasies are better known – and so almost always respected.

Love was not quite sure what Miss Dukes looked like, either, but he had been told she drove an old Morris 1000.

Several times, he had seen a woman, again of indeterminate age, wearing dark-lensed glasses, in such a car, and assumed she must be Miss Dukes.

'I apologise for ringing you,' she said now. 'But our physician, Dr Jones, has been called urgently to a serious motor accident, and his partner is also out seeing a patient. I wonder if you could possibly come and visit Mrs Green in their inability to attend her?'

'What has happened to Mrs Green?' Love asked without notable enthusiasm. He stood watching the sun slide down gracefully behind a green tracery of trees at the end of his garden. An early owl hooted from a cypress. Shadows stretched long fingers across the lawn. Night lay only moments away.

If I could paint, Love thought, inconsequentially, I would paint this. Not just what I see, but what I feel about this view, looking beyond the house towards the Downs. When the Spanish Armada was sailing up the Channel, in the sixteenth century, lookouts in Devon had devised an ingenious way of using these Downs to inform the Admiralty in London of the situation, for the fastest messenger could take days to ride to London.

Along the top, locals laid huge bonfires of brushwood and dried fern at two-mile intervals. When the Armada was first sighted, the fire nearest to it was lit. Watchers along the coast, waiting by the second bonfire, saw the flames, and at once lit it. So the line of fires went on into the heart of Whitehall. Within twenty minutes of the ships being sighted in the Channel, their Lordships in the Admiralty were informed of Spanish intentions.

Miss Dukes' voice brought him back to present problems.

'Mrs Green is unconscious, Doctor, and seems to have lost the power of speech. I am very worried. She went to bed this afternoon complaining of a headache. I think she is seriously ill, or I would not have telephoned you like this.'

'I'll be right over,' said Love at once. He went into his surgery, collected his medical bag, came out, climbed into the Cord. The lanes were deserted this late in the evening, and he made good time, the beat of the car's twin three-inch exhausts booming back reassuringly from high grassy banks on either side.

This was the nearest thing to human flight Love ever experienced and, at ten miles to the gallon, he often thought it must be nigh on as expensive. But to hell with that; he had no ties, no old parents to support, no wife with a charge account at Harrods, no children at boarding school. He was on his own and, after Maureen's death, he meant to stay that way.

Being single meant more to him than simply being alone: it meant being an entity, a complete person, without ancillaries, anchors or any encumbrances. With a wife, there could be complications, pointless involvements with dinner parties and friends of hers who weren't necessarily friends of his. Gradually, what had at first joined them could end by simply tying them, strangling individuality. And although he liked children, he did not think he liked them well enough to devote his life to them.

Some friends of his years at Oxford or Barts expressed surprise that he should like to run a country practice single-handed, when he might be a consultant at a London hospital, or be one of a group in a far larger London practice. But when he looked at their faces, pale from too many hours indoors, maybe furrowed by worry, with large mortgages and high school fees to pay, he felt they offered unassailable reasons for staying where he was, as he was. Love had no intention of surrendering the citadel of his independence. Some time, no doubt. But not quite yet. He could – and frequently did – echo the words of Sir Thomas Browne: 'In brief, I am content, and what should Providence add more? Surely this is what we call Happiness.'

Love swung the car briskly into the drive at The Hall – and then jammed on his brakes. The two rusting iron gates were closed. Someone had tied them together with a length of wire. If he had been travelling fast, he would have hit them head on.

Love unwound the wire, pushed open the gates on their

creaking hinges, and drove on more slowly towards the house. Weeds in the centre of the drive stood as high as the Cord's bonnet. When he reached The Hall, he saw that its windows were almost obscured by creepers. The setting sun briefly painted dull glass panes the colour of blood. Tiles fallen from the roof, where seeds had taken root, crumbled in broken gutters. Months, probably years, of rain cascading down the walls had left long green streaks of moss and slime on the stonework.

Love stopped outside the oak front door, climbed out, pulled a bell chain. The bell clanged faintly in distant recesses of the building. He waited. Footsteps pattered on stone flags inside the hall. Then came the creak of a bolt being withdrawn, the rattle of a safety chain. The door opened, and a woman faced him.

She was about five foot seven inches tall, and wore a dark green dust coat. She had a deeply tanned complexion, and even in the dusk she wore spectacles with unusually large blue tinted lenses. She could be the person he had seen in the Morris 1000 – if that mattered.

'I am Miss Dukes,' the woman explained. 'How kind of you to come so quickly, Doctor.'

She led the way through a wide hall, up a flight of oak stairs. Cobwebs stretched across sconces on panelled walls; dust lay undisturbed on each side of the stair treads, and between the banister supports. More dust had settled, thick as scurf, on the shoulders of rusting, unpolished suits of armour. A grandfather clock on a landing had stopped at five minutes to nine; but when – and in what day or night?

Time also seemed to have stopped in this house. Nothing looked clean, spruce, smart. From the walls, faded portraits looked down on moth-eaten carpets covering unpolished floors. This was not a home, thought Love in distaste. Despite Mrs Green's rumoured wealth, The Hall was no more than a shelter from the elements.

Miss Dukes knocked timidly on a panelled door, as though she expected a rebuff, paused for a moment. There was no response. She shrugged and led Love through an anteroom and on into a bedroom.

Beneath a silk coverlet, a woman lay, propped up uncomfortably against a padded silk bedhead with stuffing burst out in several places. Her eyes were closed, but her mouth sagged open. Her face was pale and sallow as a waxwork. It was difficult to say how old she was: Love put her in her mid-fifties, but he realised he could be ten years out, either way. The room was very dark. Leaded windows were almost opaque with dirt. In wall lights on either side of the bed, tiny bulbs shone feebly through pink silk shades linked by cobwebs. Love looked around for the main switch; this was Miss Haversham country.

'Mrs Green doesn't like a lot of light,' Miss Dukes explained quickly.

'I do,' Love replied shortly. 'I have to examine her. I can hardly see anything in this gloom.'

Miss Dukes pursed her lips disapprovingly, touched a switch. Half a dozen electric bulbs of low power glowed in a candelabrum.

'Tell me what happened exactly,' Love said, as he opened his case, felt Mrs Green's pulse.

'She has been poorly for some days, Doctor. She complained of a very bad pain in her chest, and shortness of breath. But, as you may know, she never liked to consult a physician.'

'I didn't know. You say she is Dr Jones' patient?'

'Yes. But I don't think she ever visited him. Not to my knowledge.'

'I see.'

Love raised Mrs Green's left eyelid. Her eye was unfocused, its pupil dilated.

Love lifted the coverlet from Mrs Green's hands to feel her pulse. He was surprised to see that they were the hands of a woman used to hard work. Somehow, he had imagined that she would have lived a pampered life, but her fingernails were commendably short. Although she had, for whatever reason, lived almost like a prisoner behind high walls, clearly she had not been idle here. As he felt her pulse, he saw a wedding ring hang loosely on the third finger of her left hand.

Perhaps, as with others who felt unwell, she had been afraid to consult her doctor in case he gave her bad news which she did not want to hear? Many patients preferred to live in a world of make-believe and self-delusion rather than to face reality, until – as now – it might be too late to do so.

He had frequently been called to the deathbed of someone whose life could easily have been extended, if only they had consulted him earlier. The two words 'if only' emphasised the danger of delay.

Seeing Mrs Green's wedding ring made Love wonder about her husband. What had Mr Green been like? What had he done for a living? And where – and when and how – did he die? Or was Mrs Green divorced, or perhaps even abandoned by her husband, and so had created the comforting fiction of widowhood and mystery for reasons of her own pride?

Some locals had told him vaguely that her husband had been what they called 'a foreign gentleman'. On the few occasions anyone claimed to have seen her, she wore dark glasses and a hat pulled down over her face.

Mrs Green unexpectedly opened her eyes, and stared vacantly across the room, almost in terror. As she made out Love's features, she put up one hand in an attempt to draw him closer to her. She was trying to focus her gaze on him.

'I am a doctor,' Love explained gently. 'Can you tell me how you feel?'

Mrs Green's mouth opened slightly, closed, opened again. She frowned with the intensity of the ailing engaged in futile concentration. Love thought she understood what he had said. Clearly, she desperately wanted to speak to him, to tell him something, but the ability to talk had left her.

Her mind could still send urgent messages, but her muscles had lost the will to respond. He recognised the signs: he had seen them too often in his career for there to be any doubt.

He was looking at a dying woman. He must get her into hospital at once, and even then, he would not give much for her chances of survival.

'Where is the telephone?' he asked Miss Dukes.

'Downstairs. She would never pay to have an extension in the bedroom.'

'Please ring for an ambulance,' he told her. 'Tell them it's an emergency. Give my name. I don't want to leave her for the moment.'

As he waited, he thought briefly of the combined efforts and complementary skills that would unite in an attempt to save the life of this recluse, who for so long had seemingly shunned human contact. Telephone operators. An ambulance crew. Oxygen. Possibly, a life support machine; the help and knowledge and experience of so many people she had never met. But still he had the feeling that even their combined efforts would all be in vain. Again, words of Sir Thomas Browne came to mind, as they did so often: 'We labour against our own cure. Death is the cure of all diseases.'

The ambulance arrived as Love was scribbling a note for the duty doctor at the hospital. Miss Dukes stood by his side at the front door as the ambulance crunched carefully away down the overgrown drive. They watched its tail lights disappear up the lane. Soon, even the sound of its engine died away. The evening seemed very dark, very silent.

'Do you think she has any hope of recovery?' Miss Dukes asked him.

'*Dum spiro, spero*. While I breathe, I hope,' replied Love enigmatically. 'But I have to be honest with you, Miss Dukes. I do not feel sanguine about her chances. Has she any relatives you should inform?'

'None, so far as I know. Her husband left years ago, before you came here, I think. I don't know where he is now. Perhaps not in this country, or even in this world, Doctor.'

'It is sad to face death on your own,' said Love musingly. 'Usually, there is someone who cared, perhaps just one person, who waits to say goodbye at the lych gate of eternity.'

'I have been with her for many years, Doctor. I will visit her every day while she is in hospital.'

'Of course.'

'Is it a stroke, do you think? Heart trouble?'

'I am sure Dr Jones will keep you informed,' Love replied diplomatically. 'I will leave a message for him. I am off on holiday tomorrow, you see.'

'To Australia, I understand?'

'Yes. How did you know?'

'I read a paragraph in the local paper about your trip. It said you were going to see someone who has an old car like yours.'

'That's right,' Love agreed. 'I am.'

He picked up his bag. Suddenly, he wanted to be away from this crumbling house, away from dust and decay and fear on the face of a dying woman. He wanted to be in the sunshine, in the company of the young, not here in the deepening dark, with old people, old secrets.

'You are going to Cairns, in Queensland, so it said in the paper?'

'That's right. After a stay elsewhere.'

'Then I wonder if I could ask you a great favour?'

Miss Dukes paused. Love waited. So many people frequently wondered whether they could ask a favour from their doctor, great or otherwise. Usually, it was something they did not care to ask officially; perhaps to acquiesce over actual details of an illness for a doubtful insurance claim; to agree that fading eyesight was strong enough for a driving licence. What great favour could Miss Dukes want?

'If I can help you, I will,' Love replied carefully.

Miss Dukes picked up her handbag, took out a photograph, handed this to Love. He held it up under one of the sconces in the hall to see more clearly. He was looking at the picture of a young woman. In the dim light, he could just read the name written underneath: Annabel Crawford. He handed the photograph back to her. She put it away carefully in her handbag.

'Mrs Green's niece,' Miss Dukes explained. 'Her only relation.'

'So she has someone? And she is in Cairns?'

'She was, Doctor. But only the other day a letter arrived saying Annabel had died. A drowning accident. She was very keen on swimming and scuba diving. Apparently, something went wrong. I don't know what.'

'Did Mrs Green know that?' Love asked her. 'It could have contributed to her collapse if she did.'

'She didn't,' said Miss Dukes firmly. 'I kept it from her. I was in the habit – on her instructions, of course – of opening her letters and dealing with her correspondence. Her eyes were very weak and, as I told you, she disliked consulting doctors. A good pair of spectacles would have helped her enormously.'

'So you kept this news from her?'

'Yes. As I told you, she had not been very well for several days.'

'Who wrote to her from Cairns?'

'A Mr Stevenson. He was at the funeral.'

'In what capacity? Is he a clergyman?'

'No. Someone she had met.'

'A boyfriend?' asked Love. 'Is he young, old?'

'I don't know, Doctor. But here is his letter. Read it.'

Miss Dukes crossed to a bureau, took out a piece of paper, on which were a few typed lines, handed it to Love. He read: 'Dear Mrs Green, I am very sorry indeed to have to tell you that your niece Annabel has been involved in a fatal accident, swimming some way off the coast.

'I saw her laid to rest in the cemetery and I will endeavour to forward you more details of the accident, as soon as they come to hand. Yours sincerely, George Stevenson.'

Love scribbled down the address in his diary, handed back the letter.

'When was it posted?' he asked. 'There's no date on the note.'

Miss Dukes shrugged.

'I have no idea,' she admitted. 'We always throw away envelopes. They only add to the litter in this house, and there's so much already.'

'I will certainly look him up,' said Love.

'Thank you. And if you could arrange for her grave to be looked after, I would be very grateful. And so would Mrs Green, of course. When she recovers, I will have to tell her.'

'Of course,' Love agreed, adding a mental qualification: If she recovers.

'You have written to Mr Stevenson?'

'Oh, yes. But I haven't had a reply yet. Not been time, really. But I will hear, I'm sure. The trouble is, I know no-one in Cairns, and it's so far away, and I haven't the money to fly out myself.'

'Have you telephoned Mr Stevenson?'

'Yes. But there was no reply.'

'I see. Well. Keep on trying. Someone must answer eventually, I feel sure.'

Love walked towards the front door.

'I do hope Mrs Green does get better,' said Miss Dukes suddenly. 'If she doesn't, I don't know what I will do. I'm absolutely on my own. I regard The Hall as home, and, of course, I have no claim to it.'

'But she has now no relatives she could leave it to?'

'Not so far as I know. But when money's involved, forgotten relatives often do turn up. Or she might have left everything to a cats' home – you never can tell what people will do, Doctor.'

'Never,' Love agreed.

He said goodbye, climbed into his car, pondering on the anomalies of life. Here, a woman of wealth was dying alone and possibly quite unmourned, while another woman, to whom a few hundred pounds could set her mind at rest, would soon be unemployed, and possibly without a home. Life was very unfair to some people, Love thought. But then, hadn't it always been – to everyone?

He stopped in the lane, pulled the creaking iron gates together. As he tied them up with the piece of wire, he glanced back at the house. It was now in total darkness, not a glimmer of light anywhere, simply a solid block of stone, the slate roof silvery under a rising moon.

He felt disturbed, ill at ease, not his usual urbane self. The visit had depressed him unreasonably. But – why? Something struck a wrong note in his mind, like a cracked bell. But – what?

He was accustomed to deaths and loneliness for those left behind, but this was not what concerned him now. Could it be the house itself? Like all old houses, especially in the country, where life moved at a more leisurely pace than in towns, The Hall seemed a repository of many secrets. But – whose, and what?

Why had Mrs Green shut herself off from the world? Would grief at her husband's disappearance produce such a strong reaction? Or could there be some other reason? Did she not go out because she feared being seen – and recognised?

As Love wound out the Cord's retractable headlamps and drove home slowly, with midges dancing in their amber glare, he remembered another house barely half a mile from The Hall, where he had experienced precisely the same sensation.

Two spinsters in their seventies lived there. One morning, the elder sister asked him to call. She met him in mourning black, and in silence led the way up the stairs, past the bedrooms, and up a wooden ladder into the loft.

In the centre, on uncarpeted boards, was a narrow bed with an iron frame. On top of a grey blanket lay the dead body of a very old man.

His hair was white and thin and long, reaching to his shoulders. Death had drawn back his lips from greenish stumps of teeth. His fingernails were unclipped, broken talons, like the claws of a wild beast. He wore a pair of serge trousers, old-fashioned boots with string for laces, a shabby home-knitted khaki cardigan.

'Who is this?' Love asked, trying to keep horror and revulsion out of his voice.

'Our brother, Reuben.'

'I didn't know you had a brother.'

'Nor does anyone else, thanks be to God.'

'What do you mean?'

'What I say, Doctor. For Reuben has lived here in this attic since 1940, bless his soul.'

'But that is more than half a century ago,' said Love in astonishment. 'Why?'

'He was at Dunkirk in the Army. He came back, and then he deserted. We didn't live here then, so when we moved here no-one knew us – or that we had a brother. Our father was a hard man. He said that in the First World War deserters were executed by firing squad. And that would happen to dear Reuben – if he was discovered. We all had to save him from that fate. So we kept him hidden here.

'He only went out at night, and even then, he kept his face covered. Now all that we ask is that you give us a death certificate, Doctor. We will then arrange for him to be buried elsewhere. And his secret and his shame will have died with him.'

Was Mrs Green's secret – if, indeed, she had one, or maybe her shame – also about to die with her?

CHAPTER FOUR

THE PRESENT: LISBON, PORTUGAL;
LONDON, ENGLAND

As the Qantas 747 Four Hundred airliner settled down to its cruising speed of five hundred and seventy-two miles an hour above Portugal, Love sat back comfortably in his Club class armchair, debating whether to have a second rum and lime juice.

Thirty-seven thousand feet beneath him, a man he had never met, would never meet, but whose immediate actions would influence Love's future immeasurably, watched the 747 from a hilltop outside Lisbon – and wished desperately he was up in that aircraft or, indeed, in any aircraft.

He was in his early thirties, tall, slim, dark, with a spade shaped beard. He wore sun glasses with lenses of the type that darken as the sun grows brighter. He was concerned to keep his eyes shielded, not so much from the glare of the sun but from other people's gaze.

It is relatively simple and straightforward to disguise anyone's face so that even their family will not recognise it at a casual glance. But eyes are altogether different. They show alarm, recognition, fear: they are the windows of the mind. And the man knew that such signals could instantly alert an enemy who might not notice a face altered by adept surgery.

He stood in the shadow of an old castle, the Castilho da St Jorge. He had been in Lisbon for two weeks, living in a small flat in the Serpa Pinto area. Part of this section had been burned out several years earlier by a great fire. Multi-storey blocks of flats and shops were now only blackened shells, held up by scaffolding, as crutches support a cripple. A temporary road had been built across mounds of rubble, simply to reach other ruins. All around were empty buildings, gutted, roofless, occupied by rats.

This was a quiet place for anyone to live who did not wish to advertise their presence. The Englishman who rented the flat spoke perfect Russian and Portuguese, and his guest – called Luis in Portugal and to be Louis in England – had come to trust him. On the Englishman's advice, Luis had grown the beard to disguise his appearance, and with his dark glasses he felt reasonably sure that no-one would recognise him.

This was of the highest importance, for he had defected from the GRU, Russian Military Intelligence. Despite *glasnost* and *perestroika*, Luis did not feel confident that he could ever run far enough away; the KGB was an open society compared to the GRU. No-one volunteered for this; you had to be invited to join.

An invitation was, in fact, an order. And once you were enrolled, after the most rigorous checks, investigations and training, you could never resign. You were there for life – or death. You might die on service, or you could be dismissed for a number of crimes. If you were, then you also died.

GRU headquarters maintained an entire town outside Kiev, ringed with barbed wire and guard posts for its members not on active duty, or waiting between assignments. This town was totally self-sufficient; it even had its own crematorium. The only way anyone left the GRU was through the furnace and out of the chimney.

If you were already dead, this ending did not affect you. But if you were not, if you had been accused of treachery, slackness, loose talk about your job, this means of resignation affected you most painfully. You were strapped down on a metal stretcher and slowly propelled into the roaring blue flames. Your end was recorded on video – to be shown as a warning to new recruits. Luis remembered his own reaction at seeing this video years earlier, and he still felt sick at the memory; hence his concern that he should never be recognised by any of his former colleagues.

He knew that the Englishman was in some branch of security or the Secret Service of his own country. He had never asked, and he would not expect to be told the truth if he had asked. But on most mornings for several weeks past Luis had sat with him and sometimes two or three other men who spoke English, but who were clearly not English, and had answered their questions.

Now and then Luis would look up from the table around which they sat and see the tape-recorder spools turning slowly, and the long serpent of tape, metres and metres of it, registering everything he said. He knew he was killing himself every time he spoke – if his treachery became known. Sometimes, he wished he had stayed where he was, and then he remembered he had no option.

He had welcomed the chance of a posting to Macau, the tiny Portuguese enclave that hangs like a pimple on the coast of China. From Macau he had been sent to Lisbon, and here he had made his decision. He must go *now*; such an opportunity might never come again. He was due to return to Russia within weeks, and he might never be posted overseas again. Also, the fact he was being recalled before the end of his period of overseas duty was in itself unusual, and therefore sinister.

Too often, operatives called back early found themselves in the crematorium within hours of their return. So he had telephoned the British Embassy – and asked for asylum. The request was greeted coolly. Whoever answered the telephone suspected that this was either a trap or a hoax. However, Luis gave his GRU number and his name, and also the name of his immediate superior in Macau and was told to ring back within an hour.

For the next hour he sat in a café, well away from the window in case any colleague in the Lisbon residency might see him. Then he had telephoned a second time. The response now was not laid back, casual, uninterested: he was immediately given the address of a bar in a side street where a man and a woman, dressed in blue jeans and white sneakers, would buy him a drink.

This was the beginning of freedom. Now he waited – why, he had no idea – for the moment when he could leave Lisbon. He was told he would go first to England and then maybe to Canada, somewhere he could fit in easily, with other expatriates; Poles, Romanians, Russians, where his accent would not be unusual.

But for the past two days Luis had been left on his own. He thought that perhaps the Englishman wanted to test him. He also realised that having told them all he knew, he could now be considered expendable. Luis accepted he had nothing left to bargain with; his knowledge had been his key to freedom, and he had given up that key. Now all he could do was to trust men he barely knew, not only with his life, but with his death.

On both days he drove out of town in the little Seat the Englishman owned, so that he could try to think, while his mind churned like a demented millrace. He could not drive anywhere directly. Habit made him take the most circuitous route, doubling back on himself, choosing narrow alleys and tunnels, over one-way bridges – because any vehicle following him had to stay right behind, not weaving in and out of other traffic, and so was easier to see.

This complex routine of throwing off any tail was known as 'dry cleaning'; but after only ten minutes, Luis felt confident he was on his own. He reached the Castilho through a maze of narrow streets with tramlines along which single-decker trams banged and rattled, past houses crouching together as though for comfort.

Luis had been sleeping badly, starting up wide awake at the creaking of a board, the rattle of a window in the wind blowing up from the Tagus river. He had been taught never to fight from an inferior position. It was always essential to find a site where he could look down on the enemy. He realised that psychologically this was what he was doing now, up near this castle on the hill-top. His enemies were not here, of course; but he still felt safer than down on the ground.

The hilltop, he was surprised to find, was flat, and the size of several football pitches, with stone slabs dotted across stretches of grass. This was parched because of the unusually hot summer; throbbing pumps sprayed gouts of water across it, turning bare, dusty ground into mud. Here and there lay huge round stones, like giant cotton-reels, with other stone blocks around them. He had no idea what they were for until he saw a group of schoolchildren sitting on them, using the centre stone as a table for their sandwiches.

A perimeter wall overlooked Lisbon, and ancient cannons pointed blindly across the Tagus towards the sea. Far down the hill, from where he stood, Luis could see the backs of little houses, shacks of corrugated iron, a bird in a cage at an open window. Vines had been trained to conceal bare walls, around little squares of garden where chained dogs slept out of the sun.

The reds of the tiles and the whites of the walls added to the unreality of the scene. They could be disguised block houses, or shelters for sentries, but, of course they weren't – were they? Far beneath, along the rim of the river, now shrouded by morning mist, toy cars moved through streets no wider than strips of ribbon.

Luis walked around the castle, feeling the sun comfortingly warm on his back. There was a restaurant with advertisements for Ola ice-cream, 7-Up, a blue and white *telefone* notice, postcards in wire racks. Inside, a television screen flickered. The music sounded familiar and he paused, peering into the dim interior.

A Russian circus was performing. Two lions faced each other, sitting obediently on huge drums. Their trainer lay down on the ground between them. He held a long whip in his hand, and his eyes never left the baleful green eyes of the lions. A roar of approval greeted him.

The picture changed. A girl in a spangled costume stood on her hands. A man bent down, put brick after brick under each hand until, still upside down, she was now twelve feet in the air. A one-wheeled cyclist crossed a high wire, swung off on to a trapeze to delirious applause.

Everyone seemed tremendously brave and agile; and yet what they did was dangerous and ultimately pointless. Like his own career, he thought. He had accepted years of risks – for what? Not even for the applause of an audience of peasants. He wondered which performers were the KGB agents, watching the others, and who were there from the GRU, watching the KGB. Maybe he would recognise some faces if he stayed and watched? After all, he had nowhere else to go, nothing else to do but kill time. He winced at his choice of words; he had been involved with too many terminations, to use the official phrase. Was he also a murderer of time? It seemed a strange, bizarre idea; but, of course, it was true.

He went into the café, ordered a black coffee, sipped it, still watching the screen. He could never work in a circus, he thought. The performers were all afraid to grow old; then they would have no work apart from cleaning out the cages of the even less fortunate animals. Their muscles soon became thick and stiff, so that, after a certain age, every performance was a new dread, offering a new danger.

In close-up, the faces of the girl acrobats looked tired and drawn as they swung off one trapeze, dived and deftly caught the hands or feet of a partner. My life is just as meaningless, he thought. Is it any better than theirs? I've come over to a world of plenty, but I have brought the fear of retribution with me. I have not so much run away from one danger but into another, equally deadly.

He finished his coffee, walked outside, suddenly ill at ease. How much longer would he have to wait to get out of here? Why was he suddenly feeling so restless, nervous? Was it only because of the waiting?

A coach was disgorging a crowd of tourists, mostly Japanese, or Chinese. He wasn't sure which. He always had difficulty in deciding, even in Macau. Probably they had as much difficulty deducing his nationality – which would be no bad thing. They were small men with plump faces, oily hair, shiny suits, every one festooned with cameras, lenses, view-finders. A dark-skinned man came towards him. He was fat, his face polished with sweat. He wasn't Chinese or Japanese, just in the same coach.

'Very good view up here,' he said in Portuguese.

Luis nodded. He could pick out some of the words but not all.

'You're not Portuguese?' the man asked quickly, frowning.

'No,' said Luis. 'English. Tourist.'

'Ah, you know Hong Kong, yes?'

'I have been there. But I was living in Macau.'

As he spoke, admitting this, he suddenly wished he hadn't. But why not? The man was friendly enough.

'You know Macau?' he said. 'Ah. I know it well myself. Have business there. In the Rua da Boa Pesca. Tell me, what's the ship down there in the harbour? I saw it when we came up. I think I have seen it in Macau harbour.'

'I don't know. I'm sorry.'

They walked together round the side of the castle. Two attendants in blue dungarees and blue caps with shiny peaks were slowly unloading tarpaulins from a pick-up. The Portuguese were not noted for speed at work. They paid no notice to anyone else.

Luis and the tourist looked over the wall towards the river. Little ferries were gliding to and fro like toy boats in a bath. The mouth of the Tagus, where it ran into the sea, was now the colour of straw. Suddenly, as clouds moved away from the sun, the water turned to gold. An iron statue of St George, holding his shield and sword, glittered in the bright sun.

They walked on slowly. The tourist spoke.

'Macau. Ever been to Bombay?'

He spoke as though he was making a statement rather than asking a question.

Luis shook his head.

'Never. Not India. Pakistan, yes.'

'I think you know someone who knows Bombay,' said the man slowly.

He was standing very close to Luis now. Luis was surprised at the vehemence in his voice, astonished to see his face suddenly contorted like a mask, not the face of a cheerful man. Was he going to have a fit, a stroke?

'You're wrong,' said Luis. 'Karachi and Rawalpindi I have been to, yes. Not Bombay.'

Suddenly he wanted to get away from this stranger with his cameras and his conversation. Why had he battened on him like this?

'Ah,' said the man, 'Perhaps I am wrong. Perhaps I have confused you with someone else. A Mr Rodinsky? Do you know Mr Rodinsky?'

Luis shook his head. He said he did not know him, but he knew of him. Everyone did in the GRU. He was held up as the antithesis of everything each member should aim for. Rodinsky was a traitor; Rodinsky had defected. He was the Russian equivalent of Burgess, Maclean, Philby. But what did this man know about this secret, private matter? Could he possibly know that Rodinsky was his father?

'I am sorry,' the man was saying. 'I must have made a mistake. But let me photograph the scene, yes?'

He lifted his camera.

'And you in it, of course. That always makes a better photograph, having a person in it, not just a place. Please, just stand still for one moment.'

Before Luis could object – and he wanted to object most strongly – the tourist came closer. When he was only feet away, he pressed a button.

Luis did not feel the bullet. He did not feel anything. Just for a second, before he could register pain, or even surprise, before he could begin to move, he saw the tiny mouth of the pistol muzzle, cunningly built into the camera. Then he was dead.

Luis fell forward slowly. The man caught him expertly, glanced quickly over his shoulder. No-one was in sight; only the two attendants. They now came towards him walking slowly, not hurrying, as though on cue. They picked up Luis' body, carried it over to the tarpaulins, lowered it down carefully, put a second tarpaulin on top of it, and a third over that. Then one took out a small plastic bag from his pocket, bent over the body, handed the bag back to the man with the camera.

As they all walked to the far side of the castle, near the coach, the other tourists came round the side of the walls, chattering like excited birds.

The tourist climbed into Luis' car, paused for a moment while he selected an ignition key from a bunch at his belt, and drove away. He did not look back. The two janitors climbed into their pick-up and also left, following him down.

Some of the tourists had discovered they did not like heights. Looking down at the river and the city so far beneath made them feel dizzy. They found the café and sat down thankfully inside it, ordering drinks, watching the TV, so comforting in its soporific predictability.

The circus trainer, who had lain down so bravely between the two lions, now stood up. Facing the camera, he waved goodbye with a smile on his face. His act was over.

Colonel Douglas MacGillivray, the deputy head of the British Secret Intelligence Service, was used to being called a chronic melancholic, and indeed he secretly rather enjoyed this description.

He felt that it showed character, an ability to face facts as they so often were – unpleasant, unfortunate, or both – and not as he might wish events to be in an ideal world.

When friends or colleagues accused him of invariably taking a pessimistic view of any problem, large or small, MacGillivray would reply, and never altogether facetiously: 'You forget, I have much to be pessimistic about.'

This was, of course, so often true – as it was today – that

usually no-one took the conversation further. Instead, they would diplomatically direct it into other less stormy channels: politics, the opera, even gardening.

MacGillivray accepted that the head of the British Secret Intelligence Service, General Sir Robert L . . . ., would naturally gather any glory going after a successful coup. Sir Robert could – and did – cherish future expectations, such as lucrative non-executive directorships of distinguished public companies, on his retirement. To MacGillivray, equally understandably, would come the blame for any failure. His professional life was a continual struggle to cover a steadily increasing number of targets with resources – human and financial – that just as constantly seemed to lag behind.

Now that the Soviet Union and Eastern bloc countries, the main focus of Western Intelligence attention for years, had apparently decreased in importance, with *glasnost* and *perestroika* and a growing acceptance that Communism was not a political panacea assuring wealth for all, but an unworkable and broken creed, other targets had appeared in unwelcome numbers.

MacGillivray remembered from his school days how, in the Greek myth, the mouths of Hydra were filled with poison. This he felt also seemed to apply to his present and unexpected opponents. Their posturings took up much time and effort and money. Their dangers were difficult to recognise and assess, and, like moving shadowy targets, even more difficult to hit.

MacGillivray sat at a desk in the front room of a top floor flat in a block overlooking the British Museum. He appeared more melancholic than usual as he brooded on the latest conundrum for which Sir Robert wanted a quick and finite answer – and another problem that puzzled him alone.

MacGillivray was a tall man with a hard face and reddish hair, thin on top, going grey around his ears. He had pale blue eyes of the shade that often goes with that colour of hair, and a pale pinkish complexion, rather as though the skin had been lightly sandpapered.

He wore a suit of brown Lovat tweed, a shirt with a big check, a loosely knitted tie and polished Lobb brogues.

He looked as he wanted to look, dressed for the life he would like to have had; landowner of a Scottish estate, owning mile upon mile of rounded hills, purple with heather, rolling on into distant mists. Instead, he had a wife in delicate health, a flat in West Kensington and the nearest he usually got to the country, he would say sarcastically, was a trip to Parliament Hill Fields where he ran a subsidiary office.

MacGillivray sometimes felt he was like a modern-day dragoman, reciting 'Where my caravan has rested', for his own office regularly moved about London and its periphery. While the administrative headquarters of MI5 and MI6 remained static in huge office blocks in London, known by name to every taxi driver, and pointed out to foreign tourists as items of general interest like the Tower or Westminster Abbey, the more sensitive departments never stayed for long at any address.

They might occupy houses or apartments for a few weeks or months, or work from what outwardly seemed to be an import or export office, or a travel agency, some legitimate enterprise where the arrival and departure of men and women at unusual hours would not arouse interest or curiosity. Then they would pack up and move elsewhere.

He was used to this impermanence, with the regular transfer of truck loads of metal filing cabinets with treble locks and magnetic catches, and heavy curtains containing flexible magnetic shields to defeat any long-range microphones that might be directed on the windows from a parked car across the road.

MacGillivray had long ago grown to accept the dust that so quickly accumulated in these temporary offices. No-one below the equivalent rank of an army captain was ever allowed inside them; they were thus rarely cleaned thoroughly. Dust covered shelves; grey mounds of cigarette ash grew unchecked in ash trays. The lime green Wilton carpets, chosen by the procurement branch of the Ministry of Defence, always seemed scuffed and trodden down, as though too many people wearing muddy boots had walked over them.

A green light flickered above his door. He pressed a button beneath his desk. The door opened on a magnetic lock and his secretary, Miss Jenkins, came in. She carried a tray on which, like a trophy, she had placed a large mug of black coffee. MacGillivray drank black coffee at 10 o'clock precisely each morning; not at five minutes to the hour, or five minutes past it, but, as he always said, using a boxing analogy from the time when he was Army heavyweight champion, right on the nose.

He and Miss Jenkins had worked together for more years than either cared to recollect in public, and sometimes MacGillivray felt a small spasm of male guilt concerning her. He still knew so very little about her.

Despite her Welsh name, Miss Jenkins had graduated from the University of St Andrews in classics, either during or just after the Second World War, which meant he could actually gauge her age within a few years, but somehow he did not want to do so. If he knew exactly how old she was, he would also know when she was due to retire, and this would mean change. He did not like change; every change, he felt, seemed to be one for the worse.

'Change and decay in all around I see', he thought as he stirred the coffee.

'Who said that?' he asked Miss Jenkins.

'Who said what, sir?'

Like him, she was resistant to change; they had never got on to first name terms.

'Change and decay in all around I see.'

'It comes from the hymn "Abide with me".'

'Ah, the benefit of a Godly upbringing,' said MacGillivray. 'Now, here's a line that's been puzzling me all morning. It niggles me, like a stone in a shoe. I heard it in a play on the box. Who wrote: "They say. What say they? Let them say."'

'It's certainly in the Oxford Dictionary and in Stephenson's, sir. But not the author. The words were found engraved on a ring after the disaster at Pompeii.'

'What disaster? Football trouble?'

Miss Jenkins smiled bleakly, to show she accepted that he had made a joke, but not one she considered worthy of him.

'No, sir. When Vesuvius erupted in 79 A.D.'

'But who *said* it, who *wrote* it?'

'That well known poet, Anon,' she replied. 'But it's also found, as late as the sixteenth century, carved above old stone doors in parts of Scotland.'

'I don't remember seeing it carved on any old stone doors in my part of Scotland. I rather like the sentiment, however. No doubt whoever wrote it had known their share of criticism. He – or she – could be someone who worked then for the equivalent of Six.'

Miss Jenkins nodded to show this point was taken, but she did not reply. Instead, she placed a pink folder on his desk by the mug of coffee. As she did so, MacGillivray looked at her hands, innocent of rings, the fingernails without varnish. He remembered that Miss Jenkins had once told him she lived with her mother, who must now be in her eighties, if she was even still alive. But again he did not like to ask.

At the same time, she had said they had a cat, and a budgerigar in a cage. The cat would sit looking up at the bird for hours, hoping that one day, one happy day, through accident or careless mischance, the cage door might be left open after the bird had been fed. Out it would fly trustingly – to settle within reach of the cat's waiting claws.

Strange, thought MacGillivray, how this situation is paralleled so closely by secret agents, spies, traitors, every day and night of every year, and probably in every country in the world. They imagine, quite foolishly, that, like the budgerigar, they are safe. Then one day their cage is left open. Someone makes a mistake, and others, who have been watching this particular quarry for months, or even longer, instantly go in for the kill.

'What's this?' MacGillivray asked, indicating the folder.

'Mr Parkington asked if you could help him with a few details, sir,' she said.

'Parkington? Oh, yes, he's due here, isn't he? I'd forgotten.'

'He's actually here now, a little early, sir. Shall I make him a coffee?'

'Please. And show him in.'

MacGillivray stood up to shake hands with the man who came into the room. He was in his mid-thirties, broad shouldered, with a buccaneerish air about him. He looked as though he would be more at home on the quarter deck of a pirate ship, leaving some Bahama bay where he had been carousing with Captain Morgan or Blackbeard, than in a London office. And indeed he would have been. But, like MacGillivray, to wish was not to have, or to be. Parkington wore a shirt with the top button missing; his tie had frayed around the knot.

Parkington was an orphan. He had been brought up by an uncle, a grumpy bachelor who had little patience with a boy who hated schools as much as they disliked him. Finally, Parkington had scraped through the Regular Commissions Board, and from what was officially described as 'undercover work' had moved into the more shadowy world of departments known only by initials or numbers.

He had been married several times – he would sometimes say he had forgotten how many. But he had the gift, rare in any philandering husband, of always keeping on good terms with discarded wives or mistresses. He was basically a loner, and content to be so described.

His suit, although creased now and unpressed, had been made by a good tailor, and MacGillivray noted with approval that his shoes were always clean. MacGillivray could never stand anyone who wore dirty shoes. That meant they could be slack and slovenly on more important matters. Richard

Mass Parkington had once been one of his most favoured agents, and had never been slack or sloppy in his work. If anyone left his cage open, he would be too clever, too shrewd to come out. He was a pro, he liked to say; the amateurs were playing away.

But, like so many others of his calibre, Parkington had wearied of the work. Long hours, indifferent pay, constant arguments about expenses had eroded initial enthusiasm, and he had retired.

'I want to go while I'm still able to walk away,' he had explained to MacGillivray at the time. 'I don't want to be carried out – or hang on for a pension just big enough to pay for a breeze-block retirement bungalow in Worthing, with a postage-stamp sized garden.

'I don't want to end my days going down to the local every night with a few old timers, all living in the past, all waiting for the undertaker's Daimler to arrive and the church bell to toll. To hell with that expectation. I'm going now.'

So he had retired early, and immediately an insurance company, the Midland Widows, whose directors kept a look-out for people like Parkington with a knowledge of Intelligence activities and good contacts in that field, offered him a job as a supernumary consultant.

Parkington often said he did not know then just how supernumary he actually was going to be, for in a company priding itself on the generosity and variety of its pension schemes, he claimed to be one of very few on the staff without a pension.

Because of his association with MacGillivray, the cases about which the Midland Widows consulted him were never simple ones. Other employees might call on policy holders who claimed that their shops had mysteriously burned down (with all their books and stock), just when they were about to go bankrupt.

Parkington was only asked to enquire into more serious and expensive cases. Millions of pounds could be involved. Wills might be unexpectedly altered to bequeath huge estates

– thousands of acres, rows of houses, fortunes in shares – to total strangers or unlikely organisations that sought to prove the earth was flat, or that all the secrets of the universe were engraved on an oddly shaped stone in a field near Calais.

Parkington still occasionally undertook Intelligence assignments on a free-lance basis for MacGillivray. He only charged his expenses for these, and so, in return, MacGillivray would sometimes pass across to him, quite unofficially, details about a dubious client of the Midland Widows whose name came up on their computer.

Thus they could help each other. Everyone was pleased, including the Treasury, which hated to pay for anything if it could conceivably be acquired for nothing.

They shook hands. Miss Jenkins came in carrying a cup of coffee for Parkington.

'I've put something in it,' she explained conspiratorially.

This was a measure of Spanish brandy from a bottle she kept in a drawer in her desk. She would tell anyone who expressed surprise that she should store a bottle here among the ink erasers and packets of paperclips, that it was for medicinal purposes only. And in her opinion, Parkington qualified in this instance as a medical case. He could do with feeding up, looking after.

Miss Jenkins liked Parkington. She could imagine being married to him, and indeed, lying in her narrow bed, in her unfashionable flat in South London, with the cat in its basket by her feet, she often did. She would have made something of him, she told herself. She would have stopped him drifting and drinking so much; made him settle down, build a proper career. He'd got the talent, he'd got the physique; in fact he'd got everything – except ambition. But then, she often thought, if I changed him so much, then perhaps I wouldn't like him so much – or indeed at all? And, worst of all, then he might not like her.

As she went out of the room, MacGillivray pressed another button on his desk. The green light glowed outside the door to show he was not to be interrupted.

'I've been able to help you a bit,' he said to Parkington, and pushed the folder across the desk to him. Parkington opened it, skimmed through the typed notes inside. They described how a man named Luis – no second name, only this one – had been found dead under a batch of tarpaulins near a castle frequented by tourists outside Lisbon. His body had been hidden there, under a hot sun, for several days. Finally, the smell had caused a janitor to lift the tarpaulins. Fingerprints of a stranger had been found on the ignition key of a Seat car Luis had been using. Attempts were being made to match them against millions of others on file.

'Don't take it away and don't make a copy,' MacGillivray told him. 'Just memorise the parts that interest you.'

'I know the rules,' Parkington replied. 'You're absolutely sure of these facts?'

'I'm as sure of the facts as one can ever be, yes. They've all been checked out.'

'Puts a new complexion on things, then?'

'If my experience is anything to go by, no doubt a worse complexion than before,' said MacGillivray lugubriously.

'Cheerful Sunny Jim country today is it, then?'

'Yes,' MacGillivray agreed. 'Sunny Jim country. Seen the papers?'

'They say, what say they, let them say?'

'How odd. I was just asking Miss Jenkins about that quotation only moments ago.'

'I know. She told me on the way in.'

'Oh. I thought you were quoting from your own knowledge.'

'It is my knowledge now,' said Parkington. 'I totally agree with the quotation. Stuff them all.'

'You wouldn't say that so loudly if you were still with the old firm,' MacGillivray replied. 'People are asking questions, and my Minister wants to know exactly what is happening, because the Prime Minister will soon be on to him. I'd like to know what's happening myself. The problem may have some bearing on what you have been reading, though I doubt it.'

'Let me be the judge,' Parkington told him, sipping the coffee appreciatively. He liked brandy; Miss Jenkins had good taste. Pity about her looks, though. 'Do you a trade if I can help?'

'Of course. But let me fire some facts at you first and see what you think.'

'Fire away,' said Parkington.

MacGillivray took another folder from a drawer, opened it.

'I'm paraphrasing a newspaper report,' he explained. 'It's datelined Toronto, Canada, last week. A fifty-seven-year-old bachelor who lived alone in an apartment in Bloor Street was found dead in his living room.'

'Now renamed his dying room,' said Parkington. 'But death happens to the nicest people. Even to fifty-seven-year-old bachelors in Bloor Street. Maybe especially to them.'

'Spare the wit. Just listen. He had been electrocuted. Police broke down the front door when neighbours told them piles of newspapers were left outside, and found a short in a reading lamp. The story put out was that he had been electrocuted.'

'Except', Parkington pointed out, 'in Toronto the voltage is a hundred and ten, not two forty like here. That couldn't kill a healthy man – or even a weak one.'

'Exactly. And there was a very unpleasant side to the whole thing. His little fingers and his ears had been cut off. That was not publicly revealed. It seems like some kind of ritual killing, but what kind beats me.'

'Who was he? Anyone known to us?'

'Yes. He was a former GRU colonel who had come in from the cold.'

'With *glasnost* and *perestroika* and so on, there's no cold now. It's all warmth and happiness. We're all friends. Aren't we?'

'Some of us, yes,' MacGillivray agreed. 'But this man and the fellow Luis in Lisbon came over when it really was cold.'

'Had they been of any use to us?' asked Parkington.

'Enormous use,' said MacGillivray appreciatively. 'We've had a number of KGB people defect, but almost none from the GRU. It's just too risky for them. No excuses are accepted.'

'I thought we looked after such people when they came over?'

'We did.'

'*Did*. Don't we now?'

'Not to the same extent. It's all a matter of manpower and resources for surveillance. I needn't remind you we haven't unlimited amounts of either. With *glasnost* we've had to cut down. You will remember when you were here, we were always being told to reduce expenditure, save money. Now, it's much worse. The Treasury's on our back like The Old Man of the Sea.

'One way to save was to reduce the number of people looking after ministers who have been involved with Northern Ireland and who the IRA would like to eliminate. Another way is to pull back on the guards we gave these turncoats. It saves money.'

'But not lives?'

'Agreed. The lives of civil servants are unaffected.'

'So what do you think?'

'Since you ask me, I would say these two people were knocked off by some person or persons who had a grudge against them.'

'Did they ever work together?'

'Yes, out of Marseilles. But not just in France. That base covered quite a big area. They would go across to North Africa, Pakistan, India. They travelled under all kinds of aliases, with different passports.'

'Did they ever do any specific job together?' asked Parkington.

'Only one, as far as I know. They formed a sort of ad hoc court of inquiry into a rather curious affair that happened in Bombay.'

'What was that?'

'Three GRU men were allotted a certain task – and then everything went wrong. A relief to know it happens to the other side, as well as to us. Afterwards, one man disappeared. The second was badly wounded. The third – who had nothing to do with it at all except to wait in a car – was blamed as though the catastrophe was all his fault.'

'A not unusual apportionment of blame,' said Parkington drily. 'What happened, exactly?'

'I'm not too clear. I've not seen all the transcripts. They never caught the fellow who cleared off – they would have killed him, of course, if they could. The other two would normally have been cremated. Instead, they had a hard time in the uranium mines.'

'That's death too, usually, isn't it? Cancer?'

'Frequently, yes. But I don't know what happened to them. Not many survive that, for there's no protective clothing, nothing. Anyway, that's all I know – so far,' MacGillivray admitted. 'But we keep on trying. And if I hear anything that affects you, I'll let you know.'

'Same with me,' said Parkington. 'We'll be in touch.'

'By the way, we've a new name and number now for outsiders like you to use,' said MacGillivray.

He took a visiting card from his pocket, handed it to Parkington.

'Mr Douglas Kerr,' he read. 'Service Director, Quendon Motor Factors Ltd.'

The address was of the flat where they were sitting, opposite the British Museum.

'You like Scottish names?' said Parkington.

'Of course,' MacGillivray replied stoutly. 'And especially I like the motto of the Kerr clan. That's what made me choose this name. It has a relevance that speaks for both of us.'

'Which is?'

'Late, but in earnest.'

CHAPTER FIVE

THE PRESENT: SALISBURY, WILTS, ENGLAND;
DARWIN, NORTHERN TERRITORY; CAIRNS,
NORTH QUEENSLAND, AUSTRALIA

Miss Dukes had never attended a crematorium service and so was not quite sure what to expect. Worse, there seemed no-one who could help her, for she was the only mourner.

The duty clergyman asked her what service she wanted. She told him, something short but dignified. There was obviously no need for an address or a eulogy for her benefit, since she clearly knew far more about Mrs Green than the clergyman, who had never previously even heard of her. The service was bland as butter, tailored for those of every faith and of none.

Finally, a tape played the Dead March. The coffin moved away slowly and silently on rubber rollers between two maroon curtains that parted automatically and then closed behind it. The whole business had taken only a matter of minutes.

She could imagine the burners' baleful blue flames about their terrible business, and wondered whether they consumed the coffin as well as what it contained. She had heard stories of unscrupulous undertakers who decanted the body, then knocked down the coffin into its component planks and put it back into stock to be sold a second or a third time. Every trade had its tricks, and profit was the universal spur. It intrigued her that for very paltry sums people would act in such a way. Thank goodness that such considerations would never again affect her. They had once, but that was long ago, a time not in her mind now, but somehow always in her memory.

Miss Dukes walked out into the afternoon sunshine. Everything had gone well so far, she thought with relief. She could not help glancing back towards the ominous chimney above the building. There was no smoke yet. That would come later, probably after dark when it could billow up unseen into the night sky. Were the bodies burned singly, she wondered, or in groups? What terrible secrets went up in that smoke and thankfully were lost forever in the clouds?

So many religions favoured burning or its equivalent. In Bombay, the Parsees had their grim towers of silence. There, the dead were carried up steep staircases to be stretched on metal racks high in the air. Walls shielded the bodies from public gaze as vultures and other carrion birds swooped down to pick the bones clean.

And not so far away from the Taj hotel in the same city was the Hindu crematorium, also shielded by a high wall. Instead of the chill impersonality of this English crematorium, a strong not unpleasing smell of scented wood hung for a hundred yards around it whenever a body was being burned.

Her thoughts were so focused on such recollections that she did not see a man standing in the crematorium vestibule until she had almost passed him.

He was tall and thin, and wore a black tie and black armband. He could also be a mourner – but for whom? Mrs Green's cremation was the only one that afternoon.

'Miss Dukes?' he asked her. He had a gentle, educated voice. He could be a crematorium official or, dread thought, a newspaper reporter.

'Yes,' Miss Dukes replied cautiously. 'What do you want?'

He held out his hand. She shook it, studied his oddly pale face, his small brown eyes, dark and expressionless as raisins. He was not English, of that she was certain, although he did not have a foreign accent.

'I have not had the pleasure of meeting you before,'

he said rather stiltedly. 'I am Mrs Green's nephew. Paul Kent.'

'I didn't know she had a nephew – or indeed any relations,' said Miss Dukes, peering at him intently now through her tinted spectacles.

'Oh, yes. We are not a very close family – unfortunately. And now it's too late to be close to her, may she rest in eternal peace. I did not even know her address until I saw the announcement of her death in the paper.'

'I put it there,' said Miss Dukes. 'It seemed fitting.'

'Quite so. I apologise for arriving too late for the beginning of the service. The traffic was heavy and, as always, they were working on the motorway.'

'As you can see, I was the only mourner,' said Miss Dukes. 'But at least you did come. Your aunt would have been pleased. Family ties count for a great deal.'

'Would you have time for a cup of tea with me?' Kent asked her. 'I'm spending the night in Salisbury. I have some business further west tomorrow.'

'That would be very pleasant,' Miss Dukes agreed.

'Come in my car,' he said. 'You can leave yours here. It'll be easier for parking.'

He did not speak on the short journey. Miss Dukes watched him surreptitiously. He seemed curiously ungainly, clumsy, with big feet and hands, a suit that did not fit too well, a collar that rasped on a thickish neck, pitted with large pores. He drove the car jerkily, as though he was not accustomed to it, but then it could be a hired car, and a make with which he was not familiar.

They took tea in his hotel lounge. Couples around them sipped from dainty cups and spoke in whispers, as if they were in a church. The air felt stale and tired; the windows were rarely opened. Miss Dukes sipped pensively, wishing she was back home.

Suddenly, she longed to be away from this small, cold country of even colder people. She yearned for the sun and a wide and sparkling sea. She had not swum in a really warm sea for years; and when she was a girl she was the best swimmer in her school, and such a fine diver that the top board in the school swimming pool always seemed far too low. She could have gone on to great things; she might have dived in the Olympics if only . . . if only.

She forced such thoughts from her mind, concentrated on this young man. He was eating an egg sandwich, brushing flecks of yolk from the corners of his mouth with the back of his hand.

'My aunt was a pretty lonely person,' he said.

'Yes,' Miss Dukes agreed, meekly. 'When did you last see her?'

He shrugged.

'Years ago. Time goes so quickly. It must be five, maybe six years. Perhaps even longer.'

'You didn't visit her in Bishop's Combe, though, did you?'

'No. It was in London. She was up for the day, I think.'

'Are you on her mother's or her father's side?'

'Her mother's,' he said, and then leaned forward in his chair.

'Matter of fact, I wonder if you could help me over something to do with my aunt?'

'If I can.'

'Well, I was in communication with her over a project we hoped to do together.'

'What sort of project?'

'One involving business in another country.'

He paused, obviously not wanting to be too specific, yet wondering whether he was being specific enough.

'So how could I help you?'

'Very simply. I would be most grateful if you would be kind enough to allow me to see some of the correspondence about this. Now she has been unfortunately called to higher service, I cannot of course go ahead with it with her – but it would not be right or proper for me to go ahead with any other partner, as I have the chance to do, in case my aunt

81

had expressed a wish to pass her share on to someone else. Perhaps to you, Miss Dukes?'

'That seems unlikely. Why ever should she do that, Mr Kent? We were not related. And I have never heard her mention any business connection with you.'

'But you have lived with her, been her companion for years? My aunt had the highest regard for you. She said so herself, in as many words.'

'I am touched to hear it. But much as I would like to help you over this matter, I regret that I cannot. I have seen all her correspondence since we have been living here in Wiltshire. And I cannot recollect anything whatever to do with any business overseas with you or indeed with anyone else.'

'Perhaps she only hinted at it, didn't mention it directly? Kept it to herself?' Kent suggested hopefully. 'She could be like that, you know.'

'Oh! I do know,' Miss Dukes agreed, pouring out more tea. 'But I do not recall even any hint about such a project. However, if you leave me your address, I will get in touch with you should I find anything that relates to this. I have to clear out everything, so I will have all her correspondence through my hands.'

'She had a lot? I mean, she has left a lot for you to go through?'

'Not really. She was a very methodical person. As you know, she had a tidy mind. All her letters are in the study downstairs. It's only a tiny room, right next to the front door. Was a cloakroom once, I believe. So it's not very difficult to find things in it, fortunately.'

She wiped her mouth with a paper napkin to show that she considered their meeting to be at an end. Kent took a card from an inner pocket, handed it to her.

'I had better take you back to where we met,' he said. 'Rather a gloomy place to say goodbye. I hope our next meeting will be more cheerful.'

'I hope so, too,' said Miss Dukes politely. 'And more successful from your point of view.'

They drove to the crematorium in silence, shook hands. Miss Dukes climbed into her Morris, waited until Kent had left, and then set off on the road to Bishop's Combe.

From time to time she slowed, glanced in her rear view mirror, in case he was following her, but there was no sign of his car. She put her own car in the garage, locked the doors and let herself into the house.

It smelt fusty and unlived in; a house of memories curling at the edges like yellowing forgotten photographs in an old, unlooked-at album. She checked that the downstairs windows were closed, and then went into a small sitting room. She sat down in a shabby easy chair with the stuffing coming out, turned on the television to a programme she did not even watch.

Voices, music, the sycophantic laughter and applause of coached and prompted studio audiences as one programme succeeded another, provided companionship of a kind. At least it seemed better than silence. She would move now she was on her own. Mrs Green had left the house with all its contents to her. She would sell up and move on; where, she had not quite decided. That might depend on Mr Kent. She would wait and see whether or when he paid her a visit. She rather thought he would.

Outside, shadows grew darker and longer. The overgrown lawn turned from green to black. Soon, the old house slept, and eventually so did she, sitting upright in the chair, while comics on a tiny screen told jokes she did not hear, and dancers performed routines she did not see.

A noise, tiny, almost imperceptible, but alien because it was not part of the electronic entertainment, suddenly awoke her. She switched off the set with the remote control button and sat up, listening intently.

The room was now totally dark. Miss Dukes had not drawn the curtains, and outside, through windows almost opaque with dirt, she could see the moon. Branches trembled in silhouette as a night wind blew in from the Plain.

She heard the noise again, more clearly now; a metallic

scraping like a claw or a hook on metal or stone. Someone was trying the little window in the hall. It should have been repaired or replaced, of course, but then so should so many other pieces of equipment – locks, hinges, plumbing. Now, none ever would be.

Miss Dukes stood up, moving with surprising speed. She opened her handbag, took out a small pearl-handled pistol, of the type known as a ladies' pistol, cocked it, walked out into the hall. This was L-shaped and she stood well back in the smaller part, facing the front door.

A man was climbing in through the window. In the feeble light of the moon, she could see he wore canvas shoes, thin wash-leather gloves, a scarf and a woolly cap. He landed lightly and silently in the hall on rubber-soled shoes, turned to close the window.

An amateur would have left it open in case he had to leave in a hurry. But then an amateur would not wear canvas shoes, gloves, a scarf and a woolly cap. He was a professional – and she noticed that he closed the window carefully in case a draught might waken a sleeper. He turned from the window, paused for a moment, then took a confident pace to the right, into the study.

Miss Dukes waited for a count of ten and then followed him to the doorway. She switched on the light.

'Stand right where you are,' she told him calmly. 'Don't move one inch, or you are dead.'

The man was bending over a metal deed box, his gloved fingers fumbling with the lock. He stood up slowly, looked at her. She recognised the eyes, the big feet, the clumsy hands.

'Take off that scarf, Mr Kent, or I will shoot it off. Do it slowly. And again, don't try anything foolish.'

Kent put up his right hand, pulled away the woolly scarf and cap. She could see sweat glistening on his forehead.

'You must excuse me,' Kent said unconvincingly. 'I tried the door. There was no reply.'

'I don't excuse you. Neither do I believe you. One, the

door was shut. Two, you didn't try it. But, even so, I rather expected I might see you.'

'What do you mean?'

'That is why I told you Mrs Green kept her letters in that box. She didn't. Everything is in the bank.'

'So you know about her letters?'

'I know about them. And now I want to know about you. You are no relation of hers. She had no relatives. So, who are you? Who sent you?'

She told herself she knew the answer before she asked the question, but she still wanted to hear what the young man would say.

'Someone you wouldn't know. A business associate. A Mr Lowe.'

'You mean Mr Lo, L-o?' Miss Dukes asked and saw Kent's face muscles tighten. He did not reply. Miss Dukes knew then that her suspicion was correct.

'How did you meet him?'

'I was living in a rooming-house in Toronto. He came to see me. I don't know how he knew I was there. He said he knew Mrs Green. There was a debt she owed him. He wanted it collected when I came to England.'

'Why didn't he collect it himself?'

'"A rich man does not do a poor man's errand." That's what he said. A Chinese proverb.'

'And you accepted that explanation?'

He nodded.

'Of course. Why not?'

'Because it is not true.'

As Miss Dukes spoke, she fired twice, aiming at his ankles.

Kent stood for a moment, rigid with pain and shock and then slowly collapsed, as his legs gave way beneath him like melting candlewax. He lay on the floor, gasping in pain, scratching the bare boards with his nails like a wounded animal.

Miss Dukes watched him for a moment to make certain he was not play-acting. Then she crossed to a small bureau, opened the drawer, took out an ornamental knife. She held it carefully by the tip of its blade through a silk handkerchief.

As Kent lost consciousness, she pressed the handle into his right hand. She had heard of Mr Lowe, however he spelled his name – and most likely that was not his real name.

He had sent several letters to Mrs Green, some posted in Hong Kong, others in Europe. In each one he claimed she owed him a huge sum of money. The letters had never been answered, so finally, but too late, he had sent a messenger. One day, perhaps, Mr Lowe would call himself. Or again, now that Mrs Green was dead, with news of her death published in the newspapers, and her cremation over hours ago, he might not.

In any case, Miss Dukes felt relatively unconcerned. By that time, she would be out of the country, all this behind her, thousands of miles away. But first she must be rid of this man with as much publicity as possible, as a warning to Mr Lowe.

She picked up the telephone, tapped out 999, asked the operator for the police. When the duty officer came on the line, she gave her name and address.

'I am a woman on my own,' she explained. 'A man has just broken into the house, threatening me with a knife. He made to attack me. I have a small pistol and I am sorry to have to tell you that I had to fire at him in self-defence. I shot him in the ankles. He is not dead, but unconscious. Please do come as quickly as you can.'

She replaced the receiver, switched on the light outside the front door and stood watching Kent until the police arrived.

On the Monday before Love was due to arrive in Cairns, Mr Robinson had two unexpected experiences which caused him great concern, and decided him to cable Love in England, asking him to postpone his visit.

Robinson had flown to Darwin to check with the lawyers certain insurance matters he had arranged regarding his scrap metal company. He finished his discussions earlier than he had anticipated, and was walking along East Point Road, which overlooks Palmerston Gardens on one side and Fannie Bay on the other, when he was horrified to see a walking corpse.

That was his first reaction, because he had last seen this man years ago, lying in his own blood in another country. He had personally knelt by his side and pronounced him dead. And yet here he was, wearing a lightweight suit, walking ahead of him on the other side of the road.

Robinson's training had taught him not only to recognise faces instantly, but also silhouettes of people from the side, the back, from an upstairs window looking down on them. At the training school, he had been made to sit for hours on a hard wooden chair, concentrating on a flickering black and white screen.

On the right arm of the chair, just beneath his fingers, was a button. Wires were connected to his left wrist and his right ankle. Dozens, then hundreds of face outlines flickered up on the screen one after the other. Half he had been shown on the previous day. Now they had been subtly altered with new hairstyles, beards, spectacles. When he recognised them, despite their disguises, he pressed the button. If he missed one, he received an electric shock through the wires. The more he missed, the stronger grew the current. After an hour, he would miss no-one.

So Robinson was convinced of the identity of the man across the street. He also knew that he had undergone the same intensive training. He had only to turn once – briefly, perhaps before crossing the road – and if he saw Robinson he would instantly recognise him. That could only mean death for one or the other.

In Robinson's mind, there must only be one reason for this person to be here in Darwin; he was following him to Cairns. He had come across the world for one specific purpose: to kill him.

To avoid recognition, Robinson turned off the pavement

into the first doorway he saw, pressed the bellpush. If anyone had answered, he would have asked to see Mr Smith, the first English name that came to his mind. But no-one answered. He kept his finger on the bell, his face away from the street, until, cautiously, he half turned and saw the man pause outside the doorway of a small hotel.

Robinson turned away, facing the direction from which he had come. He took a small round mirror from his pocket, concealed this in his handkerchief, and through it watched over his shoulder as the man turned, glanced casually along the street, then went into the hotel.

Robinson found he was sweating. Fear had dried his mouth, and his knees trembled as from an ague. This man was Serov. There was no question of it, yet now he had a totally new face, and somehow almost unbelievably had recovered from his injuries. Last time Robinson had seen Serov, his face was a mass of tortured raw flesh and blood. Now, it was smooth, with an aquiline nose, bushy eyebrows. No plastic surgeon could have mended any ruined face so handsomely. Serov must be wearing a mask to conceal his injuries.

Robinson guessed he would not be called Serov now. Like Robinson, he would have a new name, a new persona and background to match his new face.

How had he spent the years since their last meeting? In hospital? In gaol? In a labour camp? However and wherever, Serov would count those years wasted, time lost out of his life never to be reclaimed. He had always been jealous of Robinson. Now he would blame Robinson for causing him such pain and hardship, and he would hate him. In their narrow world, there was only one punishment for guilt of such magnitude – death.

Of course, Serov would not know him under the name Robinson. Would he – could he – recognise his face as quickly as he feared after the months of delicate plastic surgery he had endured at the hands of so many different surgeons in hospitals as far apart as Vancouver, Cape Town, and Sydney?

One had operated on his nose, another on his ears, a third on the eyelids. The operations were carried out by strangers far apart so that none of them would know exactly how Robinson's facial appearance had changed from start to finish. This was a safety precaution, but even the most complex facial changes could not disguise his eyes. If his eyes met those of Serov, even for a moment, he guessed that Serov would recognise him – instantly and accurately.

Robinson could not follow him into the hotel and ask the reception clerk what his name was now, but he must find someone else who could. Then, instead of being hunted, he could become the hunter. He went into the lobby of another small hotel, looked through the classified section of the telephone directory in the lobby phone booth, rang three numbers.

The first private detective told him he only accepted work from lawyers he knew; divorce was his speciality. The second wanted cash up front and a written request for what services were required, and why the client needed them. The third explained he was too busy to take on any more clients, but suggested the caller enquire again in a couple of weeks.

This was useless; Robinson needed action now. He copied down the address of a fourth possibility, went out of the hotel and walked along a street behind the Esplanade until he saw a brass plate on a half open door beside a chemist's shop: *A K Hogan, Discreet Investigations Undertaken. Missing persons traced*. Robinson paused for a moment, wondering whether he should approach Mr Hogan, and, in that moment of indecision he received his second shock, as disturbing as the first.

There, only yards away, driving a car, was another man from the past, whose face he had also deliberately forgotten. How easy and convenient – and potentially dangerous – it was to lock away in the back of one's mind, in the dim vaults of unwanted memories, all recollections of a name, a face, of what had happened years ago! And how fearful was the reaction if these locks were suddenly and unexpectedly sprung – as now.

This man was at the wheel of a red Toyota, waiting for another car to pull out from the side of the road so that he could park in its place. Robinson made a quick note on the back of an envelope of the Toyota's number, pushed through the door and up the stairs. Once again, he felt he had managed to escape, literally by seconds, before he could be recognised. Fear made his heart beat like a demented drum. On a landing he saw another door, knocked on this with his fist.

'Come in,' a man inside called to him.

'Mr Hogan?' Robinson asked him as he came into a small room. It was sparsely furnished with a desk, several metal filing cabinets, two wooden chairs on a strip of trodden carpet.

'The same.'

Mr Hogan was in his mid-fifties, fat as a slug, and with the same grey colouring. He wore light-weight grey trousers, a grey shirt, stained with sweat under the armpits. A huge beer belly hung over a grey leather belt. He half sat, half lay, leaning back in a swivel chair. Big feet in dusty down-at-heel grey cowboy boots stretched out across one end of the desk. Robinson did not like him on sight, but then Mr Hogan was not in a particularly likeable business. And who could say whether any of the other private investigators listed in the telephone directory would be any more likeable?

'What can I do for you?' Hogan asked him without much interest.

Robinson sat down, uninvited, in a chair facing the desk. The walls of the room were covered with pin-up pictures cut from centre folds of girlie magazines. Hogan saw Robinson glance at them.

'Got a wife problem, have you?' he asked, not unsympathetically. 'She getting screwed by someone and you want to know who and where? You been screwing someone, and you need a witness to say you were a hundred miles away at the time? That the scene, sport?'

'No,' said Robinson. 'Nothing like that. I want to trace two persons.'

'Persons?'

'Two men.'

'Could be a police matter.'

'You advertise you're an investigator. Investigate these if you want my business.'

'Tell me more, and then I'll tell you if I want your business.'

Hogan took a cigarette from a packet. He did not offer one to Robinson. He struck a match on the sole of his left boot, lit the cigarette, flicked the match across the room.

'I'm all yours,' he said. 'Ears nailed back.'

Robinson pushed the piece of paper with the car's number on it across the desk.

'Could you trace who owns that car, where he lives, anything about him?' he asked.

'*Anything* is a pretty big request. Like what d'you want to know about him?'

'Like what he does for a living. Is he married? Single? Is the name he goes under his real name? Where does he live – and how long has he been living there?'

'That will do for a start,' said Hogan. 'I gotta have some spare time, some private life. Who's the next bloke?'

'This is more difficult,' said Robinson. 'I saw a man going into the Emerald Hotel half an hour ago. He is late middle aged, about six foot tall, grey hair, a foreigner. Or he was. He may be Australian now. His name was Serov. I don't know his name now, where he lives, or why he is here. I want to find out those things – quickly.'

'I gotta ask you why,' said Hogan. 'This could be pricey. He screwing your wife?'

'No,' said Robinson. 'I *think* I knew him some years ago. I am not quite sure.'

'No?'

Hogan sounded sceptical.

'You want to settle some old score? Is that it?'

'Nothing like that. But if he is who I think he is, I might buy him a beer.'

'There you go. So why didn't you follow him into the pub and buy him a stubby of Fosters?'

Robinson flushed. He had been foolish to say so much; but then he was frightened, and fear had loosened his tongue. He had forgotten his training, and to forget what he had learned at such cost could be as dangerous as a rock climber losing his boots. Both could mean a fall, but a fall in Robinson's predicament was almost certain to be fatal.

'I have my reasons,' he replied stiffly. 'They don't concern you.'

Hogan regarded Robinson steadily through a mist of cigarette smoke. This bloke was hiding something, that was for sure; he was also shit-scared. Even so, his money would be no worse than anyone else's. And maybe because he was so scared he would pay heavily for facts – or reassurance; even more for both.

Hogan tapped cigarette ash out in the upturned tin lid of an instant coffee jar on his desk.

'First assignment is straightforward,' he said. 'The second could be difficult. My terms are five hundred dollars in advance. Cash. Now. If it goes to more than that – and it probably will – I will bill you. Terms are payment on demand. No credit. No credit cards. No cheques. No crap. Cash.'

Robinson opened his wallet, took out five one hundred dollar bills.

'You have a deal. Provided I know the answers by seven tonight. Can do?'

'Can't promise, but I'll do my best,' said Hogan more civilly now. The sight of money relaxed him greatly. He wished he had asked for a thousand. This bloke was so scared he'd have paid it without a whimper.

'Now, give me your name and phone number in case I have to contact you.'

'No. I'll come back here this evening. Seven o'clock.'

'This isn't how I like to work.'

'Do you want the job or not?'

'I don't,' Hogan admitted. 'It stinks somewhere. But I want your five hundred iron men, so I'm doing it. OK?'

'OK.'

When Robinson returned at seven o'clock, Hogan was sitting in exactly the same position. He might not have moved from his chair, but presumably he had, because he pulled a file from a drawer in the desk, and opened it as Robinson sat down.

'First, the difficult one,' he said, without any preamble. 'His name is Singer, Peter Singer. He lives in Zimin Drive, Katherine, Northern Territory. Age, mid forties. No spouse or girl friend. On his own. Doesn't booze or screw around. Doesn't own the property either, just rents it. Says he's looking for a property to buy, in Cairns or Darwin. I haven't had time to check with real estate agents, but I can do if you want.

'He speaks good English, but he's not English or Australian. I couldn't find out exactly where he came from. But again, I could if you give me more time – and more cash. These things can be tricky and expensive to find. He arrived in Australia three weeks ago. Has moved around a lot. Could be looking for someone.'

'Does he work?'

'Not so far as I can discover. Again, it's a matter of time. Interested in printing apparently. The nosey arsed bastard I use to help in these cases went snooping around his house, saw some kind of press set-up in his garage. The windows were all curtained or painted over, but he managed to get a look-see. Singer is not there right now, by the way. He has been away from home for three days – probably looking for a property. Maybe that's what he is doing here in Darwin?'

'Maybe,' Robinson agreed, his heart beating faster than before. Singer. What a strange name for Serov to choose, with its slang implication; the name given to a criminal who decided to 'sing' – to inform on his colleagues and so save himself.

Singer was not looking for a property, of course; Singer

was looking for him. He must remember this new name, not Serov. He had been involved with printing years ago: fake documents, share certificates, forged birth certificates, passports. It was reasonable that he should continue this interest here if only as a hobby, or as a cover; an excuse to explain his journeys or his questions. But while that might be reasonable, could it be the reason?

'What about the other man?' Robinson asked.

Hogan pushed a card across the desk, with an address and a telephone number on it.

'Name of Hargreaves, Jack Hargreaves,' he said. 'A toughie. Threatened my bloke with a black eye. Thought he was snooping around too closely.'

'Which he was, and too obviously, if he got that reception.'

'Sure. But you wanted quick results, sport, so he had to take short cuts. My bloke apologised. Said he was working for a finance company and had been sent out to collect money owing on a red Toyota. There'd been a mistake. Sorry. It all ended fine.'

'But you didn't find out anything about him?'

'Not more than he's on holiday here from Europe. Might settle if he could get a work permit.'

'Doing what?'

'Photographic work. Again, some sort of printing. Mean anything to you?'

'Not a lot,' Robinson admitted. 'But you did well in the time.'

'I thought so, too. Glad you're satisfied for that'll cost you two hundred and sixty-seven dollars on top, including expenses. You want an itemised receipt?'

'No,' Robinson told him. 'List it as a bad debt. Say your client never paid, and put the cash in your back pocket.'

'Smart boy,' said Hogan appreciatively. 'I was going to do that in any case.'

'I thought you might,' said Robinson. 'And do something else for me at the same time. Forget this assignment ever happened. Understood?'

'Perfectly,' said Hogan. 'How can I remember you when I don't even know your name?'

Robinson picked up the card, walked down the stairs.

As soon as he had gone, Hogan pulled the curtains across the window. Through the gap where they nearly met, he waited until he saw Robinson come out of the building. Then he threw a coin down on to the pavement.

It landed just behind Robinson. He turned, looked up, frowning, wondering where it had come from. Hogan had a camera ready, and standing back from the window, pushed the telephoto lens between the curtains. He photographed Robinson full face twice, and once as he walked on along the road, looking back and up at the building. Then Hogan went back to his desk, put up his feet, lit another cigarette and waited for the telephone to ring.

Robinson drove back thoughtfully to his house. Until he had seen those two men, and heard Hogan's reports on them, the sun had been bright and warm. He had felt as near content as he ever managed to be. But now his peace of mind was shattered. Thoughts churned in his brain, sterile as dead leaves in a poisoned whirlpool.

To see one of these men from the past would have been bad enough, but bearable. It was unlikely the man would stay in Darwin for ever, or even for long. But to see two was infinitely more disturbing. Could this be a coincidence, and therefore harmless? Could it really be a trick of chance that sometimes did happen, like winning a football pool? Or could this be something altogether more sinister? Robinson's antennae of survival, which previously had so often alerted him to approaching danger, were warning him strongly that it was.

He sensed that two people from his past were deliberately moving in on him. And where there were two, soon there could be more, many more. His room to manoeuvre was steadily and deliberately being restricted. If two men he had once known and worked with, and who believed he had betrayed them, were already here in Australia, so close that he had actually seen them in the street, could have greeted them without raising his voice, time was shrinking all around him. Unless he moved decisively and soon, he might be unable to move at all. The past would overtake him completely, imprison him, then obliterate him.

Robinson flew back to Cairns next morning, drove straight to his house. A Chinese servant came out to open the car door. He only did this when he had some news to impart. Robinson looked at the man enquiringly.

'Any callers?' he asked.

'The telephone, sir. A Mr Singer. He said you would not know him under that name, but you had met years ago. He thought you would remember him when you saw him.'

'What did he want?'

'Just to talk to you. He is in Cairns now. Said if you did not ring, he would drive out to see you.'

'When?'

'He did not say, sir. But I had the impression he meant fairly soon.'

'If he comes, tell him I'm away. I am not at home. I am *never* at home to him. He is a bad man. I do not want to see him. Ever. Do you understand?'

As the man inclined his head to show that he did, Robinson made up his mind. He had one move left that would give him a fighting chance of survival. He did not trust the police, any police. And he had no political pull. Also, Dr Love was due to arrive within days. He must put him off, ask him to postpone his visit. This would leave him on his own to deal with these two unwelcome arrivals. His mind would be uncluttered. He could not cope with a stranger here when he had so much to do. Robinson picked up the telephone, dictated a cable. Then he poured himself a brandy, drank it neat, and another one after that.

CHAPTER SIX

THE PRESENT: ALICE SPRINGS, AYERS ROCK,
NORTHERN TERRITORY; CAIRNS, NORTH
QUEENSLAND, AUSTRALIA

At a time when people can fly to the moon and litter its craters with empty soft drink bottles, Love still secretly found it remarkable that an aircraft carrying several hundred passengers could shrink distances across the world more quickly than a fashionable psychiatrist can diminish the size of a rich patient's head and bank account.

He did not voice this belief too frequently, of course. It seemed rather anachronistic, when the children of his richer patients thought nothing of flying from London to New York by Concorde to meet their parents for lunch, and still be back home in time for supper and a late film on TV.

But although the jet engine had shortened long journeys so dramatically in terms of time, the distance covered remained the same, and so, in Love's opinion, did the pressures of travel on the human body. Agreed, one might save days or weeks in the time taken, but how many weeks or months – or even years – did airline passengers subtract from their life expectation as a result? The answer did not figure prominently in holiday advertisements. Nevertheless, he believed it was still a part of the equation of speed versus wear on the human frame; perhaps, indeed, the most important part.

Love did not know quite what to expect in Australia. On the flight to Perth he had absorbed a plethora of unrelated, isolated guide-book facts. Australia was the world's largest island and its smallest continent. Distances were so enormous that Darwin was nineteen hundred kilometres from Denpasar in Indonesia but three thousand two hundred kilometres from Sydney – and roughly the same distance from Adelaide as to Jakarta.

Even so, in a country where cattle stations were not measured by acres or hectares but in thousands of square miles, Love was surprised to read that some land in the Outback was so poor that forty acres were required to graze one sheep. Several of his patients in Wiltshire owned farms not much larger, and somehow managed to support a family on the profits. Here, a farmer might require a station approaching the size of Wales to do the same.

Love liked the plain, blunt names that told of harsher pioneering days: Cape Catastrophe, Lake Disappointment, Ninety Mile Beach. As a doctor, he also noted that because the sun was so strong, Australians with fair skins suffered the world's highest rate of skin cancer. Aborigines had their own pharmacopoeia, but because they did not keep written records, and instead handed down knowledge verbally from father to son, many ancient remedies had been lost. However, one specific, hyoscine, taken from the corkwood tree, had not. Hyoscine played a vital part in the 1944 invasion of Normandy during the Second World War. Allied troops were given hyoscine pills as a specific against sea-sickness on the rough Channel crossing.

After the cool, up-to-date, uncrowded and air-conditioned opulence of Perth airport, Alice Springs was something else altogether: flat aluminium walls, a humming air-conditioning plant. The airport harked back to a recent pioneering past, but was still alert to the future growth of tourism. The atmosphere was cheerful, friendly, uncomplicated. This seemed more typical of the Australia he had imagined

Travellers, waiting for aircraft or buses to take them into town, known as The Alice, or on to Ayers Rock, paced the floor, glancing at their watches or at a blackboard on which someone had chalked the local weather report: 'Fine. What else? 41 degrees.'

Freephones lined the wall for such hostelries as the White Gum Holiday Inn, and the Heavitree Gap Motel. Love picked up a tourist magazine, glanced casually at the advertisements. Escort agencies offered 'attractive and sensuous ladies . . .', 'class and discretion assured . . .', 'luscious ladies at your call'. There was sunrise ballooning with a champagne breakfast. Restaurants served buffalo steak and kangaroo soup. He wondered whether the Stuart Auto Museum had a Cord on exhibition, and was sorry he could not stay to find out. All seemed very different from Nevil Shute's description in 'A Town Like Alice' so many years ago.

Most of the visitors around him would be out of place in that older, rougher Alice, but then, like Love, they were not locals. They were Americans in dacron suits, young people wearing jeans, retired British couples visiting sons and daughters, and everywhere ubiquitous Japanese and Chinese strung with cameras and video machinery.

Many Qantas passengers from London, going on to Ayers Rock, were catching an Ansett NT flight that only took forty-five minutes, but Love wanted to see something of the country about which Colonel Wargrave had told him so often. He waited while a vast, blue and white coach manoeuvred into position outside the airport, then climbed in. Seats filled up rapidly. Then the driver addressed his passengers.

'We'll have a comfort stop in ninety minutes,' he assured them, above the background hum of the air-conditioning system. 'That'll relieve any of you suffering from the crossed leg syndrome.'

Thus reassured, everyone settled back in seats as large as armchairs to sleep, to read, or to watch the red desert stream past on either side of the Stuart Highway.

This road ran for 1524 kilometres, with only the slightest curves, from Alice Springs to Darwin, the capital of the Northern Territory in the 'Top End'. It was named after John McDouall Stuart who, in the mid-19th century, was the first man to cross Australia from South to North, an epic journey that took him three years. Now, an aircraft took three hours, a coach barely as many days.

The desert stretched, empty and unforgiving, an immense and seemingly immeasurable expanse of red angry earth, as though millions of firebricks had been ground to a burning, choking dust that trailed behind every truck and coach. Here and there, clumps of spinifex and melons sprouted at the roadside, coated with this fine abrasive powder.

Years earlier, long before the road was built, or the railway laid, regular camel caravans used this track. Their Afghan drivers brought sacks of melons with them. As they rode or walked beside their camels, they would chew slices of melon and spit out the seeds. These clumps of melons were their memorial. So was the name affectionately given to the railway – the Ghan. When the Afghans went home, they left their camels behind. Now, more than thirty thousand roamed wild. Some were rounded up from time to time and exported to the Middle East.

Here and there, half a mile ahead of the coach, a kangaroo loped across the tarmac road, paused to see whether it was being pursued, and then waited, head cocked on one side, until the coach went by. The only other vehicles were road trains. Huge trucks towed two or three trailers, forty-five metres from front 'roo bar' – for pushing stray kangaroos out of the way – to the end tailboard. These vehicles were so long and unwieldy they could not negotiate any but the gentlest curve; and so ran between vast parking yards outside towns along the route.

Soon the coach swung off the Stuart Highway on to another, the Lasseter. This was named after Harold Lasseter who, in 1930, led an expedition to find a legendary reef of gold believed to be out in the desert, with gold deposits worth sixty million pounds – about two billion by today's values. His search was beset with misfortunes and mistakes; he did not find any gold, only an early grave.

As Lasseter lay dying from dysentery, tended by local Aborigines, he wrote sadly: 'What good a reef worth millions?

I would give it all for a loaf of bread . . . I am paying the penalty with my life. May it be a lesson to others.'

Ironically, the local casino was called Lasseters.

The coach stopped at the roadside and a cloud of red dust instantly overwhelmed it. The driver kept the engine running to power the air-conditioning system. When he opened the doors heat rushed in like a blast from a newly stoked furnace. Passengers queued for the driver to open a trap door in the side of the vehicle and serve them with plastic cups of iced water. One passenger, a heavily built man in his forties, travelling alone, turned to Love.

'Going far?' he asked him.

'Ayers Rock,' Love replied. 'And you?'

'The same,' he said. 'Then I fly on to Darwin and Hong Kong. Your first visit here?'

'Yes,' agreed Love.

'Mine, too. Very impressive. So much space and – what I like – so few people.'

As he spoke, he took a small bottle from his jacket pocket, shook a tiny white pill into his hand, put it under his tongue. Love recognised the movement, glanced at the label on the bottle: glyceryl trinitrate. The man noticed his glance.

'Angina,' he explained. 'I take one as soon as I get a pain in my chest.'

'Very wise,' said Love.

'You recommend them, then?'

'I am a doctor,' Love explained.

'I know,' the man replied. 'I saw the name tag on your luggage.'

They all climbed back into the coach, which ploughed on through the shimmering heat. Gradually, in the distance, Love could see a brighter lighter red glow above the earth, like a setting sun. This, the driver explained, was Ayers Rock. To one side fluttered what appeared to be a mass of triangular white sails, as though a fleet of galleons had somehow become land-locked. Closer to, they were revealed as a complex arrangement of huge canvas shields built above the Sheraton and the Four Seasons hotels to shelter them from the baking heat.

The hotels were built, like Australia, on a giant scale. Space was of no consequence and their architects had made full use of this. Swing doors admitted not one, but eight people at a time. The entrance foyer was the size of a tennis court. Rooms were arranged in a hollow square two storeys high around a swimming pool. Love was glad to find that his room, No. 11, overlooked this pool; he looked forward to a swim.

As he started to unpack, he heard a faint knock on the door, opened it. An under-manager stood outside.

'I'm sorry, Dr Love,' he said apologetically. 'I hope it will not inconvenience you overly if we ask you to move to a better room – a suite, in fact?'

'This room seems OK to me,' Love replied. He did not fancy making a move; he had already been travelling for too long.

'I am pleased to hear that, Doctor, but I have to tell you that this room is held on constant reservation for a regular guest. I am very sorry it was given to you in error by a new member of our staff, who did not realise this.

'The room I would suggest you take is actually a suite – twice as commodious. I understand this is your first visit to Australia, so it will be our pleasure to accommodate you in it, as I say, at no extra cost.'

'As a half-Scot and a lapsed Presbyterian,' said Love, 'I suppose that's a pleasure I cannot deny you.'

A porter moved his luggage. Love then swam twenty lazy lengths of the pool, and spent the rest of the afternoon lying on a lounger under a sun shade, thinking kindly thoughts about Colonel Wargrave and his generosity.

A coach for Ayers Rock left at ten o'clock next morning, the driver smart in white shirt and socks, blue shorts, highly polished black shoes. A dozen tourists climbed in, mostly people who had come on from The Alice. They greeted each other with the enthusiasm of travellers glad to see familiar faces.

Within a couple of miles, the driver turned off the main tarmac road on to a rough track, corrugated like a giant washboard.

'Just to let you know we're going to keep our speed about seventy kilometres an hour,' he explained. 'If we go any slower, these bumps will shake the coach to pieces and make your false teeth drop out. So if you're wearing 'em, put 'em in a pocket, or in your purse, in case. Then you can say, as the old husband said to his young bride on their wedding night, "Hand me my teeth, I want to bite you."'

As he spoke, he accelerated. The road was wide, banked on either side. Red dust trailed behind them like a travelling cloud. Here and there, as it thinned, Love could see the desert, dotted by clumps of spinifex, acacia, honey grevillea. The heat outside was soon intense. There was no wind. Leaves on eucalyptus trees, and clumps of spiky grass were all curiously still, like scenery painted against the stage background of a cobalt sky.

Close to, Ayers Rock soared up almost vertically, a cliff face scarred by fissures, wrinkled like a gigantic brain. It seemed to exude a pounding aura of tremendous, incalculable power, as though this was some living extension of the universe, not simply a giant rock. Somehow liquid fire at the heart of the earth had spewed out this huge rock under enormous pressure and heat. Red as newly shed blood from oxidised iron in its make-up, Love realised instantly why, for thousands of years, Aborigines had been so impressed that they considered this rock a sacred place.

Against its pulsating, immeasurable strength, hinted at in every coruscation, other holy places he had seen dedicated to other religions – cathedrals, temples, mosques – seemed small and puny. In many other lands – Africa, India, Russia – the earth had vomited out crystallised carbon in a cascade of diamonds. Here, it had produced the ultimate symbol of power and latent energy; this was the Red Centre of Australia – and possibly of the whole world.

As they approached, sunlight glittered on glass windows

in rows of empty coaches, parked up against concrete blocks painted red to match the earth. Their passengers were either up on the Rock or walking around its perimeter. Love saw a notice, warning visitors about the dangers of attempting to climb Ayers Rock if they suffered from heart or circulatory problems.

'There's no First Aid,' the driver explained. 'And fifteen people have died here so far, mostly because they just weren't fit enough to attempt the climb. It may not look so steep from here, but when you're up there on the Rock, you'll think differently.

'For those who don't want to climb, we'll drive round the base, and I'll show you some of the caves sacred to the Aborigines. There's one where women go to give birth to their children, tended by an Aboriginal midwife. Another, the initiation cave, is where men tell the boys what every man should know. A third has its own water hole – but Abos won't drink from it. They say it's polluted.

'In the last century, a pioneer – William Christie Gosse – the white man who first discovered the Rock, bathed there, and they believe that ruined it for ever, so far as they're concerned. So, be warned. This is holy ground you're on.

'Its Abo name is *Uluru*, which means a shady place, though when you're up on the Rock that feels hot as a branding iron, you'll wonder why. It's the bottom that's shady, that's the point. Know what the Abos call the climbers? Mad white ants, that's what.

'On top, it's very, very windy. So if you make it and your hat blows off – let it go. Don't try to go after it. Remember, there's only one safe way down, and that's the way you went up. So, good on you, and take care. It's a long slow climb – a very quick drop if you lose your balance!'

The coach doors opened automatically with a hiss of compressed air. The tourists climbed out awkwardly, stood staring at the Rock only feet away, raw red against the sky.

A track, with a chain fixed on iron poles driven into the rock as a handrail alongside it, led up to the first peak. People were climbing up this path slowly and steadily, some painfully, in single file, holding on to this chain, pausing now and then to look back at the view, and regain their breath.

Love set off. At first, the Rock was smooth. The shoes of thousands of tourists had coated its rough surface with a fine patina of rubber and leather. But the higher Love climbed, the rougher the Rock became. A number of older climbers wisely gave up after fifty or a hundred yards. They suddenly declared loudly that they had no head for heights, and the Rock seemed so steep when they looked down – or up – that they became disorientated. They returned thankfully to the cool safe cocoons of their air-conditioned coaches.

At first, the other tourists still climbing chattered brightly to each other, remarking on the path's steepness, how fit or unfit they found they were. Gradually, such comments withered and then stopped completely. They needed all their breath for the climb.

A wind, non-existent at ground level, now began to blow. The higher they climbed, the stronger this wind became. Soon it was flattening their clothes against their bodies, bringing tears to their eyes, making speech impossible.

Far beneath them, the desert stretched away to meet the sky in a red haze of heat. Toy trucks and coaches pulled tiny fronds of dust along roads as thin as cotton threads.

Finally, Love reached the top. The Rock was not flat as he had imagined. Instead, it contained gullies, caves, giant fissures. Here and there, from seeds dropped by birds, tough shrubs had grown, and now bent obediently before the driving wind.

He stood, breathing the clear air deeply, admiring the view. Other passengers from the coach now began to go down to ground level. They had proved they could reach the top; and there was no more to see than they could glimpse from an aircraft. It all seemed something of an anticlimax. They were already thinking of the coach's next stop. As they climbed down they held tightly on to the chain. The track seemed more slippery now; or maybe this was because they were tired?

Love turned to follow them, then saw a small movement in one of the deeper crevices, about twenty yards away. The man who had spoken to him at the comfort stop on the previous day was in the crevice on his hands and knees, clearly in great pain. His camera dangled from its strap round his neck. He seemed to be gasping for breath. Love remembered his admission that he suffered from angina, hurried across to him.

'I should never have tried to climb this,' the man gasped when he saw him. 'In my jacket pocket, I've got my pills. But I can't reach them. Oh, the pain . . . Can you help me, Doctor?'

'Of course,' said Love calmly. 'You'll be all right. Nothing to worry about.'

Love put his hand in the man's jacket pocket, wondering how he could get him down to ground level. He glanced behind him to see whether any others of their group were still here, who might help him. But they had all gone. He and the man were alone, in a howling gale.

As Love turned, the man also swung round in a quick lithe movement, not the feeble reaction of an ill man in agony. He hit Love hard on the jaw. Love fell to one side, rolled over – and began to slide across the sloping face of the Rock. Steadily, he gathered speed.

Love spat out blood from a loosened tooth as he tried desperately to dig the toes of his shoes into any crack or cleft before his speed increased. He could not find one. He flattened his hands against the Rock, seeking for a fingerhold.

He felt the Rock move, rough and cold under his palms, as he slid faster and faster down the slope. Then suddenly the tip of his left shoe found a small hole and he steadied himself, swinging in a circle, pivoting on his foot.

The man must have had a spasm of some kind, he thought. He must get back to him in case he was also sliding, and in his physical condition was unable to gain a toe-hold.

Love pulled himself slowly, painfully, across the pumice-like surface. The path down the Rock was on the far side from him. The two men were alone, out of sight and sound of anyone else. Love could see him, crouched in the crevice, watching him – and suddenly Love realised with shock and horror the man was not ill at all.

He was not suffering from a cardiac or any other spasm. The man's action had been simple and direct, inspired by one intention: he wished to kill Love. Why, or for what conceivable purpose, Love had no idea. He did not even know his attacker's name. But none of these points was important now. The only thing that mattered was that man to man, up on top of this gigantic rock, with the wind screaming across it, blowing breath from his body, he had to survive by his own efforts – or he would die. No-one else was near, no-one else could help him.

As Love paused for breath, the man brought up his camera to his eyes, pointed it at Love. What the devil was he up to? Love wondered. Was he going to photograph him to use as some kind of proof that Love was fighting him?

Some inner instinct warned him he could not allow this, however innocent the action might appear.

Summoning all his strength, Love brought up his knees, and from this crouching position, he took a leap forward. The man was waiting for him, and dodged to one side. He hit out at Love again. But now Love was prepared and rode the blow. They grappled together, rolling over side by side in the crevice, wide as a shallow grave. The man crooked one arm behind Love's neck and tried to smash his head down on the Rock.

Love wriggled free, hit the man a scything blow across the side of his neck with the edge of his right hand and seized his arm. The man choked, gasped for breath, attempted to stand up, grabbed his camera again, tried desperately to point it at Love.

Above and around them, the wind howled with the strength of a storm at sea. Far beneath them, passengers from another coach were slowly beginning to climb the Rock, holding on to the chain, turning back to admire the view.

The man flung himself at Love, in an attempt to free his arm and to knock Love off balance before any others arrived on top to see them. He managed to bring up his camera, held it within a foot of Love's face. For a second, time stood still. Love could see a dark round hole just beneath the lens and realised what it was: the mouth of a concealed pistol, the opening of a tunnel to eternity. He flung himself to one side.

The bullet missed his head by inches, grazing his left ear. Love seized the camera's strap, wrenched it off the man's shoulder. The buckle broke. Love's attacker reached out instinctively for the camera – and in his sudden involuntary lunge forward, lost his balance. He slipped and fell. His head hit the rock with a crack like a rifle shot. As both men began to slide away slowly, the first of the new arrivals reached the top and saw them.

'Hold on! Hold on!' one of them cried, imagining that they must have tripped. Several men came towards them, bent double against the driving wind, moving carefully in case they also lost their balance. The man began to slide away on his own, slowly at first, and then faster.

He gave a great cry of alarm and despair as the wind filled his jacket. For a second he seemed to swell like a balloon. Then he was gone, turning over and over in the air as he fell.

The tourists reached Love and knelt by his side, panting for breath with their exertions, middle-aged faces creased with worry and concern.

'What happened?' one asked Love.

Love shrugged wearily, sick with reaction.

'I am a doctor,' he explained. 'He said he had a heart problem, and when I went to help him, he attacked me. Must have affected his brain, I think.'

'Are you all right?' the man asked him anxiously.

'I will be,' Love assured him. 'The long habit of living indisposeth us for dying.'

'Pardon me?'

'Something another doctor wrote, name of Thomas Browne.'

'Oh. Still got your camera. Bit bashed about, though. Still, you can claim on the insurance, eh?'

Love nodded, stood up and began to walk down the path, grateful for the chain to help him keep his balance.

In the coach park, the driver had been speaking on his walkie-talkie to an official on the other side of the Rock.

'Lucky he didn't take you with him, Doctor,' he said.

'He wasn't with our lot, was he?' Love asked him.

'No way. He was in the hotel, though. Came up from The Alice in the coach with you. Drove out here in a self-drive car. Someone else's problem to drive it back now. Not that he'll be worrying about that, where he is, eh? You think he lost his marbles?'

Love shrugged.

'Something like that,' he agreed. 'Heart trouble can have odd side effects.'

'So can the height. If you ask me, that blew his mind. I've seen blokes go berserk up there. It's a kind of panic. And maybe the Rock's to blame. Charged with electricity, the whole thing. Puts some people's watches out – as well as the people who're wearing them.'

Love climbed into the coach, sat back thankfully. The other passengers had heard there had been an accident, but did not know the details and did not want to ask. They looked at him sympathetically: this would be something unusual to tell the stay-at-homes in Penge and Des Moines when they invited them round to see their holiday videos.

Love's key was not on its hook at the reception desk.

'Friend of yours is waiting for you in your room,' the clerk explained. 'I heard you tried to save a man from jumping off the Rock. Good on you.'

Love said nothing. This seemed a reasonable enough explanation, if not the true one. But then Pilate had asked: 'What is truth?' And if he didn't know, why should a country physician enlighten anyone?

Love went to his room. The door was unlocked. Sitting in

an easy chair facing him, with two large glasses of rum and lime juice on a side table, was Richard Mass Parkington. As Love came in, he handed one glass to him, raised his own in a toast.

'For medicinal purposes. Physician, heal thyself. And judging by the state of your clothes, it's lucky you're still perpendicular and not a horizontal man – like the other guy.'

Love closed the door, put his attacker's camera on a side table, sat down thankfully in a chair, took a long swig at the rum.

'What the hell are you doing here?' he asked Parkington.

They had last met a year earlier when Parkington, knowing Love's interest in Cord cars, had asked him to fly to Rawalpindi in Pakistan at the expense of the Midland Widows. Someone out there owned a Cord, and wished to insure it for ten million pounds. The sum seemed so large that Parkington felt there must be a special reason for specifying this value. Love, as an expert on the make, had agreed to try and discover what this was – and came close to losing his life in providing the answer.

'Me? Working in the best interests of the Midland Widows and their shareholders – God bless them every one,' Parkington explained.

'At Ayers Rock?'

'At Ayers Rock as ever is,' said Parkington. 'I missed you in Perth, as a matter of fact, by about a day. But then I heard you were here. We can't keep on meeting like this.'

'You're not offering me another assignment like in 'Pindi, are you?' Love asked him suspiciously.

'No way. I'm offering you nothing – except a drink, which I've already put on your bill. You hold a couple of largish life policies with the company. I know, because I sold them to you. And insurance companies never like to pay out. So I'm trying to save them losing money – and you losing your life.'

'How have you done that?'

'I'll tell you. But first, you tell me. Did you sleep well last night?'

'Perfectly. The management gave me a better room – a suite, in fact.'

'I know. I asked them to,' said Parkington. 'That's how I helped you. I saw the man on the coach you've just had a fight with on Ayers Rock. That's why.'

'You knew him, then?'

'Of him. When he had a drink at the bar here last night, I took his empty glass. The Australian Security people checked out his prints.'

As he spoke, there was a knock at the door. Parkington crossed the room, opened it. A messenger handed in a brown envelope. Parkington took out an envelope of similar size from his briefcase, opened them both. Each contained blown-up photographs of fingerprints. Parkington took a magnifying glass from his case, examined them closely, handed the glass to Love.

'What do you think?' he asked.

'They're the same,' said Love.

'Correct. The two on the left are those of the man who tried to kill you on Ayers Rock. One taken from his glass last night. The other from his body half an hour ago. The one on the right is also his. That was taken from the ignition key of a car used by a man he killed at St George's Castle – Castilho da St Jorge – outside Lisbon. Not a very pleasant job for the people who had to handle that body, I can tell you. It had been hidden under a tarpaulin in the heat for nearly a week – minus its ears and the little fingers of each hand. So see what a fate you missed.'

'Are you certain about this?'

'Absolutely. We know the pistol he shot him with.'

'Didn't that show up on the X-ray apparatus at airport checks?'

'No,' Parkington replied. 'It was built into that camera you've brought in. This showed up as metal, and so screened the tiny barrel inside it that could fire just one shot. All he needed. He was a pro, of course.

'The idea was to ask the victim if they would be kind

111

enough to pose while he took a photo. The view looks so much better with someone in it. And then, bang, he's dead.'

'Who was this man he killed in Lisbon?'

'A young Russian defector. There was some pointless bureaucratic hold-up about getting him into England. He was due to leave Lisbon in a couple of days. This man got to him first.'

'And who was he?'

'To be honest, I have absolutely no idea. He's here on a British passport, name of Hargreaves. Jack Hargreaves, so MacGillivray's people say. But the passport is almost certainly stolen or forged. He also has a Portuguese passport in his luggage. But who he really is, they're still working on. Incidentally, the doctors have done some tests. Apparently, he was suffering from leukaemia.'

'What did he do for a living?'

'Described on his passport as a businessman. What his business was, I don't know.'

'Will you?'

Parkington shrugged.

'Like I say, MacGillivray's people are working on it. The trouble is, they've so much else to work on, too. But there must be *some* link between a Russian defector murdered in Lisbon and you, here, nearly killed on Ayers Rock.'

'Tell me when you find out,' said Love. 'In the meantime, why did you get my room changed?'

Parkington crossed to a cupboard, opened it, took out a bolster. He threw this on the bed. A few small pieces of fluff fell out of a small hole.

'I thought he might have a pot shot at you, that's why. I'd followed him from Perth. When you booked in I suggested to the hotel you should change your room.

'When it was empty, I arranged this bolster in the bed to look like someone sleeping there, sheets over their head, and drew the curtains. He obligingly pumped a bullet into it. I know that because I checked it against the shot he fired in Lisbon.'

'But why want to kill *me*? I have nothing to do with any Russian defectors. I'm simply out here through the generosity of a patient who liked Australia, and who left me some money in his will on condition I spent it on a holiday here.'

'And for no other reason?'

'Well, one. I have been invited to visit an Australian in Cairns who shares my interest in Cord cars. But you still haven't told me why you are here, except in the most general terms?'

'I'm following your footsteps,' Parkington declared blandly. 'On my way to Cairns, I thought I couldn't come to Australia without seeing Ayers Rock.'

'So what's happening with you in Cairns?'

'Seeing a client.'

'To sell him a policy?'

'Not quite. But I may. I'm seeing a man there, name of Robinson.'

'Funny you should say that,' said Love, not smiling. 'So am I.'

In Cairns, Robinson had booked Love into the Trade Winds hotel, overlooking a wide promenade on the edge of the sea, the Esplanade. Flanked by long wide lawns, this road followed the curve of Trinity Bay along the shore. Love unpacked his one suitcase – he always travelled light – and sat on his balcony enjoying the sunshine. He wondered what Robinson would be like and tried, but unsuccessfully, to put from his mind the happenings on Ayers Rock.

Love had half expected that Robinson might be at the airport to meet him. But instead an airline steward handed him a sealed envelope as he came through immigration. This contained a single sheet of paper with one typed line: 'I will call at 1900 hours precisely.'

This seemed a rather curt way of describing arrangements for two total strangers to meet after a flight across the world, Love thought. But he decided he must not judge anyone or anything too soon.

Did Charles Robinson's note mean he would telephone at seven o'clock, or that he would arrive at the hotel at that hour? For some reason that Love could not analyse, he felt vaguely concerned by the ambiguity of the brusque note. Was this intentional – or did Robinson simply find it difficult to express himself clearly?

Love's plane could so easily have been delayed on its flight, but Robinson's note seemed to assume that when he made arrangements, he expected them to be kept. Nothing wrong with that, of course. Perhaps Robinson was a military man, accustomed to giving orders, and carrying them out, to a life run rigidly to time with no delays, no excuses? Even so, in this short note, Love detected a note of unease, an undercurrent of apprehension. Like someone who whistles in the dark, Robinson could wish to appear more confident, more in command than he felt. But then, in command of what – and why should this impression be required?

Love wondered whether he was reading too much into a seven word message. Yet he had interviewed too many patients over many years not to recognise minute signs of fear a layman might miss. There could be a reluctance on a patient's part to remember a certain name; the surprising and constant mis-spelling of a simple word that possessed some unrevealed importance to the person involved. Or, as here, an assumption that what they had decided must be agreed without question or quibble. These could all be signs of insecurity and inner worry – or of sheer physical fear.

Love sat, pondering the problem, looking at the view. The tide was on the ebb, and a mass of spiky grass and reeds grew in the sand it left behind. A flight of pelicans, attended by platoons of smaller birds, now came in to land on a stretch of shallow water. They strutted about importantly on the wet, shining sand, pecking at shrimps or worms.

As heat drained from the day, thousands of other birds began to chirp, twitter and sing unseen in trees around his hotel garden. Soon the whole garden sounded like a giant aviary filled with songbirds – an extraordinary and

114

most agreeable sensation. The sound of their songs totally obliterated all traffic noise.

Love had a shower, changed, poured four fingers of rum from the mini bar, added lime juice and ice. Thus refreshed, he went down to the front hall to await his host's appearance or telephone call. As in the hotel at Ayers Rock, the hall was built on a vast scale. Leather settees were dotted around a marble floor. Palm trees grew in an atrium. Although a number of people were in the shops and at the ticket desk, such was the hall's size and splendid proportions it still seemed almost empty.

Outside, beyond thick, soundproof glass doors, a stream of taxis arrived and departed. Airport buses disgorged one set of passengers festooned with cameras and overnight bags – and within minutes picked up another group on their way out to the airport for the next leg of their tour.

And then, at exactly seven o'clock, during a brief moment when the hotel approach was empty and the doors opened to allow a group of visitors to leave, Love heard the totally distinctive motor-boat rumble of a Cord exhaust. His heart quickened at the familiar sound.

Mr Robinson was on time. Love went out to meet him.

A Cord Sportsman two seater stood in the forecourt, glowing like a sculpture in metallic silver. Its scrubbed canvas hood was white as a yacht's mainsail. Robinson climbed out of the cockpit, shook hands. He had a firm grip, but was older than Love expected: a squat man, broad shouldered, with hard wary eyes, a tanned, leathery face.

He did not smile, and even as he greeted his visitor, his gaze seemed continually on the alert, now looking over Love's shoulder, now to one side or the other, as though searching for someone else he half expected, but had not yet seen.

'You're right on time,' said Love approvingly.

'I always am,' Robinson agreed simply. 'Climb in. I thought I'd show you my cars first. Then I hope you will have dinner with me.'

'That sounds great.'

115

There was no suggestion that Love might have any other ideas, any other plans. Charles Robinson had decided what should be done, therefore it must be done. But then, of course, that was surely only part of being a good host? Love was not usually so critical. Why, he wondered, was he niggling now about such obviously unimportant details?

As he sat down on the red, pleated leather seat facing the engine-turned stainless steel instrument panel, he wondered: could it be because these details were not altogether unimportant?

They could all be signs, pointing to a deeper concern which, as a physician, he felt he should recognise. And was it not just possible that one reason for Mr Robinson's invitation was to ask him to diagnose its cause – and maybe to cure it?

CHAPTER SEVEN

*THE PRESENT: CAIRNS,
NORTH QUEENSLAND, AUSTRALIA*

Robinson's house was some miles out of town, going north along the coast on the Captain Cook Highway – a long way by British standards, almost next door by the way Australians measured distance. Love noticed that many advertisements were in Japanese as well as English.

'They and the Chinese own about forty per cent of the land,' Robinson explained when he remarked on this. 'The Japs failed in their bid to take us over in 1942. But they sure have done pretty well since. And more are coming in all the time. When the Chinese government finally takes over Hong Kong, there'll be a huge influx. They're mostly good people, but it's who they bring with them who aren't so good. The Tongs. The Triads.'

'That worries you?'

'My wife was Chinese,' Robinson explained. 'She warned me about them. Otherwise I'd never have imagined their influence worldwide. But every Chinese take-away, restaurant, laundry, what-have-you, anywhere in the world pays their percentage. Either that or they go under. Some try and fight. But . . .'

Robinson shrugged dismissively.

In the blue distance, to their left, a long spine of mountains, the Great Dividing Range, wore haloes of cloud. The air felt sweet with the scent of frangipani and wild ginger. Some houses were built of timber, and stood high up on stilts, with cars and utes – utilities – parked under them.

'That's so crocodiles can't climb up and join the party,' explained Robinson with a grin. 'Fact is, some of the worst crocs around walk on two legs instead of four.'

'That's your experience?' Love asked him.

'Isn't it everyone's?' retorted Robinson, suddenly sour, his grin vanishing. Love noted that his smile was not an expression of humour, only a muscular grimace. He smiled with his mouth, not his eyes.

Then Love looked more closely at his face. Tiny wrinkles around his eyes, a tight fold of flesh under his chin were not the natural marks of age. They were artificial. Mr Robinson had undergone extensive surgery to his face. Close to, and knowing the signs to watch for – little tucks in the skin, a tightening here, an unexpected paleness there – his face seemed more like a mask.

Had Robinson been injured in some fearful car accident – or had he been wounded in a war? This was clearly not the time to ask. Many people with a disfigurement or surgical scar on their faces felt awkward about them, even when with a doctor. Perhaps this disfigurement, only partly concealed or obliterated, was the reason for Robinson's strange manner? Perhaps this was the matter he wanted to discuss?

They drove in silence for a moment. The only sound was the heavy thrum of the Cord's fat white-wall tyres on the hard road, the faint boom of its two exhausts.

'Where does this road lead?' asked Love, making conversation.

'About sixty odd kilometres on is Port Douglas. Originally, that was intended to be a major port for North Queensland in the gold rush in the last century. Then Cairns was chosen to be the r : 'erminus for the mining towns, and Port Douglas languis! ..

'Lots of retired people live up there now and it's a great tourist place. Good hotels, first-class restaurants, a marina. You can take a cruise to the Great Barrier Reef, and yachts the equal of anything you'll ever see on the French Riviera or in the Caribbean are moored there. I've got one myself moored further up the coast. Not quite the biggest, but still a beaut boat.

'Beyond Port Douglas, going north, you come to Cooktown. Like the highway, it's named after Captain Cook who discovered and then charted the whole of Australia's east coast in the 18th century. One day his ship, the *Endeavour*, struck a reef, now called Endeavour Reef. He beached there, and that's the site of Cooktown.

'Cook felt this could really be where his serious troubles started, so he called the promontory Cape Tribulation. Actually, he was too pessimistic. But it's a wise man, Dr Love, who accepts his troubles are only about to begin – and how he must surmount them.'

'I would agree,' said Love.

'Agreeing is one thing. Doing is another,' Robinson replied shortly.

'You sound as though you have some troubles yourself?'

'Haven't we all, Doctor? What does Job say? Man is born to trouble as the sparks fly upward.'

He swung the wheel sharply over to the left. Tyres squealed as the heavy car left the main highway. They were on a narrow road, cut through fields of sugar cane, leading towards distant foothills, going away from the sea. Here and there, red roofs of isolated dwellings stuck out from the mass of green cane. They stopped outside one of the larger houses.

'My place,' said Robinson. He switched off the engine. 'The end of the line, Doctor.'

They climbed out. The air felt cooler here. Behind them, beyond the fields and the highway, the ocean lay like a strip of polished pewter. Cars and trucks moved up and down the road. Brightly coloured tourist coaches flashed past with a glitter of reflected sunlight from tinted windows. A faint blare of air horns sounded clear as bugles.

Love felt relaxed. The feeling of great space, of emptiness all around, produced a profound sensation of ease and calm he had never experienced in England. There, tasteless developments of executive-style luxury homes – why were they never simply called houses? – always seemed just over every horizon. Too often, the countryside was only one tree thick. Here, it stretched to illimitable distance and people reacted accordingly; they had room to move, room to live.

'I see from your face you're just realising this is a hell of a big country,' said Robinson, watching him closely. 'All visitors from Europe take time to understand just how big it is. I know I did. Queensland is Australia's second largest State – a quarter of the whole country. That means that Queensland alone is seven times the size of Britain, four and a half times as big as Japan or Germany. A great place – and without too many people.'

'That's what someone else told me he liked about it – so few people,' Love replied, remembering the remark of the man on Ayers Rock. 'Is it the same with you?'

Robinson nodded slowly.

'One reason,' he agreed. 'You want to see the cars now?'

'I'd be pleased to. After all, that's why you asked me here.'

'How right. I apologise if I sound a bit short, but I've had some very worrying news recently. Rather set me back. Matter of fact, I cabled your home in England, asking if you could postpone your visit for a while until I could get things sorted out here.'

'I'm sorry. I didn't receive that cable, or I would have done so. Nothing wrong with your health, I hope?'

'Not specifically, Doctor. But I needn't tell you that every serious problem affects one's health to *some* extent. Some can even affect your life.'

'Does yours?'

'I'll consider that question – and my answer to it – when I know you better.'

Love shrugged. The man was very worried about something, that much was clear. So Love's first impression had been right – as first impressions usually were. He would wait and see whether Robinson asked directly for his help. Meanwhile, Love felt he was intruding here into some private problem, and he had no wish to do so. Robinson's attitude seemed in total contrast to his letters – but the cause was no concern of his.

'A drink?'

His host's question cut into his thoughts.

'Delighted,' said Love. 'Rum, if you have it.'

'I have it. And whisky, gin, vodka. Did you know, Australians are the highest consumers of alcohol in the English-speaking world?'

'I thought Poles and Russians held that distinction.'

Robinson frowned.

'Then you thought wrong, Doctor. They are not in the English-speaking world. I qualified my statement deliberately. Do I make myself clear?'

'Perfectly. I stand corrected.'

They went into the house. A large cool room with matt white walls opened from a wide verandah. A few bland, characterless prints of English gardens and thatched cottages added some weak colour. Rambling roses covered a front porch; a tiny fountain cascaded into an ornamental pond. All were of a world away from Cairns, an idealised view of England. They could have been cut out from calendars, or the tops of chocolate boxes. There were no books in the room, and no photographs. Altogether, it seemed as clinically impersonal as an airport departure lounge or Love's own waiting room.

Whoever lived here took care that their personality could not be judged or assessed by individualistic decorations or possessions. No-one looking around this room could discover anything about Mr Robinson's character, his tastes – or his past. Was this accidental – or deliberate?

For a brief moment, Love was reminded of The Hall in his own village. Of course, this was immaculate in contrast to the seedy decrepitude of Mrs Green's house, but both dwellings were houses rather than homes. Hers seemed like the last refuge of a lonely, possibly frightened, rich woman. Was Mr Robinson's house anything more than a luxurious staging post on a sunlit journey for another lonely, rich and frightened man – leading where?

Robinson mixed a rum and lime juice, again without asking whether Love wanted the drink served this way, poured a large MacAllan for himself, raised his glass to drink the spirit neat.

'To Cord fanciers everywhere,' he said gruffly. Love nodded. They drank.

'Lived here long?' Love asked him.

'Almost long enough,' said Robinson shortly. 'I believe in moving on. I was in Perth for a time. Then Katherine, doing some real estate ventures. Still have a house there. Then, Darwin.

'A cyclone in the mid seventies absolutely devastated Darwin. Population dropped from forty seven thousand to about half that number in a matter of days. It's been rebuilt now, of course. Very smart. I've still got some businesses in Darwin. But I felt I'd had enough of it from the point of view of living there permanently. It's hot and humid – and the cyclone might pay another call. So I came on up here. Thought I'd give this a whirl.'

'What's your job?'

'All sorts. Property. Finance. I run several garages. We have agencies for Japanese and German cars. And just recently I've gone into the scrap metal business.'

'You have obviously been very successful in your enterprises.'

'Ever seen the Queensland coat of arms, Doctor? No? Well, they feature an emu and a kangaroo. Both animals that can only go forward, never back. Advance, never retreat. I've followed that doctrine.'

'And you've always been interested in cars?'

'The answer is, yes. I started off as a mechanic. Then –' Mr Robinson shrugged his shoulders expansively – or could it be evasively? 'Then, as I grew older, I became less interested in crawling about under them, and having old bolts shear and bits of rusty metal fall on my face. The beauty of owning service stations if you own any old cars is that you always have people to do that sort of work for you. After all, I did it for a long time myself. Maybe for too long.'

As the whisky loosened his tongue slightly, Robinson's accent changed slightly from its broad Australian twang. It was not English now, but then what was it? South African? German?

'You grew up here?' Love asked him.

'No,' said Robinson, shaking his head. 'I emigrated from England ten years ago this very summer.'

He did not say where in England he had lived, or if he had been born there, and for some reason, Love did not want to ask him. He sensed that for reasons Mr Robinson was unlikely to explain, he was secretive about his origins. He did not answer questions as much as circumnavigate them. Maybe he was following Captain Cook's ability to avoid rocks – after hitting one? Robinson's replies seemed to relate to questions he had not been asked.

Again, they stood for a moment, not speaking. Silence hung like a shroud between them.

'Well,' said Robinson at last, finishing his whisky. 'You'd better come and look at the motors. Then I'd like you to meet my daughter, and we'll have a bite to eat. Now, drink up, and we'll go out.'

'I'll take it with me,' said Love; he did not care to be hurried.

He followed Robinson out of the house, across a concrete yard behind it. To the left was a set of high wooden gates, with metal strengthening bars behind them. Opposite this, on the right, a vine had been trained across a blank brick wall. Ahead, lay a single storey building. Robinson took from his pocket a small plastic carton, the size of a box of matches, pressed a button on its side. Doors on the building slid open electronically and silently.

'We're pretty secluded here,' he explained. 'Thieving could

be easy, so I built the garage where it's very hard to reach if you're uninvited. If anyone wants to steal one of my old cars, first they have to get into the property. To discourage them, I have electronic locks on the gates across the drive. They were open when we came in, so you probably didn't notice them.

'Then, they'd still have to cross this yard to reach the garage. And the gate and these doors have their own alarms. So I hope we will keep them at bay.'

'Who, exactly?'

'Who? Why, any bloke who thinks he can make a few thousand dollars by driving one of my Cords away. Who else?'

Mr Robinson made the question sound belligerent. He's not so much worried about the cars, Love thought. He is worried about himself. All these defences were not to protect the cars, but to protect him. But from whom – or what?

Mr Robinson pressed a switch on the inside wall of the garage. The ceiling immediately sprang into brilliant light from a dozen fluorescent tubes. In their shadeless glare six Cords faced Love. He had not seen so many in one place since he attended a meet of the Auburn-Cord-Duesenberg Club in the United States a couple of years previously.

Then, several owners, who took extremely seriously competing for a prize in the *concours d'elegance*, wore suits cut from cloth the same colour as their cars. These were all so highly restored and polished that they were not for driving, only for admiring.

They had ceased to be vehicles and were elevated to the status of heirlooms or totems; expensive talking points on wheels. What once had been an old car, fit only for the breaker's yard, was now collateral in steel and leather, chromium plate and canvas, with a value in millions.

Such showpieces were not allowed to move under their own power, but were carried to shows and what were called 'static displays' on trailers and transporters. Several owners brought their own personal mechanics to the meet with pots of paint and camel hair brushes to touch up any minute scratch or blemish that might somehow have appeared on their particular car during its journey.

The Cords in Robinson's garage were totally different. They were cars to drive, not simply to admire. They were old, agreed, but all possessed the brute force of heavyweight boxers, champions in retirement. And, as the Cord advertisements used to stress in the 1930s, 'No-one ever pushes a champion around'.

There were two saloons, a fixed-head coupé, a roadster like his own, and the one that had brought him from the hotel, and a rare L29. This early example of Mr Cord's engineering ingenuity was so-called because its engine had what then was known as an L-shaped cylinder head, and the car was first marketed in 1929, just before the Wall Street crash.

This particular model also had a much unadvertised peculiarity; a strong reluctance to climb steep hills in rain or on slippery roads. As with all Cords, an eight cylinder engine drove the car's front wheels, but since in this model the cylinders were in line, instead of V formation, there was much less weight on the front wheels. Thus, with a full load in bad weather, the wheels could not always gain traction on even a gentle hill and would simply spin uselessly.

Love walked from car to car, as Robinson explained where he had bought each one, and what restoration work he had carried out.

'When did you first become interested in Cords?' Love asked him. In his experience, men usually found a car or a girl attractive if their looks had appealed to them at puberty. Was this the case with Mr Robinson – as it had been with him?

Robinson shook his head.

'No,' he said. 'I was older. In my early twenties. There was a Cord in the garage where I worked. It fascinated me. It was so low, whereas all the other cars were high and box-shaped with spidery wheels and headlights sticking out like an insect's eyes. The Cord instantly made them all old-fashioned. It always looked fast – even when standing still.'

'In England, was this?'

'No-o. I forget now, where exactly. A long time ago. I've worked in a number of places, you know. I'm no spring chicken.'

Again, it was clear he would not be drawn, and Love did not want to appear too inquisitive.

'You're probably tired after your flight,' said Mr Robinson. 'There's plenty of time. No need to rush things. Now you've thrown an eyeball over them, come in and let's have something to eat.'

A table was laid for two in another room. A young Chinese manservant served barramundi, a white fish cut into large firm steaks, with Tyrell's Long Flat White wine; cheese, coffee, brandy. Robinson glanced up at him questioningly each time he placed a dish before him. The manservant nodded almost imperceptibly, and only then would Robinson begin to eat.

When they had finished, a girl came into the room. She was tall, dark haired. She wore long silver earrings that jingled as she moved, a white blouse and slacks. She was one of the most beautiful women Love had ever seen. Her face was serene, with a faint touch of the Orient about her eyes. She was part Malaysian or Javanese or Chinese, he thought, and this added delicacy to her skin and her features.

'Ah, my daughter,' said Robinson. 'Camille, this is Jason Love, the doctor from England who also owns a Cord.'

'I'm so glad you arrived,' said Camille.

Her voice sounded soft as a distant string orchestra. They shook hands.

Love usually appeared off-hand with women, except for one, Maureen, in a past he rarely cared to recall. Too often they seemed to him to be an expensive distraction, as he had seen many times with married friends. But Camille was the first in a long time to attract him instantly.

'Did you think I might not arrive?' he asked Camille.

She shrugged.

'I didn't know. Sometimes my father has invited people to come and look at his cars, and they agree. Arrangements are made, and then they cry off at the last minute. People are like that.'

'Not me,' said Love.

She looked at him quizzically, smiled.

'Can you prove that?'

'I hope I won't have to,' said Love. 'But I think I could. Do you drive these cars?'

'No. It's odd to have to admit it, but I don't drive. I like driving *in* them though. They're fun. Unusual. But I don't hold them in such esteem as my father.'

She leaned over and kissed Robinson on the cheek, sat down at the table.

'What are your plans, apart from looking at Daddy's cars?' Camille asked Love.

'I hope I may be able to drive one or two of them,' he said. 'Perhaps I could give you a few driving lessons?'

Camille smiled, a gentle yet secretive Mona Lisa smile.

'Perhaps you could,' she agreed.

'I've made arrangements with the insurance company for you to drive all my cars,' Robinson told Love. 'And my garages can deal with any problems you may have. It's the same with old cars as with old people. They are all right for a while, and then the most unexpected things can go wrong, and they need looking at.'

He handed Love a Yale key with a big tag cut from red plastic.

'Sometimes, in my experience, these cars get a bit hot under the collar when you drive them in town. They're not built to cope with a lot of traffic. This key opens the private door into the service entrance of all my garages. You'll find any tools there you may need. Spanners for American threads, American nuts, taps for American bolts, everything. I'll tell the staff you may be looking in.'

'Thank you,' said Love, putting the key in his pocket. 'But I hope I won't need to use this.'

'Where are you going to drive the cars, anyhow?' Camille asked him.

'I don't know yet, but I'll find a place.'

'You want to drive up and see Daddy's yacht. It's several miles farther on, up the Highway. You sail?'

'I have done,' said Love.

'I think you'd like it up there. The swimming is good. But keep away from the jellyfish.'

'What's wrong with them?'

'Ah, box jellyfish,' said Robinson, shaking his head. 'Never used to be any, now they're all over. Their sting is poisonous, deadly sometimes. You get stung two or three times and you won't know what happened to you. You would be dead, my friend.'

'Is there any antidote?'

'We've bottles of methylated spirits on posts along the beach. That's supposed to help you. If you smell of meths or petrol, I believe they shy away from you. But I wouldn't like to put that to the test. The fact is, more people are killed every year here by these box jellyfish than by sharks – which is not good news for tourists who think the jellyfish are harmless, as off the English coast.'

'What else are you going to do while you're here?' asked Camille.

'I want to visit your cemetery,' said Love.

'Unusual. As a visitor or an immigrant?'

'Strictly a visitor.'

'Going to reserve yourself a plot or something?' asked Robinson, puzzled. 'Pay now, die later, eh?'

'Not exactly. I want to see if I can find the grave of an English girl, Annabel Crawford.' He turned to Camille. 'Have you ever heard of her?'

She shook her head.

'Never. She was a tourist?'

'Yes, in a sense. I think she was out here for a while, taking jobs, moving on.'

'How did she die?'

'Apparently, a drowning accident.'

'She could have been stung by a box jellyfish,' said

Robinson, pouring himself a brandy. Camille shook her head.

'I didn't see anything about that in the paper,' she said. 'And they usually cover such items pretty thoroughly. Bad news is always good news for the Press. What's your interest in her?'

'I've never met her. Never even heard of her until the night before I was leaving. I was visiting an old lady who had been taken ill. A friend with her told me that she had received a letter from someone out here, a Mr Stevenson – I've got his address – to say that this girl had been drowned. I promised her I'd take a photograph of the grave, see that it's being looked after, and so on.'

'I can understand her interest,' said Robinson. 'The English are so strange. They are often more concerned with the dead than the living. Everything must be just so – once you're in your coffin. People who may never have ridden in a car in their life drive in a Rolls to their grave.'

'Where are you staying, Doctor?' Camille asked Love, to change the subject.

'The Trade Winds.'

He gave her his room number.

'I'll look you up when I'm in town.'

Robinson's face suddenly clouded. Love glanced at his daughter. Camille was looking at her father; her face showed worry, concern.

Robinson stood up.

'Well, Doctor,' he said. 'You've covered a lot of distance in quite a short time. I expect you'll want to make it an early night?'

'Certainly,' Love agreed, falling in with what was clearly his host's wish.

'Then I'll get the car and run you back.'

He went out. Camille turned to Love, put one hand on his.

'I want to see you, Doctor,' she said. 'Desperately.'

'What about? Your health?'

'No. My father. He's scared of something.'

'I thought he seemed uneasy.'

'It's more than uneasy. He's scared for his life.'

'You mean he's ill?'

'No. He's afraid he's going to be killed. But I can't tell you now. What about tomorrow? Ten o'clock, your hotel?'

'Right. I'll be there.'

Love heard the faint rumble of the Cord's engine outside, stood up, bowed to her.

'Until then,' he said. As he went out to the car, he heard the telephone begin to ring behind him.

Birds in trees around the hotel garden, singing as fervently as a Bach choir in a Welsh chapel, awoke Love early next morning. As he drew the curtains, a tropic sun immediately leapt into the room, fighting the shadows and beating them – but not dealing with Love's sense of perplexity.

Robinson was clearly very frightened of someone – or something. His daughter claimed he was in fear of his life. But was this really so, or was it simply a feminine exaggeration, spoken to make an impact? Well, this morning might see a development.

The light reflected from the sea was so bright it felt like looking straight into the heart of a searchlight – refreshingly different from the insipid, washed-out afterglow that passed for sun in England.

Love ate breakfast on his balcony: fruit juice, toast, black coffee. He was pleased to see that, like her father, Camille was a punctual person. At ten o'clock precisely, he saw the Cord arrive with the Chinese manservant driving. He went out to meet them.

'I've arranged for Harry Ling to do some shopping,' she explained. 'Would you care to try the car?'

'I'd love to.'

Harry Ling slid out from the driving seat. Love took his place behind the familiar cream steering wheel, looking over

130

the long bonnet, blunt as a coffin on end. He fired up the engine.

'You'll have to guide me out of this town,' he said.

'Let's go along the coast,' she said. 'I'll suggest where we can stop. This car is so conspicuous, we'll have to pull off the road.'

The town soon fell away behind them, and they were out in a countryside that could have been Caribbean; lush green vegetation, palm trees, a beach white as scrubbed bone. They drove on for another twenty minutes.

'Half a mile up, pull off,' she said. 'There's a small track leading into a picnic area. This time of day it should be deserted.'

She was right. Love turned the car so that it was facing the sea, cut the engine. Then he turned towards Camille.

'This is a strange place for a consultation, medical or otherwise,' he said, looking around at the thick, fleshy-leaved bushes, the white sand. 'But at least we won't be overheard. Now, tell me about your father.'

'Do you know anything about him at all?' she asked.

'He wrote to me several times saying he was interested in Cords, hinting – and in his last letter actually saying – that he wanted to discuss something else with me. But he never said what it was. Do you know?'

'No,' she said. 'But *I* know what I want him to discuss with you. I read your articles in the Cord Newsletter and I suggested he get in touch with you.'

'Why?'

'Because you don't know this country, or what is happening or going to happen here. Because you're a doctor, and so can keep your own counsel about things. Because it's unlikely that you can be bought. And I just like the sound of you altogether. Satisfied?'

'You make a good case for inviting me. Now, what is the problem he wants to discuss?'

'Let me tell you the background first. Charles Robinson – who I call father – is actually my stepfather. My mother was

131

his second wife. I know nothing of his first marriage, years ago. He never speaks of that, but he has a son.

'My mother was Chinese. Hong Kong. She died some years ago.'

'And your real father?'

'Dead, too.

'My stepfather emigrated from England about ten years ago. He had some money, and he started businesses here. These made a lot more money and he married my mother. Everything seemed to be going pretty well.

'Then, about six months ago he started receiving anonymous letters. Just a postcard inside an envelope, with "Remember me", "We'll meet again", and so on.'

'These worried him?'

'Not at first. When you're running motor businesses you apparently always have some customers who are dissatisfied with a car you've sold them. They think you've swindled them, that they've been overcharged or something. Once, someone sent him a dead rat in the post – with the sender's name and address on a tag!

'But these other letters seemed different somehow. On the postcard inside one of them was an Indian stamp – one rupee – stuck on the card. The letter had been posted in England. Others came from the continent – Rome, Paris, Lisbon.'

'Your father showed you these?'

'Oh, yes. I came to recognise the typing, anyhow.'

'So you think one person maybe typed them all, and then posted them from different places?'

'Possibly. Then, just before you arrived, he received a parcel that really upset him.'

'What was in it?'

'I don't know. But I saw it arrive. It was quite small. I don't even know where it had been posted. He took it away, as he always did with his letters, to read on his own. Half an hour later I saw him and he had aged ten years. His face was positively green, as though he had seen a ghost – or worse than a ghost.'

'Did you ask him what was in the parcel?'

'Yes. He wouldn't tell me. He just said, "Never ask me. I want to forget all about it. I just feel I'm being pursued. And I fear I may be caught." I said, "What do you mean?" He said, "Some people are after me. They know I'm here. It's only a matter of time before they come calling."'

'Didn't he tell the police?'

'I asked him to, begged him to. But he refused. Said it wasn't a police matter.

'Then the other day he was in Darwin. He came back so worried. He sent you a telegram, asking you to postpone your trip.'

'He told me. But I'd left before it arrived. What happened in Darwin?'

'I don't know. Something. For quite a time now he's been on edge, as though he's waiting for someone to turn up, something to happen. I've heard him cry out in the night, "They'll kill me. They won't give me a chance to explain. They're killers, both of them."'

'Do you know who he is referring to?'

'No.'

'So how can I help you?'

'I don't know, Doctor. I just wanted to see someone who had no contacts here, someone who *I* could trust, who I believed in.'

'You don't believe in people round here?'

She shrugged.

'I don't know,' she said. 'Harry Ling and his sister Anna, I trust them.'

'Who are they?'

'They're actually cousins of mine. They are waiting to go to England. Harry is going to be a doctor. He's passed some medical exams here in Australia, and he's going on to hospital there.'

'So why is he working as a sort of butler and chauffeur?'

'It amuses him, I think, to see how people treat him when they imagine he's a servant. If they meet him socially, as

133

equals, they're quite different. Maybe he'll become a psychiatrist! Anyhow, it's a way of making a little money.'

A car came down the road travelling slowly, radio playing loudly. A pennant attached to its radio aerial bore the crude proposal: 'Eat More Beef, You Bastards'.

'From the Northern Territory,' said Camille, smiling. 'They're real, arch-typical Australians there. You know, in Darwin in what they call The Top End of the Territory, a stubby of beer is a litre. Elsewhere, it's about a third as much. They're a tough lot. I like them.'

'I can see why,' said Love. 'I like everything I've seen in this country – except what you've told me now. This girl who was drowned, Annabel Crawford. You're sure you've never heard of her?'

'Never,' she said firmly.

'Well, I'd better try and find out on my own. Anything else you have to tell me about your father?'

'Nothing,' she said. 'But I feel somehow that now you're here, events will start to speed up.'

'Why?'

'I have a boyfriend who is doing a part-time job in a hotel at Ayers Rock. I spoke to him just after you'd gone last night. He rings me pretty well every night. He told me someone had fallen to his death off the top of the Rock. Apparently, some Pom out on holiday tried to save him. A Dr Love.'

'Me,' said Love.

'I guessed that. Were you trying to save him?'

Love paused before replying. He could agree that he was, which would not carry knowledge one pace further. Or he could tell her the truth. He remembered the words of Thomas Browne: ''Tis time to observe Occurrences, and let nothing remarkable escape us.'

This was one of those times.

'He was trying to kill me,' Love said.

'*Kill* you? Why?'

'I've no idea. We were on the same coach from The Alice, and I saw him taking some pills for angina. When I reached the top of the Rock, he was on his hands and knees in a sort of gully or crevice. I thought he was having an attack. He asked me to get the pills out of his jacket pocket, and of course I did so.

'By then, all the other tourists were already on their way down, and he hit me, took a shot at me, tried to throw me off the top. We had a fight. I won. I didn't mean to kill him, but it's as slippery as hell up there, with a wind like a hurricane.'

'I know,' she said. 'I've climbed it. But why could he possibly want to kill you?'

'I've absolutely no idea. Apart from exchanging a few words on the way from The Alice, I'd never seen him before. Didn't even know his name.'

'I'll give you an idea. He *knew* you were coming to see my father. Maybe everything was about to reach a climax and your arrival could ruin it.'

'Maybe,' said Love, unconvinced.

'Well, let's go back to your hotel. If I've anything to report, I'll tell you.'

Love drove into the hotel parking lot. Harry Ling was waiting for them. They changed places behind the wheel.

'How does she handle, Doctor?' he asked Love, blipping the throttle.

'Great,' said Love. 'Makes me feel quite homesick.'

He watched them drive out of sight, then walked out of the car park and along the Esplanade.

The tide was in now and groups of sea birds followed their leaders, swimming in formation up and down the shallow water. Love walked past a row of little shops selling brochures for Calm Water Cruises, Hot-Air Ballooning, Crocodile Cycles, White Water Rafting.

Filipino, Chinese, and Indian take-aways lined an arcade off the Esplanade. Visitors, mostly young, wearing T-shirts and jeans, sat at tables in the open air, eating late breakfasts or early lunches. He wondered whether any of them had known Annabel Crawford. For a moment he thought of going from table to table asking them, then decided against it. They would probably take him for a mendicant, or a nutter – or both.

And why was he assuming that she was their age, even of their generation? She could be eighteen or just as easily, thirty-eight; he had not enquired her age and Miss Dukes had not told him. She had shown him a photograph of a young woman – but when had it been taken? Was it recent or one taken years ago? He should have asked her; now, it was too late.

Further on lay a huge area, air-conditioned, with escalators to upper floors, restaurants, curio shops. Piped music played in the background, a wordless song without end. Love walked past lodging houses and hostels where other girls and young men with British, American, French and New Zealand flags sewn on to backpacks were coming out to start the day.

The temperature was increasing rapidly; soon it would be too warm to walk. Love hailed a passing taxi. He would make a quick trip to the cemetery, find Annabel Crawford's grave, photograph it from several different angles, call on this Mr Stevenson, and be back in the hotel in time for an early lunch.

At the cemetery gates, Love asked the driver to wait for him.

'Not thinking of joining them, then, sport?' the man asked in mock concern.

'Not yet,' Love assured him.

He walked through the graveyard, between rows of neat headstones, looking for the name, Crawford. Most stones were small and square, not much larger than a book standing on end. Instead of the quotations he had seen so often in English cemeteries – 'Until the day dawn', 'Peace, perfect peace', 'A happy release' – many simply bore the names of the dead, with a date for entering this world, another for leaving it. But he could not see any headstone bearing the name of Annabel Crawford.

In a small building like a ticket booth at one end of the

cemetery, a man sat at a desk reading a newspaper. The glass window facing him had a round hole cut in it like an old-fashioned English railway booking office.

'Wonder if you could help me,' Love asked him through the hole. 'I'm looking for a grave. Miss Annabel Crawford.'

'Pom?'

'Yes.'

'Visitor?'

'Yes. Not a resident.'

'Any idea when she croaked?'

'Fairly recently, I think. Can't give an exact date. I believe it was a drowning accident.'

The man put down his paper, began to thumb through a book of names. He pursed his lips, pushed the book away, pressed computer keys. Lines of names came up on a screen.

'A. Crawford, you say? Not here, sport. No A. Crawford here.'

The man shook his head slowly.

'There was a letter from a local man, a Mr Stevenson.'

'Never heard of him. Sure it was this cemetery?'

'It is the only one here, isn't it?'

'That's right, sport. The one and only.'

'So what do you think?'

The man shrugged, made a move to pick up his paper again; this Pom was wasting his time.

'I'm not paid to think,' he said shortly. 'I'm paid to keep this graveyard tidy, answer questions if I can – and try to, if I can't, like yours. Sorry I can't help you about this Miss Crawford. Maybe you should try the council, check the records.'

'Thanks.'

'Tell you what, sport. Give me your name and where you're staying. My mate will be here this afternoon. I'll ask him if he knows anything.'

Love scribbled his name and his hotel on a page torn from his diary, handed it with a ten dollar note through the hole in the window.

The man put the page on his desk under a marble chip as a paper weight, the bill in his back pocket. He watched Love walk away towards the parked taxi.

When he was certain Love was out of sight and not likely to come back, he picked up the telephone and dialled a number.

Late that evening, Love walked along the Esplanade, savouring the warmth and the glitter of lights around the bay, the always pleasurable sensation of being in a new, and to him, undiscovered city. As he walked, he turned over in his mind what Camille had told him. Why was her father so afraid – and where could Annabel Crawford be buried if not in the cemetery where he had been told her funeral had taken place?

A car overtook him, travelling slowly. He glanced at it idly, and recognised Camille in the front seat, with her Chinese driver, Harry Ling. He wondered where they were going, wished that he was the man she was going to meet. Now why, he wondered, did he assume Camille would be meeting a man? Because, in his experience, pretty women rarely set out at night with drivers to meet other women, whether pretty or not. But, of course, there might always be a first time, and he found himself hoping this could be the case here.

He walked on, conscious of being at a loose end. Now and then he stopped, reading menus outside restaurants, not because he was hungry, simply because he was killing time.

A number of cars were coming up the road towards him, and again he recognised Camille's. The car was approaching slowly, as though the driver was looking for something or someone. He stopped twenty yards from Love. Camille was looking out towards the bay; Love felt certain she had not seen him. He wondered who or what she was thinking about. The person she was going to meet – or had not met?

Harry Ling climbed out, walked towards a narrow door between two shops, pressed the bell. He turned, waiting for someone to open the door, and in that moment, four men surrounded him. They were also Chinese.

Two seized an arm, the third hit him hard across the face with the back of his hand. The fourth stood, grinning, hands in his pockets, enjoying the man's discomfiture. Then he brought up his knee into Harry Ling's groin. He doubled up.

Camille was out of the car now, shouting. A few couples, strolling along the Esplanade, stood and stared, not caring to become involved. Love jumped forward, pivoted to the right in the judo movement, gripped the nearest man's wrist in his left hand. Love kneed him in the groin, and as he lunged forward, brought up the knuckles of the first two fingers of his right hand into his eyes. He collapsed, screaming. The Chinese holding the driver's left arm saw Love coming, kicked out at him. Love dodged the blow, grasped his ankle with his left hand, brought down his right below the man's knee with the force that could break a piece of wood.

He heard the joint snap, and the man collapsed in agony.

The third man jumped at Love, taking up a Kung Fu stance. Love feinted, and as the man struck, gripped his wrist, butted him in the chest with his head, sent him sailing over his shoulder. His skull cracked like a hammer blow as it hit the pavement. The fourth man ran away.

'Thank God you were here,' said Camille, coming over to Love. They bent down at Harry Ling's side.

'He's not very badly hurt,' said Love. 'But I don't think he should drive.'

'And I can't,' said Camille.

'I can,' Love told her. He helped Harry Ling into the back seat of the car, climbed into the front with Camille. A small crowd of onlookers that had gathered now walked away.

'Would it be too much to ask you to drive us home?' Camille asked him. 'I will have a driver there to bring you back.'

'My pleasure,' Love assured her, and let in the clutch.

CHAPTER EIGHT

*THE PRESENT: CAIRNS,
NORTH QUEENSLAND, AUSTRALIA*

Next morning, Love bought a street map at the news-agent's shop in his hotel foyer, looked up the street where Mr Stevenson had his address. This was close enough to walk. He walked.

The house was wooden, of white clapboard, built up on stilts. A ute was parked to one side. Its tyres were flat, and wind from the sea had blown a thick coating of dust and sand over the bonnet and roof. By its appearance, Love guessed that the vehicle had not been used for weeks, maybe longer.

The little square patch of scrubby grass in front of the house was uncut, thick and tufted and dry. A few fleshy-leaved weeds sprouted in the drive-in from the road. Curtains were drawn across all the windows. The house looked deserted, unlived in, unwelcoming. Its forlorn appearance reminded Love of The Hall.

He climbed wooden steps to the front door. The door did not have a knocker, only a bell-push and a slot for letters. He pressed the button and heard an electric bell tinkle a couple of feet away. This was not like country houses he was used to in Wiltshire, where bells pealed at the end of long stone corridors, faint as music down the aisles of time. How different from the bell ringing in the dim recesses of The Hall, for instance. It seemed odd that in a land of immense open spaces, so many Australians chose to live in such small houses in tiny patches. Maybe the sense of enormous emptiness just beyond the garden walls had something to do with this? He waited, rang again.

It was very hot on the top step. A few flies tried to make emergency landings on his face. He brushed them away. The paint on the door had blistered and cracked. Once, it had been a rich maroon; now, after the heat of an unknown number of summers, it was greyish. Someone had pricked the blisters so that they split, showing a white undercoat.

He peered through the metal letterbox. The metal felt too hot to touch comfortably. He could see several letters and circulars lying on the mat inside. By craning his eyes he picked out one with an English airmail stamp. This might be from Miss Dukes. Equally, of course, it could be from any of the sixty million other inhabitants in the British Isles. But if the letter was from her, it did not look as though she could expect a quick reply.

He called through the letterbox: 'Anyone in? Anyone at home? Shop!'

There was no answer.

Love paused for a moment, then walked down the steps and round to the back of the house. Houses on either side had Hills hoists with washing hanging on them. The horizontal wires on the hoist in this backyard were empty.

Weeds grew thick on the little square of garden. A couple of cheap garden chairs, brightly striped nylon covers on anodised metal frames, had been left outside. He ran a hand over one. It came away rough with sand; they had probably been there for as long as the ute. He wondered who had put them out. Mr Stevenson? A friend, or companion, lover, man or woman? Why did this deserted house have a sinister air about it – or had he brought an air of mystery with him?

Love walked up six wooden steps to the back door, tried the handle. The door was locked, but on one side a small window had been pulled shut but not latched. There was no curtain, and he could see into the kitchen. He glanced behind him and then on either side.

There was no-one in sight, but of course that did not mean people were not watching him from behind their curtains. Simply because he could not see anyone, it would be unwise to assume that someone could not see him. However, this was a risk he had to take. If he didn't, he would have to wait until dusk and then try his luck on the window. A quick in-and-out job in daylight would be far easier. A glance to see who the letter was from, whether there was any note of a forwarding address for Mr Stevenson, or any friend or relation, and within less than minutes he could be back in his hotel, an iced Fosters in his hand.

Nothing stirred in the heat except the flies. Love took a deep breath, put a hand carefully inside the window, opened it. With one heave he was up and through, thankful no-one was inside the kitchen to club him over the head as he hung, half in, half out for a moment until he could get his hands on the kitchen table and pull himself in. What an absurd idea, he thought. Who could conceivably be waiting to do that to him?

Love closed the window carefully. Neighbours could have become used to seeing it shut. If they suddenly noticed it was open, it was just possible, even if unlikely, that this might concern them sufficiently to take some action to find out why.

Love was in a tiny kitchen with a metal sink and draining board, cheap wooden cupboards along two walls, painted cream, with green shelves and ribbed frosted glass fronts. He didn't like the colour scheme, and he didn't like the house. But then there was no reason why he should; he wasn't going to buy either. He hadn't got to live here. His aim was to discover who did.

Love waited for a moment, listening. He could hear nothing except the metallic tick of a cheap clockwork clock on the table. He opened the kitchen door into a narrow passage. The rooms opening off this were in semi-darkness with heavy curtains pulled. He closed the kitchen door behind him and the lock clicked shut. He turned the knob but the door would not open. He would have to leave through another window, or maybe through the front door. Belatedly, the realisation struck him that he was illegally inside someone else's house, a stranger's home. His excuse that he was looking for a Mr Stevenson, or at least his forwarding address, was ludicrous – even though it happened to be true.

What sort of reception would he give to any intruder in his house in Wiltshire who produced such a feeble explanation? The sooner he was away the better. But why was he so concerned? He was alone in the house. Wasn't he?

He walked into the hall, picked up the letters. Most looked like bills or circulars. None was addressed to Mr Stevenson. The letter with the English stamp was not from Miss Dukes; it had the name of a Manchester mail-order store on the back. A pity. He put the envelopes down carefully on the mat, just as he had found them – and then realised why he was moving so cautiously, why he had become worried in case he was discovered.

He was not alone in the house. Someone else *was* here with him.

Now Love could hear the sound of breathing growing louder. Someone was following him, walking very slowly from room to room, also trying not to make any noise.

Love backed against a wall. If he had to fight, this was the best position to be in, but he hoped he could talk his way out of a confrontation. He watched the nearest door. It didn't open. Instead, another door opened across the hall. He had not noticed this before because it was covered in the same cheaply patterned paper as the walls.

A man came through this door. He was a big man wearing jeans, a blue T-shirt, white trainers. He wore black-lensed glasses, like goggles, and thick gloves that extended some way up his wrists like gauntlets. In his right hand he gripped a knife with a long slender blade that glittered dully in the dim light. He was moving like a blind man, but was he blind? He seemed able to move freely in the dark, to use his ears, his fingers, to sense where he was. He was seeing without using his eyes.

For a moment he stood, motionless. Then he turned his head left to right, slowly, menacingly, like a gun turret. He was not looking; he was listening.

'Who are you?' he asked in a deep voice, speaking English but with an accent.

'A visitor,' Love replied.

'Then you're uninvited, sport,' the man said. 'Both doors are locked. Only one window is unlatched. So you must have come in through that. A thief. What do you want to steal here?'

'Nothing,' Love answered him. 'Just looking.'

'For whom? For what?'

'I understand Mr Stevenson lives here. I want to talk to him or anyone who knows him. Do you?'

'I don't know what you're talking about. You are making fun of me. I will teach you not to make mock of me.'

The man came towards Love now, feeling his way with infinite care along the wall with the tips of his fingers, holding the knife out in front of him. The blade was not pointing down, as an amateur held a knife, but with the blade pointing up, the end of its handle deep in the palm of his hand as a professional handled a knife. The razor-edged blade could rip Love's stomach open in the fraction of a second.

'There is no way out,' said the man grimly. 'As I say, front and back doors are locked. Who are you – and who are you from?'

Love took a cautious step to the left. The man's head turned towards the sound, picking up the small movement.

'Day or night mean nothing to me,' he went on. 'They are both dark, and I can wait. You cannot. The electric current is cut off here, and when the sun goes down, you will also be in the dark. That is my world, not yours. I am used to it. You are not. Then, in the darkness, when you are lost, you will also be trapped. I will find you easily enough. I will simply follow the sound of your breathing.'

The man was moving closer as he spoke. Suddenly, he lunged at Love with astonishing speed, seized Love's right wrist. His grip felt unyielding, metallic, hard as the jaws of a bench vice. Love wrenched himself free with the strength of despair.

The knife point dug like a spearhead into the wood of a dresser behind him, missing him by inches. The man pulled the quivering blade free, spun it in his hand, caught it expertly by the handle and grinned. He was enjoying this. He knew he had only to wait until Love tired, until his concentration flagged, or at the latest, until dark. Then he could dispatch him in an instant.

I will have to deal with this character now, thought Love grimly. But how?

Love's searching fingers found a door handle behind him. He turned it. The door opened. He moved backwards into another room, pulled the door shut behind him, hoping he could lock it. But there was no lock. The door swung open again and the other man came through.

'Listen,' said Love urgently. 'I am a doctor, not a thief. Drop that knife, and let's talk.'

'I'll drop that knife when I drop it into you – right into your guts.'

He took another step forward, struck viciously at Love. Again, Love jumped to one side. As he did so, he heard a faint noise in another room: the creak of a dry floor board. A third person was in the building with them.

He had been insane to venture into this house on his own. It was simply a trap, and he had walked right into it naïvely, idiotically. But who had set the trap – and was it expected to catch him – or someone else?

Love edged around the wall, never letting his eyes leave the other man's face, seeing his own face reflected in the black glass of the spectacles. The man twisted towards him, moving with him, listening, always listening to every sound.

His lips were compressed tightly, his face set hard as a bronze sculpture, his knife ready to strike when he was certain of his target.

Love crouched, waiting for him to come towards him again, ready now to spin him over his shoulder in the *otara* movement he had so often demonstrated to the judo class at the local Royal British Legion meeting in his village hall. That had been practice; this would be real.

The man jumped forward, knife now held close to his body. Love sidestepped and moved in to the attack.

In that brief split-second, the whole room exploded in a brilliant, blinding blaze of light. Then Love was falling down a long dark and silent well, past bright unwinking stars, beyond ageless towers of silence, down through depths of endless night.

Robinson sat back in a canvas chair under a striped sun awning on his patio, put up his feet on a wooden stool and pondered on the events in Darwin.

By an enormous effort of will, he had forced himself to put to the back of his mind his fears about the presence of Mr Singer and Mr Hargreaves. He assured himself that he had faced worse dangers in the past, and he had survived. He would do the same now. He had to. But even as he attempted to convince himself of his invincibility, doubts hovered at the edges of his confidence like evening shadows on a lawn.

He felt like a gladiator who every afternoon had to go out with his trident and net and meet a new opponent in the arena. But the gladiator was growing older with each encounter, while his opponent was always young. And one day his opponent would win, or the audience would give the old man the thumbs down. But not yet, Robinson told himself fervently. Not yet.

Slowly, weariness, almost a reluctant acceptance of the inevitability of conflict, overcame him, and he dozed.

A Chinese servant shook him awake.

'Someone at the door to see you, sir.'

'Who is it? Not Mr Singer? I told you –'

'Not Mr Singer, sir, no,' the servant assured him soothingly. 'Another person altogether. An Englishman. A Mr Parkington.'

Robinson sighed, stood up, smoothed down his jacket. He walked forward to meet Parkington, his hand outstretched in welcome. His brief sleep had refreshed him. He could put Singer out of his thoughts – at least temporarily.

'I heard from the Midland Widows' London office you were coming out to see me,' he said. 'But I'd forgotten it was today. I made a note of it in my diary – and then neglected to check. How foolish of me. I am delighted that you are here. I understand you are, shall I say, your company's chief troubleshooter, Mr Parkington?'

'I have been called many things, many times. Sometimes troubles try to shoot me. But I always endeavour to get my shot in first.'

'I hope that your visit here does not indicate you expect to exchange shots with me?' Robinson asked him with a smile.

'Not at all. My company is very pleased indeed to have your business – and especially to note how many companies you control, without making a single claim over the last twelve months. I wish all our policy-holders were like you!'

'In that respect, yes,' agreed Robinson, 'but possibly not in all respects.'

He smiled wryly to himself, knowing that the other man could not possibly appreciate the irony of his remark.

'Now, Mr Parkington, can I offer you a drink before we discuss what brings you here?'

'Rum and lime, if you have it.'

'Of course I have it, although it is not a combination I drink myself, or one I am often asked for,' Robinson replied. 'Curiously, I have had another English visitor asking for the same concoction. It must be popular there. But then the climate in England is so cold and damp, no doubt rum warms you? It contains sugar, which has that effect, I believe. But that is not necessary in Queensland, Mr Parkington.'

'Agreed.'

Parkington raised his glass.

They drank, sat down under the sun awning. Palm trees swayed slightly in a gentle breeze. The sea stretched to infinity, calm as a blue glass floor. In the distance, on the rim of the horizon, beyond the yachts of the wealthy, and pleasure ships carrying tourists out to the Great Barrier Reef, half a dozen dark ships lay in line.

Parkington had studied them through binoculars from his hire car on the road from Cairns. They were not moving. He could make out the anchor chain dipping from the bows of the first, and another from the stern of the last. He turned now to Robinson.

'Are they bound for your scrapyard?'

'Eventually,' Robinson agreed. 'The leading one is the only one with a serviceable engine. She is towing the others. There has been a breakdown. Nothing serious. But it is with old machinery as with old men. Their pace is slow.'

'Where have they come from?'

'I bought them from a ship broker in Singapore. They probably came originally from Goa on the west coast of India. That's the elephants' graveyard for all manner of cargo vessels, battleships, even submarines that have outlived their time. They go there to await other buyers. The owners of the cargo vessels have wisely written down their cost against taxes over many years, and so they can take whatever they can get for them and still show a profit.'

'Why Goa?' asked Parkington, sipping his drink.

'Convenience. It possesses a mass of mangrove swamps and estuaries along the coast. They simply run unwanted ships into the swamps and leave them until they find a buyer.'

'Aren't they looted, stripped of anything valuable?'

'Not really. Tourists may see them and steal a ship's clock, or a name plate. But the locals know that if they offer such bits and pieces for sale, there is only one place they could have come from. Sentences can be harsh, and Indian gaols are unpleasant.'

'Does your insurance on the scrap yard cover these ships?'

'Yes,' said Robinson. 'I had it worked out by your office in Darwin with my lawyers the other day. They have insured them all, not for the price I paid for them but for their resale value broken down. And, of course, their contents.'

'And all your workers, they're covered?'

'Surely. We use Chinese labour, mostly. They don't mind what hours they work. They just want to make as much money as quickly as possible to start their own business – a laundry, a restaurant, all kinds of enterprises.

'Some of them work simply to pay off debts to the Triads that relations have run up in Hong Kong, or elsewhere. Now you're here, would you care to drive up and see the yard?'

'Certainly,' said Parkington, putting down his drink. 'Ready when you are.'

They climbed into Robinson's Cord.

'I have only ever seen one of these before in running order,' said Parkington appreciatively. 'That was in England, owned by a country doctor – Jason Love.'

He glanced sideways at Robinson as they came out on to the Highway. He had deliberately not told him he and Love had met again at Ayers Rock.

'How extraordinary,' Robinson replied. 'He was the visitor I mentioned just now who'd asked me for rum and lime. He is over here in Cairns for the next few days, at the Trade Winds. As a Cord enthusiast, I asked him up, and we had dinner together.'

'I'll give him a bell when I get back,' Parkington promised.

The big car devoured the miles easily. Within an hour Robinson turned off the major road towards two tall metal gates set in a wire mesh fence twenty feet high. The gates were locked and chained. Beyond the fence, in the distance, the ocean glittered. Behind the gates, guard dogs on chains attached to sliding rings on hawsers fixed on either side of a sandy track barked a ferocious warning.

A Chinese watchman came out of a hut to see who or

what was causing the commotion. He wore a khaki shirt and trousers. A heavy night stick was attached to his belt. He recognised Robinson, saluted, opened the gates. They drove through.

At first, each side of the track was crammed with wrecked cars and trucks, piled one on top of the other as they had been dumped from the transporter. An open door banged to and fro in the wind from the sea like the beat of a distant drum. The cooling fan of a truck engine on end spun silently like a tiny windmill.

They passed rows of tractors, trucks, old military vehicles, paint dull from years of sunshine, streaks of rust baked on the metal by its heat. Then they reached the ships.

Chinese workmen, wearing blue-lensed welding goggles, floppy hats or towels tied round their heads against the blazing sun, crouched on decks fifty, a hundred feet above them. Flames leapt from their torches as they cut through slabs of metal as high as the side of a house. Arcs of blue fire from electric cutting equipment ate through girders while they worked.

Years ago, other welders in colder climates, as far apart as the Clyde and Yokahama, had fused together these plates, these stanchions and girders. None, Parkington thought, could ever have imagined how and where, and in what circumstances, under a burnished sun, his careful handiwork would so swiftly and ruthlessly be destroyed.

Out of the sea, the hulks of old cargo ships, streaked with green up to their waterlines, rose to astonishing heights. Superstructures soared taller than church steeples. From masts two hundred feet above them, the flags of Panama and Liberia flew in faded tatters.

Through holes cut low down in these hulls, tar and congealed oil and bilge water bled slowly and thickly into the mud. Sea birds wheeled and turned and called noisily to each other in the sky above the beached vessels. They settled on broken deck rails, on a bridge, on the rim of a funnel through which no smoke had passed for a generation.

'What happens to all this metal?' Parkington asked.

'We cut it into workable sizes and then it goes off by truck to the steel works. It comes out as long rods used to give strength to the concrete in high-rise buildings.'

'You have many accidents here?'

'We try not to. Some of those metal sheets look as thick as your wrist, but remember, rust and salt and sun have been eating into them for years. The men start to cut away a small piece then – wham – a slice weighing twenty tons drops out. In some old ships the hulls below water level are so thin now, you could kick a hole in them.'

Parkington glanced at his watch.

'Thanks for showing me all this,' he said. 'It's always a good idea to see exactly what we are insuring. Now, if you could run me back, I'll look up the good doctor. Oh, one last thing. When do you expect to get those other ships in?'

'We have got the space, as you can see,' Robinson replied. 'We will move them, believe me, just as soon as we can.'

Love was swimming slowly and painfully through a sea of deep Circassian blue. Gradually, this turned greener until he was in a lapis lazuli lake. The water lightened slowly, steadily, and finally receded altogether, leaving him on his back, gasping for breath on what appeared to be a hard, unyielding, rocky shore.

He opened his eyes wearily. He was lying on the bare floorboards of a room he did not recognise. Sunlight poured in through the window, striking his aching eyeballs with all the subtlety of a barbed wire lash. He closed his eyes, shook his head, opened them again more carefully.

This time, he recognised the room. It had been dark before, because the curtains were drawn, but now they were open. In the sunlight, walls blazed bright as burnished brass. He was in Mr Stevenson's house.

Gradually, fragments of memory fell into place like pieces

151

in a jig-saw. There had been a man in dark glasses, holding a knife in a hand of steel. Love had been on the point of finding out who he was when someone or something unknown had hit him on the head. Hard.

Love put up one hand, felt his scalp professionally. The bruise seemed large as a gooseberry. He sat up slowly. He did not care to move quickly. He felt that if he did so his head might just fly away from his body like a wingless bird.

He sat, listening. He could hear nothing but a vague, muted hum of traffic on the road outside. He stood up, still slowly, and leaned against the wall. His head beat like a drum. He walked out of the room, into the next room, then the one after that, and finally the kitchen. The door that had swung shut behind him was now open, and the little house was empty.

Love saw his face in a kitchen mirror. He looked grey and haggard. Not surprising, he thought wryly. He touched the bruise on his head again, gently, gingerly. Then he ran the cold tap, drank greedily from it, dowsed his face with water, dried himself on a dishcloth.

Love tried to analyse the situation as though it did not concern him at all, but only involved some impersonal third party. He had no right to be here, agreed. But he had an excuse – if he had been allowed the chance to explain it to someone who wanted to listen, or who even would listen. And what was to be gained by knocking him unconscious and leaving him alone in a locked house?

He patted his jacket pockets. His wallet was still there, his fountain pen, credit cards in inner pockets. Nothing had gone. So why had this unknown person hit him? Why not wait, find out what Love was doing there, and who he was? Unless . . . Unless this unknown person already knew who he was – and also the reason why he was in the house? Could his attacker be Mr Stevenson?

Love thought of the people he had met since he had arrived in Australia, who could conceivably be involved: Parkington,

Robinson, the man at the cemetery. But why would any of those people hit him? Parkington, he could rule out. The man with the dark glasses had been in front of him, not behind, where whoever had hit him had stood, so that absolved him. And Robinson and the cemetery caretaker seemed pretty long shots. But was there anyone else? If not, could either of them not be such a long shot?

Love tried the outside doors of the house, front and back. Both were locked and the back door bolted. So whoever had come into the house had left through the front door – or the kitchen window.

Love opened the window, climbed out into the little garden. A dog barked somewhere. In another house, a radio was playing. White washing on the Hills hoist in the garden next door hung dejectedly, like surrender flags of a defeated army. He could see no-one, and now he did not care if anyone saw him. He walked around the side of the house, out into the street, back to his hotel.

As Love turned into the hotel driveway, he saw Robinson's Cord towering above the other vehicles parked there; longer, larger than any, a Cunarder among cars.

Robinson was waiting for him in the foyer. He came out to meet Love.

'I thought I'd see if you were free for lunch?'

'Most certainly.'

'Then let's drive up the Cook Highway. Have lunch with me aboard my yacht. It's very agreeable, just two people sitting under an awning out at sea. Better than any restaurant, believe me. And we can talk privately.'

That was the key word, thought Love: *privately*. Maybe now Robinson would come to the second reason for inviting him out here? The tenseness Love had noticed in Robinson the previous day seemed to have vanished. He seemed more confident, sure of himself.

'Camille told me how you probably saved her life last night, and that of Harry Ling. I wanted to thank you personally for an immensely brave action on your part. Those men could have killed you.'

'But fortunately they didn't. Any idea who they were?'

Robinson shrugged.

'There used to be no violence here,' he replied, not answering Love's question. 'Now –' he shrugged. 'It is the way of the world, I suppose.'

He turned towards the Cord.

'You drive,' he told Love, as though there was nothing further to say about the other matter.

'See how it handles compared with your Cord.'

'I'll just have a quick wash and change my clothes, then I'll be with you.'

'You do look a bit bushed. What's happened? Rough night?'

'Rough time,' Love replied. 'I had an argument with a man.'

'Not one of those Chinese again?'

'No. Another person altogether.'

'What happened to him?'

'He disappeared,' said Love, 'and left his calling card.'

He indicated the lump on his head.

'That's on the back of your head,' said Robinson, frowning. 'Was he behind you?'

'Yes.'

'Who was he?'

'I have no idea. That's the odd thing.'

Robinson shrugged, looked up the road and then back at Love. Suddenly he seemed uneasy, as he had been previously. His confidence had diminished.

'You didn't even see him?'

'There were two. I got sight of the other man. He wore dark glasses and had hands with the strongest grip I've ever come across.'

Love explained what had happened in Mr Stevenson's house. Robinson listened in silence, made no comment. Love thought it odd that he did not even look surprised.

He tried to put possible reasons for this out of his mind as he gripped the familiar cream-coloured steering wheel, glanced along the long bonnet, fired up the engine.

'You'll have to guide me where we're going,' he said.

'That's easy. Just head north. Aim out along Sheridan Street. That's the main drag out of town.'

High-rise buildings, blocks of flats fell away. Here and there, in between them, were small houses, shabby, unloved relics of the past before development started.

'Deros,' Robinson explained. 'Derelicts. A few of our coloured brethren may have 'em, or drop-outs. But it's nothing like Darwin. They call them the long grass people, for outside the Post Office, they sleep rough in the long grass, or on park benches. Crocodile Corner, they call that, because they put the bite for a hand-out on anyone passing by, any visitor like you, who doesn't know the background.'

'It's a pretty rough background Australia has, isn't it?'

'Of course. It's a pretty rough country. It's big. That means you have to be tough to survive. Look around you now.'

Love did so. The sea on one side, cane fields on the other, the empty road stretching straight ahead, hot tarmac shimmering under a merciless sun.

'Up North, just beyond where I live, on the Palmer River, where they found gold a hundred years ago, Port Douglas was the port built to ship the gold out. Then, as I told you, when the railway came, they developed Cairns.

'They brought in a whole load of Chinese to work in the mines in those days. The Abos used to grab the odd one from time to time – some were cannibals then. And they liked the flavour of Chinese meat. Because they ate rice they reckoned they tasted better than Europeans. The Abos would tie them up by the pigtails, to keep them alive until they wanted them. In India I've seen people hang up chickens by the legs until they're ready to eat them. Same idea, different meat. Of course, that was a hundred odd years ago.'

'Things have changed?' said Love.

'In the way people kill each other, yes. The instinct is still there, though not with the Abos.'

'With the Chinese?'

'Why do you ask that?'

'I just wondered. Might they be getting their own back?'

'They might just be,' agreed Robinson slowly. 'You think a Chinese hit you?'

'I've no reason to. All I know is that, as you can see, someone did – and he or she didn't pull their punch.'

They drove on past Port Douglas with its marina, the Sheraton Mirage and country club, and green expanses of short-cropped, freshly watered grass on its golf courses. Again, everything was built on a splendid scale: a hundred and twenty-one hectares of garden and golf course with seventy full-time gardeners at work to make sure every edge was trimmed, every weed removed. An Arcade had forty shops and boutiques, selling expensive motor cars, fishing gear, the latest fashions. Bond Street by the beach.

They drove on for several miles. Then Robinson touched Love's arm.

'Pull in to the right about half a mile ahead,' he told him.

Love swung the big car between two gateposts topped with stone pineapples, along a gravelled drive newly planted on either side with palms. Chinese gardeners with tractors and mechanical diggers did not even look up as they passed.

'You own all this?' Love asked, impressed.

'With others, yes.'

Love parked outside a large building in the colonial style; tall pillars, white walls, tiled roof. Its height and elegance gave a sense of serenity and unconscious superiority. The message of the house and grounds was simple and unarguable; we are rich, and we intend to stay that way.

A yacht lay at anchor, close to the quay, still as a painted white ship on a painted stage.

'It's safe to leave the car here with the hood down?'

'Of course. They're all my people. The place is well guarded. Come on deck. I'll join you in a rum today.'

The yacht's white hull dazzled in the sunshine. A vast area of glass on either side of the state rooms flashed like a huge heliograph as they approached. On the top deck superstructure a radar aerial turned continuously. In the stern Love saw two shielded domes for the satellite communications system, a crane to winch aboard the two speed boats she carried, or a car.

'A hundred feet long,' said Robinson proudly. 'We carry pretty well everything – eight sets of scuba gear with a compressor. A 'chute if you want to para-fly and be towed behind in the air. Jet skis, under-water aqua-scooter and video camera. TV, of course. Video, stereo, water skis. She can sail a distance of seven thousand miles on one filling of fuel. That means almost anywhere in the world.'

'Sounds like a floating home,' said Love. 'You use her a lot?'

'Not nearly enough,' Robinson reflected. 'My business keeps me pretty well land bound. Maybe I will in the future.'

'It's always tomorrow the rich are going to enjoy themselves,' said Love. 'I've noticed this. Tomorrow and tomorrow and tomorrow. But somehow never today. Why not now? It is always later than we think. Someone said that the rich are like people who build a private golf course – and then find they have no friends to play against.

'Maybe you should follow the advice of a seventeenth-century physician, Sir Thomas Browne, whose opinions I respect.

'"Be substantially great in thyself and more than thou appearest unto others, and let the world be deceased in thee. Measure not thyself by thy morning shadow, but by the extent of thy grave."'

Robinson looked at him sharply.

'Maybe you are right, Doctor,' he replied. 'But once you start in pursuit of riches you have to keep running, otherwise the morning shadow can soon overtake you.

'A man bathing near the shore in the roughest sea can

survive the biggest waves. But if he ventures out of his depth and suddenly a big wave comes in, he can be swamped.'

'Is that your situation?' asked Love.

'To some extent. I believe that people, or events, or sometimes both, are always on your back – like predators – or at best, just behind you. As you found with whoever attacked you.'

'Time's wingéd chariot hurrying near?'

'I wouldn't mind the wingéd chariot. It's who drives the chariot that causes me sleepless nights.'

'Like now?'

'Like now let's have a rum each. Then we'll order lunch. Would you like to eat on deck or in the dining room?'

'On deck,' Love told him.

'Good. That is also my preference. Then we can see and be seen.'

He picked up a telephone, spoke to the bridge.

'We wish to leave in ten minutes. Go out for twenty miles and drop anchor.'

Harry Ling appeared with a menu.

'I think you might enjoy some crab legs to start with,' Robinson suggested. 'They're rather special out here. Then, if you want to stay with food from the sea, how about a lobster? Good. White wine? I would suggest a Brown Brothers' Victorian, a dry muscat. Whatever you want, I think you'll find we carry it aboard.'

'You're pretty well stocked?'

'Like a small town,' Robinson replied. 'When you've been poor and hungry you never forget those things, Doctor. You surround yourself with the artefacts of wealth, more food than you can eat, more drink than you could ever hope to consume. You cannot tolerate the prospect of ever being short of anything again. Not ever. Do I make myself clear?'

'Abundantly.'

Somewhere in the deep hidden heart of the vessel, engines started with a distant, powerful hum. A faint tremor filtered through the scrubbed deck beneath their feet. Crew members in immaculately pressed white duck uniforms cast off fore and aft. The yacht turned her elegant prow, sharp as a sword blade, out towards the open sea. The engines accelerated. The bows of the yacht lifted very slightly, almost imperceptibly, as the power of twelve thousand horses thrust her through the waves.

Love and Robinson sat in canvas chairs on the after deck, seeing land fade behind them. Soon it was no more than a white streak of sand with a line of green forcing it down into the water. Then even that vanished altogether.

They anchored. Two stewards brought out a table with a starched linen cloth, set out silver cutlery and three glasses for each place. Love waited until they had finished. Then, sitting back in his chair, he looked quizzically at his host.

'As a physician,' he said, 'although not yours, I must say you seem more relaxed than yesterday.'

'I am,' said Robinson. 'I had a visit yesterday from someone who knows you.'

'Really? Who's that?'

'Richard Mass Parkington. The Midland Widows.'

'I know he is in Australia. We met in a hotel at Ayers Rock.'

'Really? He did not tell me that. But he remarked on the Cord – and I remarked on the fact that, like you, he drank rum. Not the most common drink here, Doctor. Are you working with him out here?'

'No. We have met in the past on several occasions. The last time, when he asked me to confirm the provenance of a Cord in Pakistan.'

'Really? I believe he was once involved in what is loosely called Intelligence?'

'Possibly,' said Love non-committally.

'It is wise not to speak too much of such private matters. When we met first, I felt I could trust you as a physician. Now, having thought more deeply on the matter, I would like to trust you in another way.'

Robinson paused, dredging for the right words. Love sipped his drink, watched him. Robinson went on.

'I asked you to visit me in Cairns for two reasons, Doctor. One, because I liked what I had read about you in the Cord club magazine. You seemed a straightforward person.'

Again, he paused.

'And two?' Love prompted him.

'I wanted to tell someone I believed I could trust totally about a matter that's causing me great concern.'

'A medical one?' asked Love.

'No,' he said. 'A private matter. I want your help, Doctor. And I am prepared to pay for it.'

'In what way can I help? Never mind any fee. I am your guest. In mediaeval times it was the rule of chivalry that so long as a guest had food from his host undigested in his stomach, he was honour bound to take part in whatever enterprise his host suggested. I think that is a good rule. I will abide by it.'

'Thank you. I've made enquiries about you from a number of people. That's how I learned you had once been involved, however peripherally, with Colonel MacGillivray. Possibly that's also where Parkington first met you.

'I don't know, and you are unlikely to tell me. But I am in a position in which you are probably the only man I *can* trust who can conceivably help me. I suggested having lunch aboard the yacht where it is safer than in a restaurant.'

'Safer? In what way?'

'I present less of a target here. I'm surrounded by people who I pay well, who – up to a certain point – I feel I can trust. You noticed that Chinese steward in my house and here?'

'Yes.'

'As Camille may have told you, he's my nephew, a third-year medical student. He's going to England to complete his training. He and his sister Anna are both working for me. She is my confidential secretary.

'You mentioned one old custom from mediaeval times, Doctor. I will tell you of another. Kings and prelates used

160

to employ people who tasted their food before they ate it, just in case it was poisoned. Harry, the steward, is their modern equivalent.'

'He tastes – or tests – everything before you eat it?'

'Yes. He volunteered to do so. I did not ask him.'

'But who would want to poison you, Mr Robinson?'

'No-one would specifically *want* to poison me or to shoot me. But they could wish simply to kill me, to take me out, be rid of me. I fear such an attempt. What I am asking you, Doctor, is your help to prevent me being murdered.'

CHAPTER NINE

Ten thousand miles away, Colonel MacGillivray sipped his ten o'clock cup of black coffee, and without any pleasure regarded Miss Jenkins across the room.

'From your general demeanour,' he said, 'you would appear to be the bearer of bad news? Why can't someone bring me some good news for a change?'

'Perhaps this *is* good news, just disguised,' Miss Jenkins replied hopefully. She did not like to see the colonel depressed. She always felt that this must in some way be her fault.

'Then tell me how good its disguise is.'

'I think you had better read this yourself,' she suggested, handed him a buff folder, bound in pink tape. He opened it, read the two sheets of paper it contained, closed the folder, handed it back to her.

'These have just come in from our liaison officers with Special Branch and Five,' Miss Jenkins explained as though this knowledge would in some way raise his spirits.

'I know,' he said dourly. 'It says so. There is no need for you to tell me as well. Now, why do *you* think they want me to see this?'

'I think, Colonel, because we have had a query from Mr Parkington about Mrs Green. I passed it on to Five and the S.B. in the usual way.'

'Who the hell is this Mrs Green?' asked MacGillivray irritably.

'A rich widow who died in a Wiltshire hospital. She was attended by Dr Love on the night she died.'

'Dr Love? The same medical practitioner who was involved with Parkington in Pakistan over that Cord car worth millions, apparently?'

'The same.'

'That figures,' said MacGillivray shortly. 'Something went wrong then because he was involved, didn't it?'

'Not exactly then, Colonel. Everything was wrong before he arrived. Actually, to be fair, he was largely responsible for putting things right.'

'Who wants to be fair, Miss Jenkins? Life is unfair. Why should we try to be different?'

'In the case of Mrs Green, Colonel, he was only called in to see her because her own doctor was unavailable.'

'Then she dies. Now we have a break-in to her house, and her spinster companion apparently shoots this intruder out of hand! Odd behaviour, surely, in a maiden lady of presumably gentle birth. Fortunately, she has a licence for the pistol. Said she needed it for shooting rodents.'

'This particular rodent came in through a downstairs window on two legs, Colonel,' Miss Jenkins interrupted.

'So I am aware. He said his name was Kent, which has an English ring to it. Hops, oast houses and so on. But Five ran his details through the computer and it seems his real name is Kravinsky, which has a more Russian ring.

'He is understandably uncommunicative about his past, but his fingerprints establish his identity. Like the man who died in Bloor Street, he was once in the GRU. It seems that a colleague misbehaved in some way and two colleagues were blamed, simply because they were working with him. For that misfortune, they spent years in the uranium mines – where Kent was also serving a sentence for a misdemeanour so petty that here he probably wouldn't even have had his wrist slapped. Then, under Gorbachev's new policies, they are all released before their time.'

'I can't see what he could possibly hope to find relative

to his experiences in a widow's home in Wiltshire. And it is unlikely she would keep much money there.'

'I don't think he was necessarily after money. But whatever he was looking for he didn't find. Perhaps, of course, he wasn't really looking for anything that had any bearing on his sentence. Maybe someone simply used him, wanted to frighten Mrs Green for some reason.'

'If so, they left it too late. Kent arrived after her death.'

'So that leaves Miss Dukes, who seems unusually handy with a pistol for a maiden lady.'

'I am also good with a pistol,' replied Miss Jenkins frostily. 'I am a member of a shooting club.'

'Of course you are. But then you are special, Miss Jenkins. Miss Dukes may also be special, but in ways I cannot even imagine. Be so good as to ask S.B. to run her details through the Police Computer. If they come up with nothing, then perhaps one of their young men could pay her a call, either announced or otherwise. See whether he can find anything at all that could conceivably throw light on this business.'

'You're much more cheerful, Colonel, now that you feel we are getting somewhere.'

'I rejoice that you think so. But actually we may just be running on the spot, confusing motion with progress.'

'In that case, maybe Dr Love could help us. After all, this has taken place in his home village.'

'Then find out all the details you can, my dear, and fax them out to Parkington in Australia for the good doctor to see.'

Love looked at Robinson in surprise. This was what Camille had also told him. But did the fact that two people said the same thing necessarily mean that it was true? For a moment, neither man spoke. Sea water clucked gently against the yacht's polished hull. The noise sounded vaguely disapproving, disbelieving. Just beneath the surface, blue and gold angel fish fluttered past; then a shoal of damsel fish, with five light and dark rings round their bodies, and multi-coloured parrot fish, with mouths like the beaks of birds.

Sharp as daggers, they flitted this way and that in the clear sea.

'Are you serious?' Love asked, breaking the silence.

'Deadly serious.'

'Have you been to the police?'

'No.'

'Why not?'

'I've no proof. And I might have to tell the police about things they have no right to know. And what could they do in any case? Have you ever thought, Doctor, why people are often reluctant to give evidence in a trial against a dedicated man of violence, a real hoodlum? Agreed, he may be sent down, *if* the jury hasn't been nobbled, *if* the judge isn't corrupt.

'But what happens to the witness when the trial's over, whether the crook's been found guilty or not? Nothing for maybe a month. And then, one day a fellow stops him in the street, asks the way to the airport or some such thing. And as he starts to tell him, the stranger brings a potato out of his pocket with a razor blade buried in it.

'Last bloke I heard of who had this done to him needed twenty-five stitches and lost the sight of one eye. People with a grudge can wait a long time to pay it off. They often actually enjoy the wait, because then they pay the grudge back so many more times in imagination.'

'Is that the case with you?'

'It could well be.'

'Well, who *is* after you?'

Robinson looked away, poured himself another rum. He was clearly reluctant to continue. Doubt and fear showed in his face, clouding his eyes. Had he already said too much? Had he given away a secret which he felt he should not entrust to anyone?

'Every week in my surgery people come in with something that worries them,' said Love gently, to prompt him. 'Some-times it's a sex problem. They think they've caught some social disease, but they don't want to admit it. When I was young and in the Army, if a soldier had a dose of pox, he'd always claim he'd caught it off a lavatory seat.

'The MO told them firmly that only padres and majors could *ever* catch it that way. No-one of less rank. He couldn't help them unless they were honest with him. I can't help you unless you tell me everything. Half is no use.'

'I accept that,' said Robinson. 'But before we start, I want you to know that, as I've said, I'm not asking advice for nothing.'

'To hell with that. I'm pleased to help you.'

'And I'm pleased to pay. I won't offer you money, Doctor, but I know your interest in Cord cars. You have seen my Cords and know I have two of the type in which we drove here. I intend to make one over to you.'

'That's far too generous,' said Love. 'There's no need whatever for you to do this. I haven't helped you yet. I may not be able to help you at all.'

'You're listening,' said Robinson simply. 'That's help when you're on your own. Take the car, and no more argument. I'll write a note about that when I get home this afternoon. You can pay me a dollar if you like, so you can say you bought it, in case there's any gift tax or nonsense of that kind.

'Now to my problem. I don't know whether you know much about money, Doctor, but with everyone I've met who has made a great deal, there's always one secret chapter in their lives, one incident they're reluctant to talk about; something they dread may appear in a newspaper article about them. Do I make myself clear?'

'Abundantly,' said Love. 'What's your incident?'

'Years ago, I took money that wasn't mine. I used it. I didn't just double it, I increased it several hundred times. No-one knows about this episode in my past, any more than they know how other, much richer men than me, *really* started.

'Some of them married for money. Others murdered for money. Most swindled for it. Money is like a seed. You can throw away a packet of seeds and have nothing to show for them. Or you can plant them and grow a bed of flowers.

So with money, if you've got the green fingers of the true financier – what some rather foolishly call the Midas touch – you can make it grow amazingly. But you have to have some in the first place. I had none. So I took what I needed.'

'Do the people you took it from suspect you?'

'No-one suspected me. Or so I thought. But you never can be quite sure. I've brought you out here because I am convinced that no-one can spy on us, no-one can hear what we are saying, or even see us here.

'But really, in the last analysis, I am deluding myself. Satellites – French, American, Russian – are whirling round the world all the time. They can photograph so clearly you can actually read the figures on the Cord's number plate taken from, who knows – twenty, two hundred miles up? Our faces are probably now on someone's monitor screen. And if they can lip read, they'll know what we are talking about.'

'Maybe,' said Love. 'But it's still unlikely that anyone was reading a satellite print-out when you took this money you say wasn't yours.'

'Agreed, Doctor. But someone in a bank, in a clearing house, in an office, might have seen a letter. They could have seen my name against a deposit account and added up two sums, and reached one conclusion.'

'That's all hypothesis.'

'Agreed, again. What is not hypothesis is that in Darwin last week I saw two men from the past.'

'You took the money from them?'

'No. But as a result – if only as an indirect result – they suffered greatly because of my action. If I had seen one man, that could be coincidence. But to see these two, on the same day, in the same city, that's no coincidence, Doctor.'

'So what did you do?'

'I went to a private detective. He found out very quickly who they are. They're living in Katherine, in the Northern Territory.'

'That's quite a distance from here,' said Love, remembering Colonel Wargrave's stories.

'We're used to distances in this country. A thousand miles is nothing – a couple of hours' flight.'

'So you think they're up here on some revenge project?'

'Yes. Either for themselves,' he paused. 'Or for someone else.'

'You know who else?'

Robinson shook his head.

'No.'

'You trust the private detective?'

'I don't know.'

'Why do you say that?'

'When I was leaving his office, a coin dropped right on the street behind me. It must have come out of a high window. I looked up at his office window. The curtains were pulled. But there was just a glint of something.'

'Like what?'

'Like a camera lens.'

'So you think he could have photographed you, then gone to see the two men and offered them a picture – for a fee, of course?'

'I didn't give him my address.'

'He could find it easily enough,' said Love. 'So could they – once they have your photo.'

He sat for a moment, thinking.

'You wish my help, you say?'

Robinson nodded.

'I do.'

'Then I would like to tell Parkington what you have just told me. Is that allowable?'

'If you feel you have to,' said Robinson reluctantly.

'I do,' said Love. 'Now tell me something else. Who knew I was coming to see you in Cairns?'

'No-one,' said Robinson at once. 'I typed the letters myself.'

'Did you keep a copy?'

'Oh, sure.'

'Well, then, what about Anna? Could she have looked at it?'

'She *could* have done, but I think that most unlikely. Why do you ask?'

'When you're a doctor and faced with a difficult diagnosis, you make a list in your mind of all the possible things that it could be. I'm doing that now.'

'And what is your conclusion?'

'First, I think I should get back to Cairns and have a word with my friend about some possibilities.'

'I'll tell the captain we want to sail immediately,' said Robinson. 'What's the other conclusion?'

'I am sorry to say this, Mr Robinson, but I must be frank with you. You are not being totally frank with me. This is not the whole story, Mr Robinson, only a small part of it. Unless I know it all, I cannot help you, much as I would like to do so.'

Robinson stood up, walked along the deck for a few paces, stood looking out to sea. Then he made up his mind, turned back to Love.

'All right, Doctor. I will show you something which may convince you my fears are real.'

Love followed him through a state room, splendid with white leather settees and armchairs; gold candlesticks glowed on a polished rosewood table. Robinson unlocked a small door at the far end. This led into a tiny anteroom, with a small desk, a single wooden chair. He carefully locked the door behind them, then took another key and opened a door built into a bookcase and concealed by the spines of dummy, leather-backed books. It belonged to a refrigerator, empty except for a small plastic bag. Robinson spread a newspaper on the desk, put the bag on this, shook out the contents. Love stood looking at two frozen human ears. Beneath them was a small visiting card. On this was typed in block letters: 'You will hear from us again.'

'I received these some days before you arrived.'

'Have you told anyone about them?'

'No.'

'Whose are they?'

Robinson shrugged. He looked very pale.

'I have no idea.'

'Who sent them?'

'I wonder if Mr Singer or Mr Hargreaves could be involved.'

'Why?'

'Because, as I have told you, they have no reason to like me.'

'That isn't reason enough to cut the ears off some man, living or dead – unless he was also involved in some way. And they were taking revenge on him.'

Robinson did not reply.

'Have you had any other parcels like this?'

'Yes. One. A few days earlier. It contained the little fingers of a man's hands.'

'What did you do with them?'

'Threw them into the sea.'

'Have you been in touch with Singer or Hargreaves?'

'No. But Singer has telephoned my house. I told Harry Ling to say I was never at home to him.'

'They are still in Australia?'

'So far as I know, yes.'

Love replaced the two ears and the card in the bag, put them back in the refrigerator.

Robinson had moved across the little room and was standing with his back to him. Love could see that he was weeping. He had not expected this; he felt suddenly immensely sorry for him, and personally inadequate: Robinson was clearly on the edge of despair. Love put a hand on his shoulder in an attempt to comfort him.

'You think you can help me, Doctor?' Robinson asked him anxiously.

'I will certainly do my best,' Love promised. But even as he spoke, he knew that Robinson had still not told him the whole truth, perhaps not even the major part of it. And until he did so, he could remain in mortal danger, and there was nothing that Love or Parkington could do to help him, nothing at all.

And as Love watched the land grow larger as the yacht came in towards the shore, he thought of something else. Mr Robinson's worries were keeping him from making further enquiries about the grave of Miss Annabel Crawford.

Robinson turned to face him.

'You wonder why I weep, Doctor, and I sense from your attitude that you feel I am still not being totally frank with you. Am I right?' he asked.

Love nodded.

'Yes,' he agreed. 'Quite right.'

'Then I will tell you the reason for my grief. The ears – and I suspect the fingers – are not from a stranger. They are from my only son, of my first marriage. I have had an anonymous note to say that one or other of these men – or maybe both of them – killed him in Lisbon. That way they wanted to get at me. Just as those Chinese on the Esplanade hoped to get at me through Camille. That is why I am so grateful you are going to help me, Doctor. With you, I have a good fighting chance. On my own, I am as good as dead, and worse, so is Camille.'

Love came into his hotel room, poured himself four fingers of rum, added lime juice and three cubes of ice from the bedroom refrigerator. He looked through the classified pages of the telephone directory, then dialled a number.

'*Marlin Coast Enquirer* here,' a man's voice answered cheerfully. 'Thank you for calling. Can I help you?'

'I hope so,' said Love. 'Your newsroom, please.'

'One moment.'

A click of connections; another voice, more harassed.

'Hullo, there. News editor speaking.'

'Hullo there to you,' Love replied. 'I'm ringing to ask your help and also to give you a story. My name is Jason Love. I'm an English doctor over here on vacation. I'm trying to find the grave of an English girl, the niece of an acquaintance of mine. She died round here quite recently.'

'What did she die of, sport? Not old age?'

'No. Apparently a swimming accident. Drowned. I just don't know how, exactly. That's what I want to find out. Her name was Annabel Crawford. She was the niece of a Mrs Green of Bishop's Combe in Wiltshire, England. I wonder if your paper has run any report of her death and funeral? I promised her aunt I would make arrangements for her grave to be looked after.'

'Hang on a minute, sport. Annabel Crawford, you say? Stay with me while I tap out the name.'

Love waited, sipping his drink. In the distance, in an unseen newsroom, he could hear people talking, the click of typewriter keys. A radio announcer was giving details of an earthquake in Afghanistan, and a road train that had run out of road outside Darwin, allotting equal time to both catastrophes. Then the news editor was back.

'Sorry, mate. Nothing. Nix. Nothing at all.'

'Could you put a piece in the paper saying that if any of her friends are still around, I would be happy to meet them – buy them lunch or dinner?'

'Why not? Makes a story on a dull day.'

Love explained where he was staying.

'By the way,' he added. 'I've already asked the only contact I have here – Charles Robinson. He knows nothing at all about Miss Crawford.'

'Why should he? Reckon he knows more about old cars.'

'Right,' said Love. 'We share that interest.'

'A very rich man,' said the news editor, his voice hushed with the respect the mention of money induces in some people.

'Glad to hear it,' Love told him. 'And I hope you have some luck.'

'Good on you, sport. And thanks again for your call.'

Love replaced the receiver, looked up the number of the local radio station, dialled it. The operator put him through to the producer of a talk-in programme. He repeated his request, and was told it would be broadcast within the next five minutes.

Love poured himself another rum while he waited to hear this on the radio in his room.

If anyone in Cairns knew anything about Annabel Crawford, how she had lived, how she had died, where and when she was buried, they would at least know how to contact him. And if they didn't, Love reckoned that she could have made no friends or even acquaintances. Or that, if she had, none of them wished to come forward and admit they knew her.

Or could there be another reason altogether, which sounded so bizarre and unlikely that Love hardly liked even to consider it?

Parkington sat at a desk in a back room of the Midland Widows office in Darwin. An air-conditioning machine hummed beneath windows that looked out over a stretch of grass and then the ocean. The view was magnificent, but he was not concerned with this; he could see this spectacular stretch of coast any day. What he wanted to see now and could not, was some link between seemingly totally disparate events.

On the desk in front of him lay a sheaf of fax messages, spread out in order of arrival. They had come from Quendon Motor Factors in code, some in response to a request from him for certain details, others offering information MacGillivray had collected on his own initiative. All had travelled in a circuitous route, by way of a boat-building yard in Vancouver, a chemical plant in Johannesburg, a tourist office in Melbourne. Broken down on his portable decoding machine, hooked up to the office computer, they added little to his total knowledge but something to his confusion.

It was his custom, when working for MacGillivray, or the Midland Widows, to absorb all manner of facts about seemingly unconnected people, places and incidents. Most of his cases, he would say, were like a train that you could join at several points on its journey, but in the end you reached the same destination. But where exactly was this train of events leading him?

He had asked for every known detail on the National Police computer about Mrs Green. Back came the news she was unknown under that name. Nor was there any trace of her birth, of a Mr Green, or their marriage. So far as records were concerned, and the department known as Traces, which collated all manner of seemingly irrelevant facts about everyone – parking fines, police court appearances, income tax enquiries – Mrs Green did not exist at The Hall or anywhere else.

Of course, Parkington knew that she did. But under what name? And why would anyone choose to live under a pseudonym in virtual seclusion with a companion? Possibly, because she had a secret. But again, this possibility only provoked another question: What sort of secret?

MacGillivray had produced some details about Miss Dukes, but none of any obvious relevance or value. She was in her fifties, had a medical history of heart trouble, had been employed by a south coast hotel as a receptionist, then worked as the housekeeper for a retired dentist until his death, and then for Mrs Green.

Nothing there that Parkington could see with any bearing on his problems.

It was the custom for some Australian security authorities to work, as they put it diplomatically, 'in close liaison', not only with the police but also with certain private investigators. On the desk were several photographs passed on to Parkington by his Australian colleagues. They had been taken of Charles Robinson by a Mr Hogan in Darwin. Robinson had apparently engaged Hogan to investigate the backgrounds of two other men – a Mr Singer and a Mr Hargreaves.

MacGillivray's department had never heard of Hogan, but produced a few sparse details about the other two. Singer was a Pole; Hargreaves, a Bulgarian. They had both been in the Russian GRU, working on forged documents – passports, birth and share certificates. For some reason not known, they had fallen into disfavour and served for several years in a uranium mine. With *glasnost*, they were released and allowed exit visas. But why should they go to Australia, the other side of the world? The answer could be that, as Love had suggested, they wished to frighten Robinson or to meet him.

As Parkington suspected, Robinson also had a Russian background. He had defected in the 1980s, an act of betrayal that had caused shock waves within the entire GRU.

Could Robinson's defection have caused these other two men, possibly with others, to be arrested and condemned to the mines? Had they travelled to Australia to extract revenge, or could there be some deeper, more complex reason?

Hargreaves was dead and Singer had disappeared. As Parkington would expect from a professional, he had left no clues as to his whereabouts.

And what about Dr Love? He was seeking Mrs Green's niece, or someone she claimed was her niece. But Mrs Green – who had apparently never existed under that name – was dead. Her companion, Miss Dukes, according to MacGillivray, was not at home. So where was she? Everyone seemed to be moving away or moving on. Parkington felt he was the only one to be staying put, marking time.

He shuffled the papers around the top of the desk, as though by so doing he might physically fit the missing pieces together. At last he came to a conclusion; not a finite conclusion, but he hoped that it might at least be on the way to that, a further step on a journey whose destination he still did not know. He put the papers in his briefcase, went out through the front office.

'See you again soon, sport?' asked the manager hopefully, a cheerful young man in a sharp suit and horn-rimmed glasses.

'I hope,' said Parkington. 'In the meantime, can you give me a lift to the airport? I want to catch the next flight to Cairns.'

'No problem.'

When the plane landed, Parkington hired a cab and drove out to the cemetery. He walked up and down the lines of neat gravestones until, as though by chance, he reached the hut where the caretaker sat reading a newspaper. He looked up as Parkington put his head down to the speaking hole in the window.

'Care to earn a hundred dollars?' Parkington asked him, musing, as he did so, how easy it was to be generous with someone else's money.

'Doing what?' the man replied.

Parkington pushed a visiting card with the Midland Widows crest across to him.

'Helping me with an insurance enquiry,' he said. 'Nothing lethal.'

'Well?' asked the man. 'Where's the money?'

Parkington took out a fifty dollar bill, pushed it through the hole.

'The other fifty is yours when you help me,' he said.

'I'm helping you,' the man assured him.

'A Pom came in here the other day, asked for the grave of a Miss Annabel Crawford. Right?'

'Sure, I remember him. But there's no grave here for anyone of that name.'

'So what did you do when he left?'

'Do? Nothing.'

'For fifty dollars,' said Parkington, 'who did you tell he had been here?'

'Tell? I don't know what you mean.'

His eyes were suddenly shifty; he would not meet Parkington's gaze.

'I want to know who you rang,' said Parkington. 'I am investigating a serious case. I can easily check it out through the telephone company, but you could save me a lot of time – and maybe yourself some trouble.'

'What sort of trouble?'

'Trouble that comes from not having fifty dollars.'

'Shit!' said the man. 'Here's the number.'

He took a piece of paper from his jacket pocket, handed it to Parkington.

'Who answered?'

'No-one. An answering machine.'

'So what did you say?'

'That Dr Love had been looking for this particular person's grave.'

'Who asked you to do this?'

'A woman. Said she had known this girl who wasn't buried here. This doctor fellow was a nutter who was pursuing her. She wanted to know when he arrived in Cairns. She suspected he would come here.'

'An odd story,' said Parkington.

The man shrugged.

'It's an odd world, sport. How about that fifty dollars?'

Parkington handed over the note.

'If the woman rings again, contact me. There's another hundred in it for you if you do.'

'Right, Buster,' said the man and suddenly looked past Parkington.

'I must go. Funeral party coming in.'

Parkington walked out, past the hearse with banks of flowers, the black cars behind it filled with mourners. Someone who might not have enjoyed too many rides in a large car in their lifetime was now making their last motor trip in style. Parkington thought there must be a moral here somewhere. But he could not see what it was.

Love came into his hotel. As he collected his key from the desk, the clerk gave him a message.

'A Mr Parkington has been telephoning you,' he said. 'Twice. He said it was important. You have his number?'

Love nodded. It was his experience that when people left a message and said it was important, the matter was generally of more importance to them than to the person they were trying to contact. Pondering on this matter of

177

relative values, he went up in the elevator, opened the door of his room.

A woman was sitting in the seat under the window, overlooking the garden and the bay, where she could see who came in and out of the room. She was wearing a white T-shirt and faded jeans. From her complexion, she looked as though she spent a lot of time out of doors: her skin was deeply tanned by sun and sea. She was in her thirties, but, he thought, not too far into them.

'Dr Love?' she asked, standing up as he entered the room.

'The same. Refuse all substitutes. And you?'

'Annabel Crawford.'

'But I thought you were *dead*?' Love said in amazement. 'I've just put out a request in the local paper and on the radio for anyone who knew you.'

Annabel smiled.

'As in the case of Mark Twain, rumours of my death have been greatly exaggerated,' she replied. 'I heard on the car radio that Dr Love, a Pom over here to meet an old car enthusiast, was looking for anyone who had known me.

'He didn't ask to see *me*, for he believed I was six feet under. I rang the radio station and the DJ gave me your hotel. The clerk told me your room number. They were cleaning the room, so in I came – and here I am.'

'This must be the most unexpected revival since Lazarus confounded the undertakers,' said Love. 'And you are much better looking. In fact, as a doctor, I can truthfully say I have never seen a healthier corpse!'

She smiled.

'I hope not too many of the corpses you have seen were once your patients?'

'Far too many,' Love admitted. 'Like most doctors, I bury my mistakes.'

'Well, no-one's buried me – yet. I can't understand how this absurd rumour ever started. Is this some sort of joke, that I'm supposed to be dead? I've been out in Australia for months. My mother knows I'm here.'

'Your *mother*? How does she come into this? Miss Dukes told me you were Mrs Green's niece and had been drowned in a bathing accident.'

'Wrong on both counts. Mrs Green isn't my aunt. She is my mother.'

'I didn't know that,' said Love slowly. 'I only met her once, when I was called in to see her. Anyhow, Miss Dukes is definitely of the opinion you are dead. I have even been to the cemetery to try and find your grave. I suggest we ring her – now – to give her good news for a change.'

'Why for a change? What do you mean?'

'You probably won't have heard, but Mrs Green – your mother – is seriously ill. I had her admitted to hospital just before I came out here.'

Annabel's face creased with concern.

'I had no idea,' she said. 'No-one told me.'

'Hardly surprising – since Miss Dukes had heard you weren't around to tell. Speak to her now and find out how your mother is.'

Love dialled the number of The Hall, waited for five minutes, holding the receiver up to his ear, willing someone to answer a telephone ringing in a crumbling house on the other side of the world.

Here, in a sun-filled room overlooking the ocean, he remembered dust on suits of armour, weeds in the drive, a house of perpetual twilight. The Hall must be empty, he thought, or else Miss Dukes would have answered. She might be out shopping. Anything.

He checked his watch. Ten past noon. That meant it would be between two and four o'clock in the morning in England – he never could remember when summer time began and ended. Even so, summer time or winter time, no shops would be open at that hour in Wiltshire. He replaced the receiver.

'No answer. We'll try later. She could be asleep and hasn't heard it. No – a better idea.'

He dialled another number. A sleepy voice answered.

'Dr Jones.'

179

'Jason Love here. I am in Australia. Sorry to ring you at this ungodly hour.'

Jones' Welsh voice became petulant.

'Well, if you're sorry, why do it, man?'

'To give your patient Miss Dukes some good news. Do you know where she is? I have with me a relation of Mrs Green, who would like to speak to her. Miss Dukes believed this relative was dead. I want to tell her that she's very much alive, and by my side, wanting to talk to her. Mrs Green will be glad to hear that too, I know.'

Love deliberately did not explain the relationship; Mrs Green might not have told Jones she had a daughter. Maybe this was her secret, the reason she lived as a recluse: she was ashamed.

'Miss Dukes is not at home,' said Jones, more awake now. 'She's gone on holiday. But, of course, you won't have heard? Mrs Green died. Actually, she was dead on arrival at the hospital. Cardiac arrest. Went out like a light, so the ambulance men said.'

'I am sorry to hear that. Was there an inquest?'

'Yes. Purely routine, though. I spoke to the chap who did it. She was cremated the other day. Left instructions in her will that was what she wanted.'

Dr Jones paused.

'But there was one odd thing. They took a blood sample. The result was delayed for some reason, and only arrived after the cremation. And it didn't tally.'

'What do you mean exactly?' Love asked him. He guessed what this meant, but he felt he needed someone else to spell it out for him.

'The sample was AB negative. But Mrs Green had a rare type of red blood cell – beta thalassaemia – as you know, mostly found in people from the Med. or other hot countries.'

'How did you know this? I thought she had never consulted you?'

'Check. She hadn't. But she'd seen a doctor before she

came to Bishop's Combe. It was in her medical records that came with her. Must have been a mistake somewhere in her records. It's easy enough to happen – as we know, eh?

'Anyway, Mrs Green has left Miss Dukes the house and some money in her will. She didn't expect to be left anything, so this was a welcome bonus, and she's gone off indefinitely to get used to having some money – and being free of that life of drudgery. From what she's told me, Mrs Green was a Tartar.

'Anyway, give me your address in Australia just in case she calls me – although I think it's unlikely. She was very chipper when I last saw her, I can tell you. But I have no idea where she is – or how long she'll be away.'

'Thanks. And good night. Or good morning.'

Love replaced the receiver, turned to Annabel.

'Did you hear any of that?' he asked her. 'I was speaking to your mother's physician.'

'No. What did he say?'

'I am very sorry to have to tell you that your mother has died. A heart attack. Very quick, so he said. I am not really surprised. When I saw her she was unable to speak.'

'And I didn't even know she was ill. How odd and yet not unusual, I suppose. We were never really close.'

'I don't remember seeing you in Bishop's Combe,' said Love.

'I was only there on fleeting visits. And these grew rarer as I grew older.'

They stood in silence for a moment. Love opened the mini-bar, took out a bottle of Taittinger champagne, poured out two glasses. They raised them.

'To better times,' he said, watching Annabel for any sign of grief. Sometimes, people could appear to conceal their feelings totally – and then break down hysterically. Annabel seemed to have accepted the news of her mother's death stoically, almost as though this was no surprise, that she had been expecting it.

He could not remember Mrs Green's face clearly; in any

181

case she had been very ill and her features were drawn, her eyes pleading. Annabel's face was not particularly like hers then, and yet it appeared vaguely familiar.

Sir Thomas Browne's views came to mind. 'It is the common wonder of all men, how out of so many millions of faces, there should be none alike. Now, contrary, I wonder as much how there should be any.'

As Love poured out more champagne, pondering Sir Thomas' words, the telephone rang.

'Dr Love?' the caller asked him.

'The same. What do you want?'

'This is Radio Cairns. I have just done a piece on a missing or dead person, Annabel Crawford, giving your name and hotel as the place for anyone who knew her to contact. Don't know whether you heard it? You did? Good.

'We've already had a few calls here at the station, but nothing absolutely positive so far. I'm just checking to see whether the broadcast has produced any leads for you?'

'Indeed, yes. More than that. It has produced Miss Crawford,' Love told him. 'Alive and very well.'

'Well, that's *great*, sport! 'Strewth! Unbelievable, eh? Resurrection morning! Shows the pull of the station – which is a helluva useful boost for us with advertisers. Could we borrow Miss Crawford for ten minutes? I'd like to do a quick interview with her, and then run her back to your hotel – or wherever she wants to go – if that's all right.'

'You'd better ask her,' said Love, handing the receiver to Annabel.

She agreed.

'He's actually speaking on a car phone,' she explained to Love. 'He and a technician are right here outside the hotel.'

'Shall I come down with you?'

'No need. They'll have me back in a quarter of an hour. Less if we do the interview in the car, which he hopes he can.'

'Then let's have dinner together tonight. Unless you have a date?'

Annabel laughed.

'I have now,' she said.

'Where are you staying?'

'Backpackers' hostel on the Esplanade.'

'I've walked past it. I'll see you there at seven,' he told her.

He followed Annabel out to the elevator, waited until it arrived.

As he came back to his room, the bedside telephone was ringing. He picked it up.

'Hullo, sport,' said a breezy male voice he recognised instantly, 'Radio Cairns this end. Dr Love?'

'Yes.'

'You rang me this afternoon. We put a message out on the show. Thought I'd check to see if you'd had any response to that Pom girl.'

'Yes. She turned up,' Love said. 'Wasn't dead after all.'

'Great. We'd like to do a piece with her in the studio, if that's OK? I can send a car over for her.'

'But you've already sent one.'

'You're kidding. We've only one car here, and that's right outside my window in its parking slot. I can see it now as I'm talking to you.'

'Well, someone who said he was from Radio Cairns has just collected her. He rang only minutes ago. She's just left.'

'There you go. Must be some mistake, sport. But when she comes back, please give me a bell. You have my number.'

Love replaced the receiver. Annabel had been discovered – and had disappeared. He stood looking at his half-empty glass of champagne. He could see no bubbles rising in it now. Somehow, it seemed to have gone flat.

Love remembered his surprise at seeing Mrs Green's work-worn hands and the wedding ring loose on her finger. But of course, it wasn't her ring.

The theory that had seemed so implausible he had not cared to consider it, was true. Mrs Green hadn't died. Miss Dukes had.

* * *

The door of Parkington's hotel suite was half-open. Love went into the room. Parkington was sitting in an easy chair in his shirtsleeves, four fingers of rum in a glass by his side.

'I hear you rang,' said Love. 'If it's good news, I'll stay. If it's bad, goodbye.'

'You sound a bit fraught,' said Parkington soothingly.

'I wouldn't disagree,' replied Love. 'And I will tell you the reason for my fraughtness.

'The night before I flew to Perth, I was asked to visit a Mrs Green in our village. She was in a coma and obviously not a good insurance risk, so I got her into hospital double quick.

'Miss Dukes, her companion, had heard I was going to Australia and asked me to check that the grave of Mrs Green's niece, Annabel Crawford, who had been drowned here, was being cared for, and so on. I couldn't refuse, could I?'

'Thousands would,' said Parkington. 'I for one. Immediately.'

'Well, I didn't. And what happens? First, as you know, some man, whose name I still don't know, for reasons I can't even guess at, tries to kill me on top of Ayers Rock. Next, I pay a visit – admittedly uninvited and through a kitchen window – to a Mr Stevenson who apparently wrote to Mrs Green about this accident.

'I don't find Mr Stevenson, but someone else who attacks me with a knife. Then someone else altogether – again I've no idea who – knocks me out. Added to which there is no grave for Annabel Crawford in the cemetery.

'I tell the local radio station and the local newspaper that I would like to meet anyone who knew her – and less than an hour ago she turns up in my hotel room, *alive and well*.

'Minutes later, the radio station rings to ask if she will do a broadcast describing how she heard I was looking for her. She agrees and goes to meet the D.J. Then the radio station rings again to ask exactly the same thing. So the first call was a hoax. But – by whom, and why?

'I speak to Mrs Green's doctor back in Wiltshire. She has died – but a blood test taken by the hospital doesn't tally with her records. So either they are wrong – or, as I believe now, Mrs Green isn't dead. Mr Robinson, meanwhile, and his daughter Camille both tell me he is under some kind of threat of death, and can I help him? Believe me, Richard, I can't even help myself.

'That's my story. Now, what's yours?'

Parkington poured out another glass of rum and lime.

'I came out here to see Mr Robinson, who is a Midland Widows policy holder. He has a number of businesses, garages, properties, a scrap metal business. A lot of money is involved.'

'But surely you didn't come to the other side of the world just because of that? I thought you were called in to investigate troubles. What you tell me is prosperity.'

'Agreed. But ten years ago the Widows had quite a few troubles. Through their American branch, they had insured a ship – the *Kansas Rose* – and its cargo from Boston to Karachi and Bombay. It was packed with all manner of things – armaments, bullion, fish manure, explosives, turpentine, oil – a real dog's dinner of a cargo. Tied up in Bombay's docks just before the monsoon, with all hatches battened down, and the heat terrific, the whole lot caught fire and exploded.'

'Sabotage?'

'No. Spontaneous combustion. We paid out millions. After that, this ship and various other vessels, which were blown out of the water by the explosion, were towed away to some graveyard of old useless ships in Goa. And that, we thought, was that.

'We keep a list of all ships we've insured and what happens to them, where they are. The *Kansas Rose* was sold to a broker in Singapore, then re-sold to Mr Robinson here.'

'Where is it now?'

'Right here. Off Cairns. One of the six you can see on the horizon. She's going to be broken up.'

'But again, *that* didn't bring you here, Parkington. Not on its own.'

'Agreed, again. But when you consider Mr Robinson's background, the story becomes a little more complex. He's not just a hard-working New Australian, who's made a fortune. He was originally Russian, name of Rodinsky. A major in the GRU, Army Intelligence, which is more secretive and infinitely more ruthless than the KGB.'

'Even so,' said Love. '*That* didn't bring you round the world. So what did?'

'He was in Bombay when that ship blew up. And he defected within days. So there could be a link. Our people pumped him dry of what he knew, which was a great deal. Then they gave him a cash handout, a new name, a new face, a new passport, a one-way airline ticket to anywhere in the world – and told him to get lost. Quickly. And forever.

'He came out here, in my opinion, because it's the farthest away he could get from England without starting to come back. Various other defectors have started up in business and made whole new careers, usually writing or lecturing about their experiences. They have done fairly well, but Robinson has done splendidly. Not on the money we paid him, which, as you can imagine when the Treasury is involved, was very little. But he seemed to have money, so he could buy his way into things. And he did and was an almost instant success.

'Now, the thought crosses my mind, did he somehow get some money from selling something he found on that ship? Or did he find some? *If* he was even there. All these are pieces of a jigsaw that don't quite fit together – yet. I want to find out the missing bits. You follow me?'

'I'm beginning to,' said Love. 'I know he's frightened of something. Very frightened. He has asked me to help him, but he's not given me the whole story. None of what you tell me now, for instance.'

'That figures,' said Parkington. 'Would *you* tell a stranger everything, if you were in his position?'

'If I needed help as badly as he says he needs help, I would.'

'There's another point he may or may not know, which could – and indeed should – be worrying him. Another defector was murdered in Lisbon last week. He was Robinson's son – killed by the same man who tried to kill you on Ayers Rock.'

'So who was he – and why attempt to murder me?'

'I'm using the Colonel in London to feed whatever facts he can to me. From that fellow's fingerprints he's not a newcomer on the scene of violence. Quendon Motor Factors have a long file on him. He's a professional killer. Again, he was involved in some way, as a member of the GRU, with Robinson in India. He's got an English name now, or he had. At least he'll be buried under one – Hargreaves.'

'But why me?' said Love. 'He wasn't even one of my patients who didn't like my treatment.'

'Lucky for you he wasn't. But in my view it's the old equation: friend of my enemy is my enemy. He knew you were going to see Robinson. He didn't know why, but the fewer allies Robinson had, the wiser it would be for him, if he wanted to pick him off, to pick you off first.'

'But how would he know I was going to see Robinson?'

'How do people know anything? Someone tells them. Someone told him.'

'But who?'

'We'll find out. Then we'll know the answer. Perhaps to this. Perhaps to the whole conundrum. But he was certainly determined to get you.

'He put a shot into your bed at the hotel in Ayers Rock. But when he learned you had not even been in that room, he knew he'd lose a lot more than face if he missed you a second time. He'd already set you up, by claiming he suffered from angina. So if you saw him apparently in pain, you would immediately think he'd had an attack. He was a pro, remember. And a pro always plans a back-up just in case the first attempt fails.

'So having established you were going on the coach to the

Rock, he got out there before you and was waiting for you up on top.'

'Robinson told me he had seen two people from his past in Darwin,' said Love reflectively. 'Just seeing them there frightened him. But, I wonder, were they meant to?'

'I don't follow you,' said Parkington.

'You know the story of the Baghdad merchant whose servant went into the bazaar and saw Death standing there? He thought Death jostled him and he was afraid.

'The servant ran to his master and begged to borrow his fastest horse, so he could ride far away to Samarra. The merchant agreed, and then as soon as his servant had ridden off, he went down to the bazaar and, sure enough, he also saw Death and he asked him: "Why did you jostle my servant?"

'And Death replied: "I didn't jostle him. I was simply surprised to see him in Baghdad today. For tonight I have an appointment with him in Samarra."'

'So you think those two men deliberately let Robinson know they were in Darwin – because *they* had an appointment with him in Cairns?'

Love nodded.

'So what else do you think?' said Parkington, watching Love closely.

Love put down his drink.

'I think I have been deliberately set up by someone I don't know, for reasons I can only guess at. But there is a link between so many apparently unrelated incidents.

'In my view, Mrs Green is the key person. When Annabel Crawford turned up in my hotel room I rang Mrs Green's house. I assumed that although she would probably be in hospital, Miss Dukes would be there. She wasn't. There was no answer.

'I then rang Dr Jones whose patient Mrs Green was. He told me she had died. So I had to tell Annabel her mother was dead. She took this very calmly. But the more I thought about the matter, I realised there was no reason why she shouldn't.'

188

'What do you mean?' asked Parkington.

'Because Mrs Green wasn't dead at all. Miss Dukes was.'

'How do you know?'

'Dr Jones told me Mrs Green had a very rare blood group. The person who died didn't.'

'How did she die?'

'Natural causes. There was an inquest. I asked specifically what had caused her death. In layman's terms, it was heart failure. Nothing sinister.'

Love walked to the window, stood looking out at the sea.

'And here we have a young woman who says she is Mrs Green's daughter. Believed to be dead, now suddenly alive and well and in my hotel room, wondering what the fuss is about. Then, as quickly as she appears, she disappears.'

Love turned to Parkington.

'Doesn't this lead you to two positive conclusions?' he asked him. Parkington shook his head.

'Can't say it does,' he admitted.

'The first conclusion is that Annabel Crawford doesn't exist.'

'But you bloody well saw her. You just said so.'

'I saw a woman who *said* she was Annabel Crawford. Which leads me to my second conclusion. The woman I saw, who claimed to be Annabel, was actually Mrs Green.

'If Mrs Green – for whatever reason – wished to disappear, and her companion, Miss Dukes, is mortally ill – what would be simpler than to change identities? Mrs Green dies, Mrs Green lives – under another name.

'I only saw the patient once, remember, in a dim room at night, with feeble lights. She had a darkish skin, which I put down to the general gloom. Annabel Crawford also has a dark complexion. I put *that* down to the sun here.'

Parkington poured himself another rum.

'You don't sound too surprised,' said Love. 'Aren't you?'

'Not entirely. Perhaps because I have had some faxes from the Midland Widows London office and Quendon Motor

Factors in reply to specific questions I put to them. But before I go into that, there's only one person who can help us put all this in context. That's Robinson.

'Let's put it right on the line to him. No half truths, no excuses. He either tells us everything he knows or we go home and let him handle his own problem. Which, if he is speaking the truth, could be terminal. I intended to see him again, in any case. So we'll just do that sooner rather than later. And together. And – now.'

CHAPTER TEN

*THE PRESENT: CAIRNS,
NORTH QUEENSLAND, AUSTRALIA*

As the Cessna gained height, Cairns airport shrank to the size of a toy. The aircraft's owner stretched out luxuriously in his seat, watching palm trees swiftly diminish to upturned green feather-dusters.

In moments like these, when his private aircraft took off or was about to land, and he instinctively braced his pudgy legs against the floor, Mr Lo invariably felt a faint twitching in his thigh muscles. He always remembered why.

As a very young man, after the Second World War, Mr Lo had pulled a rickshaw seven days a week through the streets of Hong Kong. He could still feel tenseness in his arms, now relaxed against the padded rests of his seat, when his muscles would tighten in those faraway days, as he took up the strain of the weight of a plump European passenger.

Then, like a beast of burden on two legs, he would lean forward under his plate-shaped hat, and pull with all his strength. Once the rickshaw was going steadily on the level, perhaps along Victoria Park Road, by the edge of Causeway Bay, he could pad along like a horse, his mind switched off except for remembering the destination. But going up hills, he had to lean forwards at an angle of forty-five degrees, and going down he had to throw all his weight – in those days very slight – against the solid burden behind him. Otherwise, the rickshaw could literally run him over and then career away out of control.

There were no rickshaw-wallahs now, but those who had run between the shafts, those few who were left, remembered, and Mr Lo most of all. Many of his contemporaries saved their tiny tips and bought a share in a stall in Stanley Market, selling fruit or vegetables, or in the bird market in Hong Lok Street, where they specialised in the singing birds the locals kept as pets. But that life, existing at the most on two bowls of rice a day, with a few scraps of fish, was not for him. He knew that then well enough. But how to translate this knowledge into wealth?

He was a spry, muscular youngster, and one day an older man, a Chinese, obviously wealthy and influential, asked him to deliver a small parcel to another part of the city. Mr Lo did so quickly and willingly; the fee for pulling an empty rickshaw with this tiny package beneath its seat was the same as for pulling two fifteen-stone passengers.

The man approached Lo a second time, then a third time, to carry out similar errands. Soon, what had begun as an occasional journey became daily, then several times a day. Lo carried out all these commissions promptly, efficiently, and without any delay or disturbance on the part of inquisitive policemen. Why should an empty rickshaw refuse potential passengers who hailed it? Mr Lo always had an excuse – a loose spoke; a broken spring; he was going home.

Sometimes, if the policeman became tiresome and wanted to examine this faulty spoke, Mr Lo would give him a five or even a ten dollar bill, folded and refolded to the size of a postage stamp, and then he would be waved on his way.

The man who had originally approached him always repaid these sums he paid out, and Mr Lo never cheated him, never claimed he had given a bribe when he had not. He knew that the man was a senior member of a secret organisation – and reasoned it was not impossible that policemen who stopped him were also on this man's payroll, and were testing him, checking his honesty in preparation for his possible promotion to greater responsibilities. And so it turned out.

Finally, the man asked him to call one evening at a room

above a café near the Jade Market, off Nathan Road. The man was not alone. A number of older men with grave faces and hard eyes and bland cheeks were with him in this private room. After many questions and his answers, they had a final query to ask Mr Lo: would he care to become a member of a Triad?

He knew about Triads, of course; almost everyone knew of them and feared them. These secret societies with strange names and varying degrees of power had existed in mainland China and on the islands for centuries. But until Mr Lo began the three days of complex, sometimes terrifying initiation ceremonies, swearing the thirty-six oaths, learning the twenty-one rules, the ten prohibitions, the ten punishable offences, he had no real conception of their enormous power, or their influence and ruthlessness.

He had to accept that, for certain serious misdemeanours, such as betraying a fellow member, he could be put to death. For other offences, such as hiding when colleagues were forced to fight, he might have both his ears cut off. If he gave away secrets of the Triad, he would lose his ears and in addition receive seventy-two blows.

The rules were harsh, but the rewards were great – a share of the percentage levied on Chinese businesses and businessmen around the world. Mr Lo's dedication brought him promotion to a rank known as a 426 Red Rod; Red Rods were killers, enforcers, strong-arm men. All senior Triad members were known by their numbers, with every number divisible by the mystical figure of three. So Mr Lo was on the road to riches.

He soon discovered what had been in the little parcels he had carried so regularly and efficiently, and as shipments of heroin increased, so did his responsibilities and his wealth. He always carried out his orders without quibble or question. He would torture, mutilate or murder; all were simply assignments to accomplish quickly and successfully – as once he had trotted between rickshaw shafts at the obedient bidding of his fares.

On Triad matters, he travelled to England, to the United States, to North Africa and Pakistan; and here, for reasons totally out of his control and command, he experienced his first – and nearly fatal – failure.

As a result, he had to endure contumely, abuse, a harsh beating, all without complaint. He knew he had barely survived the threat of severe mutilation, and even of death, so great had been the loss of face this disappointment occasioned. Not simply to him, of course, but, infinitely more important, to those above him, to whom face was all.

Mr Lo had survived, but he would never be allowed to forget the narrowness of the margin by which he had escaped elimination. For years thereafter, he had been forced to undertake menial tasks until it was considered he had purged his failure.

Gradually, he again began to be entrusted with more important commissions, but never quite reaching the heights he had previously achieved. Then he found a way in which he believed he could atone for all past omissions. He discovered the name of the person whom he blamed for his own downfall, and for the unpardonable humiliation of his superiors.

And now the woman concerned was sitting by his side in the Cessna. The arm of the law might be long, but the arm of the Triads was infinitely longer, indeed so long that, as he had been taught, none could ever measure it – or escape its retribution. He had traced her to England and then to Australia. Now she was here beside him without any hope of escape.

Mr Lo turned to her, smiling. His face gave no hint of the furies raging within, as a steam boiler can outwardly appear smooth and polished, while roaring pressures inside have the strength to tow a train.

'You must wonder, Miss Crawford, why we are taking you by air to broadcast over Radio Cairns?' he said pleasantly.

'I suppose it is some sort of publicity stunt,' she replied, looking down over the coast and the sea. From this height, yachts seemed small as toy boats in a child's bath. In the distance, she could see six much larger vessels, obviously derelict. The aircraft swooped down over them. Dark decks were scored with rust, holds lacked hatches, funnels were bent, masts drooping. Anchor chains held these hulks in line as the aircraft turned above them.

'They are going to the scrapyard,' Mr Lo explained. 'Proud vessels that have sailed the seven seas, brought fortunes to their owners and livelihoods to their crews. But there is an end for all things. For every beginning, there must also always be an end.'

'You sound quite poetic. When do we start the interview?'

'It has already started, Miss Crawford.'

'I don't understand you. There's no microphone here.'

'We do not need a microphone for our conversation.'

'You mean there's one built into the aircraft somehow? Or in the lapel of your jacket?'

'I mean there is just you and me, and no audience.'

'But I was told this was Radio Cairns?'

'What one is told, and what actually is, are not always the same thing. Truth may be indivisible, but sometimes it attracts a necessary entourage of lies.'

'I don't understand you. Is this a joke?'

'Far from it. All is never quite as it seems outwardly – even in your own life, Miss Crawford.'

'What on earth are you talking about? I don't believe you're a broadcaster at all. Who *are* you?'

'My name is Lo in the Chinese, Lowe in the English.'

Annabel looked at him sharply. Lo saw how her face was suddenly grey and tired, and guessed he had defeated her. The plane banked, turned away from the ships, flying farther out to sea.

'You are not Annabel Crawford,' Mr Lo went on. 'In Bombay, you were Victoria da Souza. You were engaged to an Englishman, John Winters, who died after opening a box that did not belong to him to get at the money it contained.

'Your immediate grief was easily assuaged. You simply made off with the money.'

'I don't know what you're talking about,' she said flatly, but unconvincingly, and her voice trembled.

'My comrades in London found Mr Winters' parents in England,' Mr Lo continued. 'We checked his fiancée's name with friends among the Immigration authorities in the United Kingdom. We found the date you arrived there.

'We then checked your National Health number, and other official documents. These led to a house in a Wiltshire village occupied by a recluse, Mrs Green.'

The woman looked out of the window, not wanting to meet Mr Lo's gaze. She remembered the letters, claiming that Mrs Green owed Mr Lowe huge sums of money. She remembered Paul Kent's visit; she remembered everything, all too clearly. The worst had happened; she had been found out, her deepest secret laid bare.

'You concealed your age,' Lo continued remorselessly, savouring his victory. 'To help the illusion, you wore dark glasses, covered your face, lived in a house surrounded by a high wall, with a companion. You hired her cheaply because she was in poor health. You did all this because you feared that one day the owners of that money would seek you out and punish you.

'When your companion died, you claimed that Mrs Green had died. An odd name to choose – Mrs Green. I believe you selected this because it was so easy to remember. You took it from Green's Hotel, next to the Taj in Bombay.

'How often did the poorly paid Eurasian Miss da Souza pass that fine hotel and envy those with money to stay there, to dine there? Well, now you had the money – and the name. But you feared to show yourself. You thought you were hiding a fortune – but it was hiding you. You were its prisoner.'

'You're talking rubbish.'

'In the last analysis, most of life is rubbish. Dust to dust, that is the extent of our journey. But I have spoken enough and my time is limited – yours, I may say, is even more truncated. Now, you saw those ships?'

'Yes.'

'One is the *Kansas Rose*, which carried that money from Karachi on to Bombay. If only it had been unloaded in Karachi, many people now dead would still be alive. Our lives would never have crossed. But that is supposition, fantasy. This is fact.'

'There was a second box,' the woman said, trying to deflect Mr Lo's interest away from her, attempting desperately to play for time.

'I know. A Mr Robinson found that. He is being dealt with.'

'How did you find him?'

'Through others who wished to see him on other matters. Russians he had betrayed – or so they thought. I met them through a mutual interest in printing.'

'Printing? I don't understand you.'

She kept talking, hoping to deflect him from whatever he was planning to do, in the frantic hope she might still survive.

'Not posters or letter-heads,' Mr Lo replied. 'Fake passports. When the communists take over Hong Kong, rich Chinese will pay a fortune for a foreign passport to escape. We will supply them. Do you know that the rate is already as high as half a million United States dollars for a single Western passport? And now we can provide thousands.

'Only one thing I have not yet discovered. Why have you taken the name, Annabel Crawford? Who *is* Annabel Crawford? I have been unable to find out.'

'And you never will!' she shouted.

She snapped open her seat belt, jumped up, hit Lo furiously in the face, then leaped away, kicking at him. He had not expected this fierce and uncharacteristic reaction. His eyes narrowed with anger: she was humiliating him. He unbuckled his seat belt, seized both her wrists. A steward came running from the back of the aircraft. The Cessna dipped alarmingly at the sudden transference of weight, banked, and began to climb.

Mr Lo was momentarily thrown against the seat by the steep angle of climb, and let go of the woman's wrists.

'Hold her!' he shouted angrily.

She punched the steward in the stomach, and heaved at a lever on the door. Two oiled bolts slid back, the slipstream whipped the door wide open. Its force snapped the door's metal retaining strap. It smashed flat against the fuselage.

Mr Lo and the steward instinctively backed away from the dangerously yawning aperture. Far beneath, they could see waves glitter in the sun like corrugated glass.

The plane banked and turned again and came down lower over the sea, as though to escape turbulence. Wind shrieked through the open doorway. Mr Lo and the steward gripped the armrests of the nearest seats in case they were both flung out. Annabel braced herself against the heaving floor.

If she stayed in the aircraft she would either be thrown out – or killed by some other means. She had not seized a fortune and lived in virtual hiding for a decade to await death now at another's command. If she had to die, she would do so in her own time, in her own way. She was not certain how high the plane was above the sea; certainly higher than she had ever dived before. But the height was relatively unimportant; what was crucial would be the angle at which she entered the water.

As the Cessna turned again, she made up her mind. She took a deep breath, a step forward into the doorway – and jumped. The plane turned, began to climb steeply.

'You should have held her!' Mr Lo yelled furiously at the steward. He had failed for a second time, and this knowledge raced like fire in his blood. His superiors would not take this kindly. The steward stood, also sweating with terror. Mr Lo glanced out of the door. He could see circles of foam radiating from a dark dot in their centre. Her hair, he thought. She must be dead, of course. To hit the sea from that height would be like falling on concrete.

No matter, she had tricked him. He had wanted to question her further before he killed her. Now he would never find an answer to his question, or make her sign the money over to them, as he had intended. He sat down, face expressionless, while rage and frustration tore his confidence to pieces. The howling wind reached in through the open doorway and clutched his cotton jacket like fingers from the grave.

Parkington picked up the telephone in his hotel bedroom, dialled a number. A Chinese voice answered him.

'I would like to speak to Mr Robinson,' Parkington told him.

'I am sorry, sir. He has just gone out.'

'When will he be back?'

'I do not know, sir. He is at his garage in Cairns. Who shall I tell him rang when he comes back?'

Parkington gave him his name and the number of his hotel, replaced the receiver.

'Come on,' said Love. 'Never wait for a call that may not come. I've always heard there's no-one with endurance like the man who sells insurance. Let's prove that – *now*.'

Parkington nodded. They went downstairs, climbed into his hired car. Twenty miles along the Cook Highway, he glanced behind him, turned to Love.

'I don't want to be alarmist,' he said, 'but we've just grown a tail.'

'Pull over and see if it really is ours.'

Love looked in the rear view mirror. A blue Honda was about two hundred yards behind them, keeping its distance. Parkington accelerated. So did the Honda. He slowed. The Honda driver did the same. Parkington pulled into the side of the road, waved to the car to overtake. It slowed and then stopped behind them.

'I was right,' he said, accelerating away. 'But he doesn't seem very expert, or he would have gone on ahead then and either picked us up later, or handed over to another car.'

'Can we throw him off?'

As Love spoke, the Honda suddenly came alongside, overtook them, accelerated sharply, and then stopped directly in their path. Parkington braked heavily. Tyres smoked on the hot tarmac of the road. A white Mercedes made to overtake, then ran level, easing Parkington into the side. He stopped, shrugged philosophically.

'I was wrong,' he said wryly. 'They do know what they're about – unfortunately.'

A Chinese climbed out of the Mercedes. The driver, also Chinese, stayed behind the wheel, the engine still running. The man wore a T-shirt, lightweight trousers, dark glasses. He walked like a fighter, on his toes. Parkington wound down his window.

'Which of you is Dr Love?' the man asked without any preamble.

'I am.'

'Get out,' he ordered.

'Why?'

'Because I say so.'

He moved slightly to one side. Another Chinese had come out of the Honda and stood on his left. He wore a loose linen jacket, and kept his right hand in the pocket. Love could see what he was meant to see, the outline of an automatic against the thin cloth.

'If it's a hold-up,' said Parkington easily, 'give them what they want. We don't want to add needlessly to the statistics – more deaths on the Highway. For my money, two live cowards are better than two dead heroes.'

'We don't want your money,' the first man replied. 'Just Dr Love.'

Love had the strongest suspicion that this must be a result of him restraining the Chinese who had attempted to beat up Harry Ling. The thought brought him no comfort. If you stuck your neck out, you must expect blows to be aimed at your jaw, but that philosophy did not make them easier to accept. However, *Che sera sera*, whatever will be, will be. Love felt a strange almost resigned acceptance of the situation. What he could not escape he would have to endure. At least he could accept that these men had some kind of excuse for what they were doing – which was more than he could say for the man who had attacked him on top of Ayers Rock.

Trucks overtook them, hooting impatiently. Cars slowed. Drivers, thinking there must have been a road accident involving three cars, glanced back ghoulishly, hoping for a sight of blood or mangled bodies on the road, then raced away, disappointed.

As Love opened his door, climbed out of the car, he wondered at his chances if he tried to fight his way out. That might just be easier here than later. The man with the gun shook his head, guessing his thoughts.

'Don't try it, Doctor,' he warned. 'You're two against six. You could get badly hurt. And no-one here to give you any medical attention at all.'

He leaned over the door, removed the ignition key, turned to Parkington.

'Wait here. Two of our friends will stay with you. So if you have another key, don't attempt to use it. They are armed.'

Love climbed into the back of the Mercedes with the Chinese. The car set off quickly, going south, branched off on to another road. Soon the trees grew dustier, and then they were running through an emptier land with clumps of spinifex, and only here and there a eucalyptus tree.

'Who are you?' asked Love.

The man did not reply.

Love sat back, closed his eyes. It felt hot inside the car, with a faint scent of joss-stick smoke. He had been a bloody fool, acting in a quixotic, lunatic manner, going to Harry Ling's defence. He should have realised how many thousands of Chinese there were here, how tightly knit they were as a community. One man, a stranger, had no chance whatever against so many.

Even if he had flown out to another city, maybe even to another country, Love realised that his description would have flown with him. Somewhere, days, weeks, even months ahead, and perhaps thousands of miles away, a stranger would stop him in the street, possibly ask him for a light, maybe the way to the station or the airport, and as he replied – as Robinson had told him – he would feel the sudden slash of a razor across his face or a knife plunging into his stomach.

The driver slowed, swung off the road, then drove for two or three miles across scrubby grass towards a small group of wooden houses with a ring fence. Two cars and a ute were parked in the shade of a clump of trees. The blades of a modern windmill turned slowly, pumping water from a borehole.

The car stopped. Red dust instantly covered it like fog, then blew away slowly, abrasive, harsh, dry. The Chinese with the gun prodded Love out into the yard. He stretched, wondered where he'd be beaten up, and how badly, whether he would have any chance whatever of escape. Certainly, there seemed no more opportunity here than on the Highway.

A Chinese on either side of Love, a third behind him, walked him into the house. The hall was decorated with coloured photographs of Nanking, Peking, Shanghai. An electric light shone behind a three-dimensional picture of a waterfall. By some optical trick, the water in the painting seemed to flow endlessly.

The Chinese pushed Love into a side room. He heard the key turn in the door. The room was about sixteen feet square, with two chairs, a table, a chest of drawers. From framed coloured photographs on the walls, inscrutable Chinese stared at him impassively, arms folded, hands concealed within the loose sleeves of their robes. The window was barred. Love sat down.

A side door opened, a man came in. He closed the door carefully behind him. He was in his fifties, of medium height, brown skinned, oiled dark hair combed back from his forehead. He wore a silk T-shirt, dark blue trousers, leather sandals. He could be any successful middle-aged Chinese: a surgeon, an ambassador, the chairman of a large company. He exuded an aura of power, authority. He was a man who gave commands; others carried them out. Quickly.

'Dr Love?'

'Yes.'

'You don't know me,' said the man crisply. 'And we may never see each other again. But I wanted to meet you personally.'

'Why?'

'To tell you something.'

'To do that, was it necessary to force my car to the roadside, bring me here at gun-point, and hold my friend hostage?'

'I wished to see you on your own.'

'Why?'

'I understand that, a few evenings ago, you were walking along the Esplanade in Cairns when you saw a young Chinese man being attacked by others as he got out of a car. A young woman was also in the car. Have I been correctly informed, Dr Love?'

'You have.'

'You went to the young man's rescue?'

'I did.'

'In doing so, my understanding is, you caused the skull of one of the attackers to be fractured. You broke the leg of another.'

'I don't know the extent of their injuries,' Love replied. 'I did not set out to injure them. My aim was simply to persuade them to desist.'

'Precisely. And you succeeded admirably. Do you know who these men were, and who sent them?'

'I have no idea.'

'They are members of a Triad increasingly active in the area and very dangerous. Their leader is a Mr Lo. And now, you may suspect how our meeting is going to end?

You are going to get beaten up, maybe even killed for your rash actions?'

Love shrugged. There was a time to speak and a time to stay silent. This seemed a time for silence. Nothing he could say could conceivably alter the course of events. He wished he could follow the counsel of Sir Thomas Browne: 'Let not Disappointment cause Despondency, nor Difficulty, Despair.' But in his present situation, these words seemed easier to recall than to act upon.

'On the other hand,' the man continued, 'our meeting *could* have a quite different ending. I asked you here not to castigate you, but to congratulate you and to give you my thanks. I am John Ling, this young man's father. You may well have saved his life, and the life of the woman in the car, his cousin. It would be uncouth and churlish of me not to voice my deepest gratitude in person.'

'I am very pleased, and, I must admit, most relieved to hear this. But at the risk of appearing churlish, this seems an unnecessarily dramatic way of expressing your appreciation.'

'I am not a dramatic person, Dr Love, believe me. There is already too much drama in all our lives. I prefer to lead a placid existence, to follow a calm, regulated course. Sometimes others attempt to thwart this peaceful aim. But, as the English saying is, one good turn deserves another. I simply wished to see you, person to person, as soon as I could, to tell you that if I can help you during your stay here in any way, I will be honoured to be of service.'

He crossed to a wall cupboard, opened it, took out a bottle of Taittinger and two glasses.

'What about the men who brought me here?' Love asked him. 'Did they know why you wished to see me?'

'No. One must never keep one's employees fully informed, otherwise they know as much as we do – or imagine they do. And that can lead to difficulties. Would you agree with that philosophy, Doctor?'

'I would agree that in these unusual circumstances it could possibly be of value. I assume you have sometimes invited people here *not* just to thank them for kindnesses shown or services rendered?'

'That is so, Doctor. There are some who have made melancholy journeys. But then, as Confucius said, life itself is melancholy. Would you agree with that?'

'Right now,' said Love smiling, 'I would not. I take a more positive view.'

'To more positive views everywhere,' his host replied. He winked as he raised his glass.

Charles Robinson liked to drive in the early evening along the long Captain Cook Highway from Cairns, through Port Douglas for points north. This was the sort of road for which the Cord had been designed: long, straight and empty, under a bright and shadowless sun.

There was little traffic at that time on the highway. Cairns, although rivalling Townsville as North Queensland's major city, had only around ninety thousand inhabitants, and at this time of evening few of them were out driving. They had too many more attractive ways of spending spare time – swimming, fishing, entertaining or being entertained at barbecues. So, between six and seven o'clock, Robinson often had the road almost to himself, and could wind up his Cord accordingly.

For this reason, he rarely complained when – as now – he received a call to say that his presence would be appreciated at one or other of his business premises. At a quarter to six, a young man he had engaged two months earlier as manager of the paint shop telephoned him. With more people visiting North Queensland each year than lived in Cairns permanently, road accidents had steadily increased. Hammering out minor dents and repainting wings was becoming an increasingly important and profitable part of his garage business. This young man – Jackie Cheng, a Chinese from Hong Kong with a British passport – had proved an excellent workman.

'What's the problem?' Robinson asked him genially.

'Something I think you should see for yourself, sir. It has never happened before. At least, not since I've been working here. The paint shop has been broken into.'

'Anything missing?'

'Not that I can see, but quite a bit of damage has been done to that Rolls in for a respray.'

'Hell,' said Robinson despairingly.

The owner of the Rolls was a titled and irascible Englishman, who spent part of each year in Queensland. Robinson accepted that it was a curious fact of business life how, whenever anything went wrong, it invariably seemed to involve people like Sir Ralph, who reacted in an unpleasant, disagreeable way.

'When did this happen?'

'Must have been last night. The Rolls has been under a dust-cover all day. I've only just seen the damage.'

'What happened?'

'Some blokes must have come in with aerosols and blown it over in mauve and yellow.'

'But how did they get in? The garage is always locked after hours.'

As Robinson spoke, he suddenly remembered he had given a key to the service bay to Dr Love. He would not be responsible for any damage, obviously, but could he have lost this key? Or could someone else have made a copy of it – which might be even worse?

Either of these possibilities meant he might have to change the locks, because the Midland Widows would undoubtedly become agitated when he reported a break-in. They could insist on all manner of other precautions: more locks, bolts, bars on windows, a different alarm system. Come to that, why hadn't the alarm gone off? Lucky this insurance bloke, Parkington, was here. He could see for himself what had happened.

Robinson turned his mind from the future to the present.

'Can you get this paint off with thinners?'

'We've tried in one area. But the result's not very good.

As the car is due to go out tomorrow morning, the foreman thought you should see it now, before Sir Ralph does.'

'Thanks,' said Robinson. 'I'll be right over.'

He parked his Cord in the garage forecourt, entered the showroom with his master key. This door, at any rate, had been securely locked. A row of new cars glittered blue, red, silver as he switched on the lights.

Cheng met him, his face creased with concern. Robinson felt sorry for him; what had happened was not his fault.

'Where is the car?' he asked him.

'In the back, sir. We moved it out of the paintshop to try a small corner of one door with mild abrasive.'

'That won't shift paint without leaving a mark,' said Robinson irritably. Surely Cheng knew this? He followed him through the paintshop. They passed half a dozen cars in grey primer, their windows covered by sheets of newspaper stuck on with strips of masking tape, awaiting finishing coats of colour. The air extractors were switched off for the night. There was a strong, not unpleasant smell of cellulose.

Everything looked neat, well ordered, Robinson thought proudly. Big air compressors with electric pumps, rows of spray guns set out on wall racks, drums of primer, cellulose, polish; stocks of wet and dry sandpaper.

A door in the far wall led into a small vestibule with a second door on its far side. This could only be opened when the first door was closed, a necessary arrangement to prevent any grit from sand blasting operations seeping into the paint shop. A single grain of sand could ruin the most expensive, glass-like finish. A thick rubber beading sealed this door totally against the frame. The sand blasting bay had no windows opening outwards, but a small window was set high up in the wall between the two booths.

The Rolls stood in one corner, under a tailored canvas cover, behind a pick-up truck and a van.

'Let's see the worst,' said Robinson philosophically.

Cheng lifted up one corner of the canvas. Beneath this,

deep blue paint on a rear wing glowed rich and lustrous as a polished sapphire.

'Looks all right there at least,' said Robinson, surprised. 'So where's the trouble?'

'Here,' said a voice behind him.

Robinson turned. Four men faced him. They must have been standing behind the truck or the van or he would have seen them earlier. But who the devil were they? And what were they doing here?

They wore dark-lensed goggles and gauze masks over their noses; they could be spray painters. They stood, legs slightly apart, weight on the balls of their feet, like fighters waiting for the bell to ring for the start of the opening round.

There was nothing sinister about the masks, of course, but somehow the men's unexpected appearance had a strange and disturbing air of menace. Robinson felt fingers of fear stroke his heart. His mind went back to other times, in other places, when he had experienced this portent of dread. Never once had it been in error.

He did not recognise any of them as his employees. Could they be freelance workers hired to beat a backlog of work?

'Who are you?' he asked the nearest man.

'We'll ask the questions,' the first speaker replied. He held out his right hand, without taking his eyes from Robinson's face. Another man handed him a pressure blow-lamp. He opened the tap. As gas hissed through the jet, he applied a cigarette lighter. Blue flame roared from the fluted nozzle.

'What the hell are you about?' asked Robinson, curiosity overcoming concern. Surely they were not going to attempt to burn away the paint?

'I told you, we will ask the questions. And the first one, Mr Robinson, is this. Where do you keep your money?'

'Money? Whatever I have is invested. In this company and others.'

The man's blunt and offensive question demolished any hopeful possibility that they could simply be new workers on overtime or moonlighting here from other jobs. Were they kidnappers? Robinson had read about such things in newspapers, but surely he could not now be personally involved?

'What are you after?' he asked. 'A ransom?'

'No. A return. Years ago, you took money intended for other people. We want it back.'

'I don't know what you're talking about. I've never stolen anything in my life. Who the devil are you?'

'It's who *you* are and what you did then that concerns us.'

'I don't know what you are talking about,' Robinson repeated. 'I keep no money here, in any case. Do you expect me to carry huge sums about with me?'

His voice sounded strangely hoarse, as though he had been shouting for a long time against a storm and no-one had heard him, no-one at all.

The man did not reply. Instead, still keeping his eyes fixed on Robinson, he adjusted the flame with the ease of long familiarity, so that its roar intensified, its heat increased immeasurably.

Robinson watched, fascinated: the blue cone of fire had grown a red-hot centre. Almost imperceptibly, the men on either side of him moved closer to him, pinioned his arms to his sides. He could see Cheng, the spray painter he had trusted, whose work he had praised, grinning at him.

'Did you let them in? Is this your doing?' Robinson asked him, anger clogging his throat. 'What is all this about?'

To Robinson's amazement, Cheng spat at him. A gobbet of green phlegm landed on his shirt. The man with the blow torch flicked the flame lightly, left to right, using this as a marker. The flame did not burn Robinson's skin, but he could feel its warmth through his thin cotton shirt. The torch came back again, right to left, closer this time, so that now Robinson felt its heat tighten the flesh on his neck. Another inch or two nearer and he would be burned.

'Now,' said the man shortly. 'So that you can be under no delusions as to what we will do, I will tell you.

'First, I will burn off your eyebrows. Then your hair. Then

we will go down across your face very slowly, until you accept that it is in your own interest to come to an arrangement with us. While you can.'

'You'll kill me,' said Robinson hoarsely. 'Then you'll get nothing. Nothing.'

'Not so. We can quite easily kill you and still get everything you own. I have here a will made out in your name. You will sign it – we will guide your hand – to leave your entire estate to a charity. Us. So think about it. Think about it well, Mr Robinson. While you have the chance.'

He lowered the blow-lamp and then brought it up quickly.

Robinson gasped as he felt his eyebrows curl and scorch under the flame's darting tongue. He closed his eyes against the heat and waited, shoulders braced as, long ago, in other countries, he had watched other men wait hopelessly, muscles tightened, for the *coup de grâce*.

Parkington swung his car into the garage courtyard, switched off the engine. He and Love climbed out. The evening felt warm, heavy with the musky scent of dusk-blooming flowers. The garage was closed, but Robinson's Cord was parked near the main doors, so they guessed he must still be there.

'I have a key to the service department,' said Love. 'Let's go in now.'

He opened the side door, closed it behind them. They stood for a moment in the semi-darkness.

'Where's the light switch?' Parkington asked him.

'Wait,' Love replied in a whisper. 'Someone else is in here, too.'

'Of course,' retorted Parkington impatiently. 'Robinson.'

'Not just him. I heard voices. Don't put on the light yet, until we see exactly who is here. And why.'

They waited until their eyes grew accustomed to the gloom. In one corner, they could make out a car up on a hydraulic hoist, protective canvas covers over its front wings. An outside light, activated by the deepening dusk, came on. This shone through a window, on rows of bright metal spanners hanging on a wall in order of size. In one corner, Love saw a small door in the far wall. They crossed the floor towards this. Love tried the door. It opened easily into a vestibule where another closed door faced them.

Love opened this cautiously. They were in a large area, with its floor rough from a thick covering of abrasive dust. The soles of their shoes rasped as though they were walking in moccasins on sheets of sandpaper.

The same outside light lit up the shell of a car body. Its naked metal, denuded of all paint, glowed bright as polished silver. The car rested on a trolley above a grid on the floor. This was the sand-blasting bay.

Here, jets of air under tremendous pressure from powerful electric compressors would blast cataracts of dry sand from huge circular hoppers to scour away old paint and rust before a car could be resprayed. Much of the used sand then fell through the grid where vacuum fans drew it away into big ducts. This sand was deadly. A puff of it could choke a man within a minute – or blast the flesh off his bones in a second.

Against one wall stood three air cylinders, each with an air pump and a pressure gauge reading up to a hundred and fifty pounds to the square inch. Next to them were the giant hoppers containing sand and small metal shot used for blasting large areas, such as a bonnet lid, a door.

Half a dozen metal nozzles of different sizes, each with its own control trigger, were clipped neatly to the wall, linked to the compressors by thick reinforced rubber pipes. Next to them hung protective masks and helmets that completely covered the heads of the operators. Because of the dangers of the dust, each helmet had its own pressurised, filtered air supply fed in through a rubber pipe.

Love and Parkington could hear voices faintly now, just beyond the far wall. Then came a cry of pain, and in the background, a faint roaring, as of a furnace with all air vents open. High up in the wall, Love saw the small window. The sounds were coming through this.

He climbed on to a wooden box, peered through its misty glass, dim with overspray from different colours of cellulose – blue, yellow, red. In the next room stood six men. Four wore gauze masks of the type used by spray painters, which also concealed their faces. The fifth was a young Chinese in working clothes. The sixth was Charles Robinson, in his shirt sleeves.

One of the masked men held a blow-torch. As Love watched, he flicked its flame across Robinson's face, then slowly brought it back in the opposite direction. Robinson cried out in pain. The flame was now scorching him. Soon, it would burn, and his skin would begin to bubble and blister, and then folds of flesh would fall away. He was within minutes of an excruciatingly painful death.

Love motioned to Parkington to climb up on the box beside him and look through the window. He did so. Love jerked his head inquiringly in the direction of the sand-blasting equipment. Parkington nodded.

Love climbed down. He crossed to the nearest hopper. Close to, this appeared far taller than he had thought. The cylinder, six or eight feet in diameter, towered twice as high above his head, supported on three widely spaced legs.

The base of the hopper was funnel-shaped, so that the sand inside would sink to the bottom under its own weight. In the narrow neck of the funnel, a spoked wheel controlled a valve to adjust the ratio of sand to compressed air. Thick flexible hoses led from each hopper to the nozzles.

Love opened the valve to its fullest extent, climbed back on the box. He lifted two nozzles and hoses from their hooks, handed one to Parkington, held the other himself. Then he took down two sets of goggles and protective face masks. He and Parkington put them on. Then, holding the nozzles well away from their bodies, they pressed the control triggers slowly to release compressed air.

At once, needles on pressure gauges leapt around the dials.

Electric motors started with a metallic whine. Pumps pounded like bass drums. Love nodded to Parkington. Together, as in a drill movement, they raised the hoses towards the window, smashed the glass pane, poked the nozzles through the shattered glass and squeezed the release triggers with all their strength.

Robinson looked up as the window splintered. He saw the nozzles – and realising the danger, dropped down on his hands and knees to avoid the inch-thick jets of dry sand that streamed out at prodigious pressure.

Love and Parkington aimed at the men in the masks. An amber cloud of stifling sand instantly filled the entire area as the two cascades hit their targets. For a second, the men turned towards the window, in amazement and horror. They could not immediately comprehend what was happening – and then it was too late to avoid the streams of abrasive sand.

The man holding the blow-lamp dropped it at once, flung up both hands in a vain attempt to protect his eyes.

But cataracts of sand had already lifted flesh from his face and his fingers, laying bare bones and raw, red sinews. He shrieked in his agony, and dropped down into the dust, rolling about in a frantic futile attempt to escape the inescapable.

The flame from his lamp blazed uselessly by his side, burning a long, red-hot streak through the thickening carpet of sand.

More sand whirled around the vast workshop in a deadly, erosive fog. It clogged the men's thin masks, burned flesh from their hands, their necks, filled their ears, their nostrils. Their hair vanished, leaving bald, raw scalps. Bare skulls showed through strips of tortured, wrinkled skin. Folds of flesh hung from their faces like strips of latex rubber.

Pressing hands into their eyes, as though this could some-how ease unspeakable pain, or at least contain it, they fled blindly, bumping into each other in their desperate haste to reach the only exit door.

Love and Parkington released the triggers. At once, the electric motors and pumps slowed and stopped. Love climbed down, turned off the main control valve under the hopper. Then they both walked into the spray shop.

'Thank God!' cried Robinson in almost hysterical relief. He was crouched on the floor, holding his handkerchief against his face.

'How did you know I was here?'

'We telephoned your home,' Parkington explained. 'One of your staff told us. So we decided to come right over.'

'I suggest you ring the police, Mr Robinson, and explain that there has been a serious break-in, grievous bodily harm, and any other crime that comes to mind. Seeing the state these intruders are in, I wouldn't think they'll run too far or be too difficult to find. Then we both feel we must have an urgent talk with you before any other mishaps befall.'

'A very long and serious talk,' added Love.

CHAPTER ELEVEN

*THE PRESENT: CAIRNS AND HOG ISLAND,
NORTH QUEENSLAND, AUSTRALIA*

'I don't feel like driving home for the moment,' Robinson replied understandably. 'Come into my office. We can talk there. Then I'll ring the police.'

Love and Parkington followed him into a small room. Robinson opened a cupboard, poured out two rums, mixed lime juice, measured himself a MacAllan.

'At least I remember what you both drink,' he said, with a faint smile.

'I hope you also remember some rather more important things,' retorted Parkington.

'I've tried to put them out of my mind,' Robinson admitted. 'But, as you can see, others are unwilling to do the same.'

Robinson took a long drink of whisky, swilled around the remainder in his glass as though making up his mind. Then he reached a decision.

'Gentlemen,' he said. 'I have to trust you with my past. I do not know what you know or suspect, so I had better start at the beginning. I am Russian. Or I was.

'I worked in a government garage in Kiev, where they kept KGB and GRU cars. That's where I saw a Cord for the first time. It had been seized in Poland at the end of the Second World War and brought there, with several other vehicles – Mercedes, Rolls-Royces – looted at the same time.

'I was a good mechanic, and came to know several GRU

officers. As a result, I was invited to join the GRU. That means I *had* to join. No-one can ever refuse such an invitation, and once you're in, you are there for life – or death.'

Robinson paused again for a moment, as though reluctant to continue. He finished his drink and went on, speaking slowly; his memories were infinitely distasteful to him.

'I finally decided to defect because I saw how even the top people in the Soviet Union so often faced denunciation – then demotion, and then, often, death. Remember the Soviet President, Nikolai Viktorovich Podgorny? What happened to him? Tell me that. You cannot. Nor can I. No-one can. He just disappeared. Vanished. Went. Now we saw him, now we didn't. Then history was rewritten, and his part in events removed, as though he had never existed.

'What really happened to Kruschev, Bulganin, Breznev? Remember Comrade Shelepin? He was on top of the heap, head of the KGB. He was immensely important. He ran the World Federation of Democratic Youth, a communist cover which organised demonstrations all over the West where the easily duped shouted for peace, disarmament, justice – everything Russians were then strenuously denied.

'You might think Comrade Shelepin prospered and retired, loaded with honours? You would be quite wrong. He went unwillingly, in fear for his life.

'I saw Shelepin towards the end, in Vienna. He was drunk. He was always drunk, for he had been demoted. Everyone knew that he was on the way down – and then out – so no-one wanted to talk to him in case his failure brushed off on them. But wherever he went he still had a KGB bodyguard of six.

'One of them I knew, and I asked him who would kill Shelepin now? He was not a target, the man replied. "It's not to protect him we're here. It's to stop him going over the wall!"

'I realised that if this was how one so senior was treated, there could be no hope for any of us. And I made up my mind that as soon as I had a chance, almost any chance, I was getting out while I could.

216

'Because of my background I was usually given tasks involving anything mechanical. Before I went to Vienna, for instance, I was in Bavaria, apparently as an American tourist from the Mid-West, but actually following the First American Armoured Division on their manoeuvres.

'They had just received a new anti-tank missile. We wanted it. And I got it – easily. They were firing missiles with dummy war-heads, so when they hit a target they didn't explode, of course. Sometimes, the missile just disintegrated, sometimes it didn't. In either case, the Americans left the bits where they fell. No-one bothered to pick them up. Why should they? They were only scrap – to them.

'But to us they were scrap of immense scientific value. So I sat around in bars, talking to locals, farm labourers and the like. I explained I was a collector of odd military items, which was true, of course. They brought me these things they had found in fields or forests, as well as old Nazi relics and so forth. I bought them all for a few marks, or a round of drinks.

'In contrast, when *we* fired *our* missiles, the troops would spread tarpaulins out where they landed, and every tiny bit was always picked up. The Americans had so much, they didn't bother.

'They didn't appreciate that if they had been more careful, we would have had to recruit at least an American general or suborn the designers of the guidance system, at enormous cost and great risk of discovery, to supply a tiny fraction of what they allowed us to pick up for virtually nothing. We desperately wanted their advanced guidance systems. They handed them to us.

'My superiors were pleased with me, and I was given a totally new assignment in Karachi, with two others junior to me, Serov, who now calls himself Singer, and Hargreaves. His name was also different then. A ship, the *Kansas Rose*, had a very valuable cargo that the GRU wanted desperately. Not a missile, not a man – but money. Cash. Millions of United States dollar bills, packed in two metal boxes. They were going to the Chinese in Karachi and then on who knows where. Triad money. Blood money.

'The Chinese communists had tried to throw out the Triads – you can't have two secret societies running a country. But the Triads go back hundreds of years, so they're not easily disposed of. That money, taken in fees and dues from the industrious Chinese in the States, should have come off the ship at Karachi. But there was a mix-up. The *Kansas Rose* sailed on with the money still in its hold. We caught up with her in Bombay, but then the ship caught fire, blew up. We hadn't bargained for this accident. It was unprecedented.

'We searched the docks desperately for any clue, to see whether the boxes had disappeared. Nothing. Then we saw a bank official, name of Winters, collect them, and so we followed him. We'd missed the money once in Karachi. If we didn't get it now, we'd all be recalled, and that could mean death. One failure is bad. Two can be fatal.

'We followed Winters to a garage next to his house. There was an argument. He fell and split his skull on the floor. Serov was impatient and tried to tear the metal box open to get at the money. An explosive charge hidden inside blew his face and his hands away. So there I was looking at a fortune – and what seemed like two dead men.

'Dead men don't talk. The third man, Hargreaves, was a hundred metres away, waiting in our car, keeping watch. He wouldn't talk, either – because he'd nothing to talk about. Just then, a woman came in – I checked her out afterwards – name of da Souza. We saw each other, but we did not speak. I learned later she'd been hoping to marry Winters. When she saw the money and Winters dead, she didn't stay there weeping for a lost love – she just made off with the contents of one box. I took the other.

'I knew that this was my chance to defect, but I had to get out very quickly before word of this fiasco reached GRU headquarters. I went to a bank, opened an account, paid in this money, and transferred it at once to London. Then I gave myself up to the British High Commission. They weren't too keen to get involved at first, but when they'd checked I was who I said I was, they relented.

'The British Security people gave me a pretty good grilling, and changed my face for me. Then they advanced me some money, and offered me a one-way air ticket to anywhere in the world. I wanted to get as far away as I could, so I came here. New name, new face, new start. I knew about cars. I thought I could make a living from them. And I have.'

'So who is after you now?' Love asked him.

'Serov and Hargreaves were sentenced to years in the uranium mines at Zheltyye Vody, in the Ukraine, for their part in this fiasco. Serov hadn't died. He was only unconscious. Hargreaves came into the garage and found him.

'The surgeons fitted up Serov with a crude pair of steel hands, all springs and ratchets and hinges, and a number of masks to cover the terrible disfigurements on his face.

'Hargreaves contracted leukaemia in the mines. Most of the prisoners did. When they went there first of all they were told it was an easy prison. They were just digging clay for potteries. Of course, there was barbed wire and watch towers with machine guns and searchlights, but they expected that. There was also something worse, much worse. They noticed that the trees were all bare, like skeletons. Everything was grey, covered with a strange kind of dust. Then their hair started to fall out, and, too late, they realised the truth. The whole area was radio-active.

'They blamed me for their troubles – and when under Gorbachev's more benign regime they were released early, they came after me. They killed my only son in Lisbon, and another man in Toronto because they found they'd both sat on the disciplinary court that sentenced them. Then they threatened me here.'

'How did they find you?' Parkington asked him.

'Through the Triads. As you know, there are a lot of Chinese here, and more come in every week. Serov and Hargreaves got in with the Triads because they'd specialised in printing forged papers. And the Triads need any amount of forged Western passports to sell to Hong Kong Chinese.

'The Triads also have a very good reason to squeeze me. They want that money back – with interest. And their idea of interest is to seize everything I've built up.

'With Hong Kong going back to the communists in a few years, more and more Chinese want to come here, or to Britain, the States, Canada. The Triads mean to move in with them. They need the money to expand – quickly.

'They tried to seize my daughter and my nephew the other night, to use as a lever against me. An uncharacteristically unplanned attempt, it seemed to me – but they would still have succeeded if you hadn't been there, Doctor.'

'So the man with the steel hands in Stevenson's house was Serov?' asked Love. 'Why did he want to fight in the dark?'

'Because that would put you at a terrible disadvantage. In the GRU we all learned to fight equally well in the dark as in daylight. To train us, houses of different sizes were built inside a giant hangar. There were no windows in the hangar and only one door. The houses all had shutters so it was always pitch dark inside them, not a glimmer of light anywhere.

'We would be put into one of these houses, and two or more instructors would already be in there, waiting for us. We had to learn how to avoid them – or they'd beat us up badly, might even kill us. We learned fast.'

Robinson shrugged his shoulders as though brushing off such memories. He poured himself another whisky.

'Well, that is what I have to tell you,' he said. 'Now I will go home and inform the police what has happened here this evening.'

'I think we should come with you in case there's any rough stuff on the road,' said Love.

'Thank you. But I'll be all right. I'll wait here for a few more minutes, get my breath back. Then I'll go.'

Robinson watched them leave the office. Then he quickly changed into a dark shirt and trousers, let himself out of a side door and drove up the Highway to the marina where he moored his yacht.

When Love came into his hotel, the desk clerk handed him his room key.

'A young person is up in your room,' he explained.

'Person? Man? Woman?'

'A young woman.'

'Great. Courtesy of the hotel?'

'Oh, *no*, sir.'

Love went up in the elevator, opened the door of his room. In the seat by the window where Annabel Crawford had been sitting, how long ago – a day, a week, an eternity? – was Camille Robinson.

'I thought you were never coming,' she said.

'I'd have hurried if I'd known you were waiting,' Love assured her. 'What brings you here?'

'To see you, of course. What else?'

'You flatter me. But there must be something else, I think. Drink?'

'A lime juice.'

He poured her one, another for himself, added rum.

'Where have you been?' she asked Love. 'You've got sand all over your suit.'

'You haven't heard about your step-father?'

'No. What about him?'

Camille was instantly concerned.

'The Triads tried to persuade him to make his money over to them.'

'What happened?' she asked tensely. Love explained.

'My friend Parkington and I managed to reverse that situation,' he added.

'Is he all right?'

'Yes. He's all right. He should be on his way back to his house about now.'

'Is that safe?'

'I think so.'

'But you are not sure?'

'In this life, one is sure of nothing except that one day we will all be required to leave it. But I feel fairly confident. I expect Parkington will tip off the Australian security people about what's happened. He's got good contacts here.'

As Love spoke the telephone rang. He picked up the receiver.

'Dr Love?'

'Yes.'

'I am speaking from Mr Robinson's house. Is Miss Robinson there?'

'I'll hand you over.'

He passed the telephone to her. Camille listened, nodded, frowned, pursed her lips. She replaced the receiver slowly.

'There's been an accident,' she said.

'What sort of accident? To whom?'

'To my step-father. In the house. He's just got back and fallen down, apparently, and cut himself badly.'

'Who was phoning?'

'One of the staff.'

'Not Harry Ling?'

'No.'

'I'll come with you,' Love told her.

'There's no need. You look all in, covered with sand. Have a shower and an early night. I'll ring you in the morning.'

Love escorted her to the elevator, stood for a moment after the doors closed, watching the indicator flash Three, Two, One, Ground. He walked slowly back to his room, and sat turning over in his mind the events of the day. He realised he was attempting to tie up the loose ends in his mind, and at the same time avoid the thought of Camille leaving him.

Was she simply going down in the elevator – or out of his life? As he considered the options, he suddenly wondered just what she had called to see him about.

Robinson's speedboat cut through the dark, heaving sea like a swordblade, carving a wide phosphorescent swathe of foam.

Robinson crouched behind the wheel, brows furrowed with concentration.

The sea was far rougher than it had appeared from the shore. He felt acutely conscious of being out on his own, without lights, heading for the open ocean. Waves hit the slender bows of his speedboat with the regular boom of a cannon firing a ceremonial salute. The hull shuddered under their impact, and prudently he throttled back. It was pointless to run into trouble, and with this heaving swell, so very easy to do. Behind him, the lights of Port Douglas twinkled and then dimmed, like a necklace of falling stars, and then slowly dipped beneath the waves.

Wind whipped spray against his raked windscreen. Visibility was poor, for the moon had not yet risen. Robinson hoped that any other vessels in the vicinity would be carrying lights so that he could see them. He deliberately carried none; lights could give away his position, and this he dare not risk.

Almost unexpectedly, he saw ahead of him the six cargo vessels moored bow to stern. He had travelled farther and faster than he had realised, for the current was running his way. Each of the ships carried riding lights. On the vessels at the head and tail of the group revolving amber beacons warned other shipping that a solid row of metal hulls lay in line ahead.

Robinson throttled back, in case any watcher on any of the six decks could see his wash or hear the muffled thrum of his engine. He headed away from the ships, passed the last one a quarter of a mile to the right, and then came back slowly on their far side, so that they lay as a screen between him and the shore. Anyone watching from land might otherwise see their riding lights apparently go out as his boat passed in front of them. They would then know that another craft was out there – and some might even guess whose it was.

The sea was rough now, waves slopping over the sides of his boat, which was not intended for trips like this. It had been designed to carry half a dozen passengers on a sunny day, or to tow two water-skiers across a calm sea, not to venture so far out that waves hammered the hull constantly and angrily, and the nearest land lay out of sight.

Robinson throttled back until the engine was only ticking over. The exhaust bubbled and burbled like a kettle on the boil as he came in cautiously against the *Kansas Rose*.

His speedboat scraped the scarred, rusted hull that towered above him. The current carried him on towards the bows. He saw a rope ladder attached to an upper deck. Its wooden treads beat the metal plates of the hull with every wave; the old, condemned ship boomed like a vast and hollow gong. Robinson made fast the painter to a lower rung, climbed up the ladder quickly, silently.

The deck shone with spray under a slowly rising moon. Pocked and scabbed by rust, littered with metal cables and lengths of chain, it stretched ahead of him, longer and larger than he had anticipated. Robinson stood for a moment to regain his breath. Ahead and high above was the bridge, all windows broken long ago, metalwork, once white, now blackened and streaked by fire. The funnel, eaten through with rust and the effects of years of sun and sea, leaned back at a grotesque angle. Derricks hung long thin arms above an open hold yawning dangerously at his feet.

The ship moved slowly and slightly against her chains as the driving current took her. He heard the slop of water in the bilge, and the putter of petrol engines working pumps down below.

The *Kansas Rose* had been so badly damaged by the fire in Bombay that rivets had started from their holes, and several feet of oily water, foul and evil-smelling, sloshed over the base plates. The pumps could keep this level static, but they could not drain it completely. The ship should make the knacker's yard, but in her condition, after a long, punishing voyage from Goa, around the southern tip of India, and then across the Indian Ocean, the Timor and Arafura Seas, into the Coral Sea off Cairns, he realised that this was by no means a certainty.

Robinson saw a metal ladder leading down into the depths

of the hold. He crossed the deck, climbed down it carefully. The smell of exhaust fumes, combined with petrol spilled from the pumping engines, hung in the air, a choking poisonous fog. Water in the lowest part of the bilge reflected the sky like a cloudy mirror, but the false floor of the hold, a couple of feet above the base of the hull, still stood clear of water.

It was covered by a thick black scum of rotting, charred timber. Great flakes of rust a foot across, and spars and brackets that had fallen from upper decks in the fire, littered it with surrealistic abandon.

Robinson stood for a moment, then carefully moved around the side of this false floor. Here and there rust had eaten right through plates an inch thick. He felt his feet dip dangerously into unseen holes, and hastily pulled back before his weight broke the thin, eroded crust of metal. If he fell through, the jagged edge, sharp as a bandsaw, could cut his leg to the bone. He could easily die out here, he knew, bleeding to a terrible death, alone in a floating iron tomb.

Robinson took a pencil torch from his pocket, shone it carefully around the hold. Ship's ribs, glistening with damp, rose up beyond the edges of the open hatchway. The sky was now a patch of deep blue velvet pricked by stars. Robinson moved towards the bows. He had seen a spade thrown to one side. He put his torch in his pocket, picked up the spade, began to hack at the thick carpet of debris.

This proved easy enough to move, but there was so much of it, he had scarcely cleared one small square before the muck moved again and obscured the floor. He worked more and more quickly, driving the spade through black oozing slime, tossing this haphazardly left and right until he had laid bare a patch a metre in diameter. Then he paused, thankful for a rest.

He was sweating from his exertions in this pit, breathing only engine fumes and the sour smell of corroded and rusting metal, submerged for years in stagnant salt water.

Then he started again, striking the bare patch blow after

blow with his shovel. The hold magnified the sound each time he struck. It rang and echoed through the huge hull; he felt he was standing in the centre of a gigantic bell.

He put the spade to one side, took the torch from his pocket, shone it on the patch of metal. Now his heart contracted with excitement. Through layers of rust and oil and sodden calcined ash, he saw the glint for which he had hoped, and yet had scarcely dared to believe could exist.

Robinson was no longer looking at the hold of a burned-out scrap cargo vessel, covered with the rubbish of a decade. He was looking at a stretch of golden floor; a fortune, a golden fortune, and all his.

He stood up, wiped sweat from his forehead with the back of his trembling hand. He had followed his hunch and it had not misled him. In Bombay, years earlier, he had heard that bars of bullion had been blown out of this ship's open hold and over the docks. He calculated that more gold must have melted in the inferno and then poured across the base of the hull. Wood ash, debris of all kinds, would rain down, and lie feet deep, totally obscuring it. And now his theory had finally been vindicated.

Robinson stood up, mesmerised by the prospect of the wealth at his feet – his wealth, because he owned the ship and all the ship contained. He was rich beyond all accounting, all imagination.

At that moment, as he stood, attempting to realise exactly what this meant, the entire hold exploded into a blaze of brilliant light, bright as a thousand suns.

Robinson staggered back, momentarily blinded. He put up his hands to shield his eyes from this unexpected incandescent glare. In the darkness, beyond the floodlights, a cultured voice spoke with all the calm of a genial host offering his guest a choice of cocktails.

'Stay right where you are, Mr Robinson. Put your hands above your head. If you move one inch, you die.'

*   *   *

Love and Parkington sat in the back room of the Cairns Midland Widows office. Opposite, in an easy chair, cigar in hand, sat a young Australian. He wore a lightweight suit and a smile of triumph.

'Thought you'd be interested in this, sport,' he said easily, nodding towards the sheaf of papers he had handed to Parkington.

'Great stuff,' Parkington agreed, passing them on to Love. 'How did you find it?'

'Very simple. We knew this Chinese bloke Lo was flying nearly every day in his Cessna. Always with the same Chinese pilot, and sometimes with a couple of other Chinese people we've been interested in for some time. So we simply put a bug in the plane to hear what went on.

'What I've just given you is a transcription of everything said and done on his most recent flight out to sea, over those old cargo hulks, and back.

'They gave a one way trip to a woman who seemed to be either a Mrs Green or a Miss da Souza. Take your pick.'

'Where is she now?' Love asked him.

'Was,' the Australian corrected him. 'If you read on, you'll see Lo tipped her out of the plane – or she jumped. We're sending out a patrol boat to look for her body.'

'Great work,' said Parkington.

'Any time,' the Australian replied.

'Where's Mr Lo now?' Love asked him.

'He landed and we put a tail on him, but he gave our bloke the slip. He'll not go far, though.'

'Australia's a big country,' Parkington pointed out.

'Sure. It's also an island. He'll have a long way to swim if he tries to get off that way. Now, anything else we can do for you, sport? Always glad to help a Pom. My ancestors came over in the First Fleet.'

'And now you're on the side of the goodies. That's progress. Or something.'

* * *

Next morning, Love had just stepped out of his shower when the telephone rang. Parkington was on the line.

'Feel like a sea trip?' he asked him.

'Where to?'

'Hog Island. Out towards the Barrier Reef.'

'To study coral formations?'

'No. To study the architecture of a lighthouse, inside and out. Especially in.'

'What the hell for?'

'I have just had word from my contacts here that four men apparently picked up Camille Robinson last night on the road between here and her home. Early this morning, a boat with four men, believed to be Chinese, and a young woman answering to her description, landed at Hog Island. They are apparently in the lighthouse.'

'Is she hurt?'

'Apparently not. But that phone call she had was obviously a fake.'

'*Was* Robinson hurt in an accident?'

'No-one knows. He's not around. Hasn't been seen since we left him in his garage. The speedboat from his yacht is also missing.'

'I see. Doesn't sound promising. And what exactly is on Hog Island?'

'No hogs now, that's for sure. Nothing much except beach, palm trees and the lighthouse that hasn't been used for the last ten or twenty years. Camille and her escort seem to have moved out of our patch.'

'Or into a better one for us.'

'How do you work that out?'

'Easily. You and I take a trip to the island, as you suggest, and see for ourselves. It's a confined area. Like shooting rats in a barrel rather than in a field. There must be a higher ratio of hits.'

'The two of us against four – and possibly more?' asked Parkington. 'Are you serious?'

'Never more so. Where shall I see you?'

'Right here on the jetty at Port Douglas. I'll hire a boat.'

Love dressed quickly – jeans, T-shirt, canvas shoes – took a cab up the Highway.

Parkington was sitting on a bollard at the end of the jetty, smoking a cheroot.

'Ready?' he asked him.

'For whatever there is on offer.'

As Love spoke he suddenly wondered whether he had gone mad. Here he was, a country physician, unarmed and about to try and rescue a part Chinese girl he scarcely knew from at least four guards. It would be far easier to ask the Australian security people to handle this. So why the devil was he proposing such a lunatic scheme, and even looking forward to the prospect?

Could it be because the girl was Camille? He knew the answer before he asked the question. The answer, of course, was, Yes.

In a house set back from the sea above Port Douglas, two men waited by an upper window. One scanned the jetty through a pair of field glasses.

'Just as you said,' he remarked. 'The English doctor paid off his cab, walked along the jetty. He and the other man then jumped into the boat and now they're heading out to sea.'

'I told you that's what would happen,' said his companion in satisfied tones. 'These people have simple minds. They are like the marlin on this coast. Show them a big enough bait and they snap it up at once. They never pause to think. So they never see the hook.'

As Parkington accelerated out to sea, the bows surged out of the water. In the distance, they saw a faint green smudge that gradually took the shape of a long, low island, with a rim of white sand; then, green bushes, undergrowth and waving palms. Hog Island.

In the centre of the island, towering above the tallest trees, stood the lighthouse; a red, dome-shaped roof, circular walls segmented by thick red and white horizontal stripes. Parkington slowed the boat, opened the chart box, took out a pair of binoculars, handed them to Love. He focused them on the lighthouse, made out the huge glass lens, with green curtains behind it to shield the lamp and its keepers from the enormously magnified heat and brilliance of the sun.

'You're sure it's not in use?' Love asked him, lowering the glasses.

'Absolutely certain. There's a modern lighthouse elsewhere, all computerised and so on. But they have to keep the curtains behind the lens drawn during the day because the sunlight is so strong, it could cause a fire. If you remember what a small burning glass can do, in England, imagine the heat that this lens, probably forty feet tall and nearly as wide, can generate here. Like a damn great microwave oven.'

'You think it's the Triads who have Camille?'

'Yes. She's the best lever they could ever find to use against her father – probably the only one. Robinson's a tough old turkey. He's been through a lot. I wouldn't think he frightens easily.'

'Will they hurt her?'

'Not at once. It's not in their interest to do so. At least, not unless he starts being difficult. They'll let him sweat for a bit – and then show him where his interests lie.'

'So we must make them move before they're ready,' replied Love, remembering the human ears in Robinson's refrigerator. 'Flush 'em out.'

'And you still believe the two of us can do that?'

'There's nobody else,' Love told him.

'So what's your plan? We go to the front door and ask to look round?'

'That's not so far out,' Love replied. 'I do that, while you see if there's a back door. I'll tell them I'm a Pom tourist – never seen a lighthouse before. Talking to me should occupy

230

one man and give you enough time to get in. Once we're both in, we take it from there.'

'Sounds too simple to me.'

'Got a better idea?'

'No. If I had, I wouldn't be agreeing to this.'

'So let's give it a whirl. You know what they say in the Army? Time spent in reconnaissance is seldom wasted.'

'And time wasted is seldom spent in reconnaissance,' Parkington retorted.

They were coming in now on the far side of the island. A large launch, all white and red paint, lay at anchor fifty yards offshore – probably the one that had brought Camille out from the mainland.

Farther along the beach, a local prawn fishing boat was anchored, big and unwieldy, with long wooden poles poking out on either side. The fishermen had draped nets from them to dry. Love could see men working on deck. It seemed extraordinary to accept that, only yards away from this peaceful scene, a woman could be held prisoner until a ransom amounting to millions was paid.

And if it was paid, what guarantee would anyone have that she would be released? Was it really possible that he and Parkington could stop this? Two against four here – with how many more only an hour's trip away?

'Are you armed?' Love asked Parkington.

'An automatic. I always get it through customs inside an empty talcum powder tin – which shows up harmlessly on the X-ray screens. And a watch MacGillivray gave me. The sort of thing in which he places more trust than I do.'

Parkington tapped a gold-plated watch on his left wrist, then unstrapped it, handed it to Love.

Love examined the cheap dial. A moon slid slowly behind a crescent-shaped slot, the red second hand moved jerkily past the Roman figures.

'What does it do – apart from tell the time?' he asked.

'Drop it on any hard surface – the floor preferably, but a table will do – and you'll find out. There's a two-second delay, then it explodes, a kind of thunder flash. All light and noise but no great harm – except to dazzle and stun and throw unsuspecting people off balance. You keep it. I never trust these fancy gadgets.'

Love strapped the watch on his wrist.

They were approaching land now; the shallow water glinted clear as gin. Multi-coloured fish darted in droves above the sandy bottom; coral stretched out pink fingers towards the surface. Parkington switched off the engine, put the ignition key away under his seat.

He threw out an anchor, pulled its nylon rope until the flukes bit firmly into the sand. Then he and Love jumped over the side. The sea was deeper than it had appeared; warm water came up to their chests. They swam for a few strokes, then waded in towards the beach. Hog Island seemed deserted. They sat down on a fallen tree trunk, wrung water out of their shirts, tipped damp sand from their canvas shoes.

'In case anyone is watching,' said Love. 'We always act like two tourists.'

'Or two idiots,' Parkington retorted.

'Maybe. Now, on your way, ex-soldier.'

Parkington stood up, walked along the edge of the sea. Every few paces, he scuffed the shining sand, bent down to pick up a tiny shell, or flick a pebble into the water. Then, casually, as though on the spur of the moment, he wandered up from the beach and into the undergrowth towards the lighthouse.

Love waited for five minutes by his watch, then he also stood up and strolled, equally casually, in the opposite direction. Within fifty yards, he turned his back on the sea, and walked up between the bushes to the lighthouse.

Close to, this was much larger than it had appeared from the sea. It was a very solid, Victorian building, on a huge flat rock. The red and white horizontal stripes, that had seemed so bright and clearly defined from a distance, now appeared pitted and cracked and faded.

Love wondered who had built the lighthouse. Convicts?

Settlers? Naval personnel? He thought it would be interesting to have time to find out. Now there was barely time for what they had come to do – and the more he thought about this problem the less he liked his own glib proposal for solving it.

How could two men with one automatic and a joke watch between them deal with at least four other men, presumably well armed and no doubt professional fighters? And what if it turned out that someone had made a horrible mistake – and the girl wasn't Camille but someone else – and this was not a kidnap but a harmless picnic party on an island beach?

He pushed such alarming thoughts from his mind, trying to remember whether Sir Thomas Browne had said anything that could have any possible bearing on their present situation. The best he could recall came from Browne's tract on 'Christian Morals': 'Quarrel not rashly with Adversities not yet understood . . . To be sagacious in such inter-currencies is not Superstition, but wary and pious Discretion.'

Well, they were not quarrelling rashly, but they could be short on pious discretion. However, it was all too late now for second thoughts. They were on a one-way journey: their only route out lay straight ahead.

Beneath the huge circular lens that glittered in the sun, Love could see two windows, both too small to allow anyone in or out, even if they possessed a ladder long enough to reach up to them. At ground level, a tarred wooden door faced him. Around this and the rocky base of the lighthouse, undergrowth had been cleared away for a distance of perhaps thirty feet. The ground here was stony, the only vegetation a few tiny, hardy plants that clung tenaciously to crevices and cracks in the rocks.

Love lay down in the undergrowth, watching the front door. He had no idea where Parkington was – until he felt him drop down beside him.

'There's no other door,' Parkington reported. 'This is the only one. I've been all the way round. Any sight or sound from inside?'

233

'Not so far.'

'So what do you suggest we do?'

'Use guile. As David did with Goliath.'

Love undid the elastic belt of his trousers, wrapped it around his right hand. Then he picked up half a dozen small chips of rock, put them in a small pile near him.

'I'll catapult these up against the lens, then move round for about twenty yards and do it again. And so on, all the way round. If anyone is in there, that should bring them out to see what's happening. Then it's up to us to enlighten them.'

Love slid farther back into the bushes, raised his home-made catapult, pulled the belt tight with his right forefinger. He aimed half way up the lens and fired. The chip hit the glass with a melodious boom like a temple gong. He fired a second time and a third, and then, moving through the undergrowth, fired again and again.

When he had used up all the chips, Love paused and peered up at the lens. The chips had not marked the thick prisms, but they had achieved their purpose; Love saw a face peer out of a window. Then he heard the squeal of rusty metal; bolts on the front door were being withdrawn. He moved around quickly to be on its blind side. The door opened outwards, and a man stood framed in the entrance.

He was stocky, broad shouldered, and Chinese. In his right hand he held an American Ingram sub-machine gun. This was barely larger than an old-fashioned revolver, and much used by terrorists because of its convenient size, its light weight and ferocious fire power of up to twelve hundred rounds a minute. A blast from this would not simply kill Love and Parkington; it would obliterate them.

Parkington lobbed a small piece of rock at the door. It hit the wood panel just above the man's head. He ducked instinc-tively, frowned, not understanding what was happening. He could see no-one, yet someone must have thrown a stone. Or could a bird have dropped it from its beak? That seemed unlikely, so he came out and walked for a few paces on the bare patch in front of the building, to see whether anyone was lurking in the bushes.

He paused. As he was about to turn to walk back, Love, watching from the far side of the door, jumped on his back. A knee in the man's right kidney, a fist in the left; an elbow crooked around his neck until bones cracked, and he fell back. As he did so, his finger squeezed the Ingram's trigger. A clattering burst of rounds ripped a groove in the rocks as he collapsed. Love dragged him to the blind side of the window, went into the lighthouse. Parkington followed, automatic in hand.

They were in a circular room, with whitewashed walls between four and five feet thick, made of huge blocks of stone. Although the lighthouse lantern had been converted to electricity years before being decommissioned, it had originally used a paraffin burner. A strong smell of paraffin still lingered in the warm air, mixed with salt from the sea, and the peculiar mustiness of dry stone.

A circular staircase led up to two higher platforms. The shoes of generations of lighthouse keepers had polished smooth its metal treads. Living quarters were on the first and second landings, with the lantern at the top. The windows Love had seen were set into the wall to throw some light on this staircase, which even now was dim and gloomy.

Someone, up on one of the landings, and unable to see down the curved stairway, called out querulously: 'Who are you firing at? Who was throwing stones?'

Love put a finger to his lips. Neither he nor Parkington replied, but began to climb the stairs quietly, keeping very close to the wall to help their balance.

A small room opened off the first landing. Against the curved wall was a curved bookcase and a curved dresser. A ship's brass clock ticked loudly like a metronome. An old-fashioned radio and transmitter stood on a side table, near two wooden chairs and a workbench spread with tools.

Above the bench Love saw a framed colour picture showing the flags of seafaring nations as in the nineteen-thirties.

Next to this, a coil of thin rope hung from a nail, and beneath the rope was an old-fashioned rheostat.

This had a centrally pivoted brass lever with an ebonite handle that could be moved across half a dozen polished brass contacts. On it was a notice, cast in brass: 'Curtain control for standby cells.'

Under the bench stood a group of glass accumulators, connected to each other by wires as thick as a man's finger. They did not make things like that nowadays, Love thought; electronics had long since taken the place of such manual controls. These were dated as a steam engine in a world of nuclear power, but they still retained the solid uncompromising dignity of their day. And they were in working condition, ready in case of any emergency.

As Love and Parkington paused by the door to this room, the man shouted again.

'What the hell is going on down there? Are you all right?'

Love pulled Parkington into the room, then beat on the door with his fist. For a moment, there was no reaction, then they heard the ring of shoes on the metal treads of the staircase. Someone was coming down in a hurry to see for himself.

When the man drew level with the open door, Love put out his foot, tripped him. The Chinese gave a great cry of alarm and fell down the stairs, head first.

As he slid downwards over the metal treads, he forced the sides of his shoes against the wall, until he slowed and finally stopped. Parkington looked out of the doorway. The man was crouched half-way down the stairs, his face contorted with pain. His left arm hung uselessly by his side, obviously broken. In his right hand he held a Mauser pistol. He fired twice.

Parkington gave a cry of pain. His automatic clattered away uselessly down the stairs. He fell back into the room, clutching his right hand. Love could see blood ooze between his fingers. He pulled him inside, slammed the door.

Love knew he had to attack quickly now and win, or they

could both die. They were unarmed, and the man down the stairs, although injured, could take his time, picking them off almost at will, one at a time. Then their rescue attempt would have failed before it had properly begun.

Love calculated that if he left the room now, and went up the staircase, the gunman would follow him. He would know that Parkington was wounded and therefore, at least momentarily, out of the fight. But he would not know whether Love was armed or not, and so would probably assume he was. He would therefore leave Parkington for the time being and come after him.

Banking on this assumption, Love ran up the stairs, still keeping close to the wall. The next platform led into a small kitchen. Drawing pins held an oil-cloth stretched tightly on a table. Half a dozen old-fashioned aluminium pans were piled on a dresser. Love picked them up, waited in the doorway until he heard the man's breathing around the nearest bend in the stairs, only feet away. Then he threw them down, one after the other.

He heard the man shout in anger and surprise, then a blast of shots from his Mauser. The smell of cordite hung heavy as jasmine oil in the air. Then, silence. Had he fired all his ammunition – or was he waiting for Love to come out, to deal with him as he had done with Parkington, as soon as he appeared?

Love peered cautiously round the doorway; the man was reloading, a difficult task with only one arm. Then Love saw Parkington step quietly from the first doorway on the lower landing. He held the rope from the wall in his good hand, one end tied in a loop. He paid out several yards of rope, then swung the loop up and over the Chinese.

As it dropped down loosely around his shoulders, Parkington pulled sharply. The loop tightened. The man lost his balance, screamed as the rope tightened on his broken arm, and fell head first down the stairs. Parkington stood to one side to allow him to go the whole distance.

Love went on up the stairs, more slowly now. Two men

down, so presumably two to go; the odds were shortening. He climbed the final few steps, reached the perforated metal floor of the lamp platform.

The lamp filled the centre, leaving just space to walk around it, with a polished brass guard rail to prevent anyone falling against the glass that protected the filaments and arcs. Even though the lighthouse was not being used, it was clearly kept in spotless condition, ready to be fully operational at very short notice.

The lens was a huge mass of big, sharp-edged prisms that formed a thick curved wall of glass. Between the lens and the lamp hung pleated curtains of heavy dark green cloth. These were attached by hooks and rings to one circular rail at the top, and to another at the bottom. These rails were joined by vertical rods, and their rims serrated with cogs that engaged a small toothed wheel, connected to an electric motor.

When lit, the light would beam constantly out to sea. To give the essential flashing effect, the curtains, powered by this motor, would move steadily around on these rails. For one moment they would shield the glass, so that the light seemed extinguished. Then, as the curtains passed beyond the lens, the light would again blaze out until the curtains covered it again. As the curtains kept turning, at a slow and regular speed, the impression from the sea would be of a brilliantly powerful flashing light.

Love now understood the significance of the switch control lever and the batteries in the room beneath. Even if the main source of current failed or was switched off – as now – the row of batteries could take over. This was a fail-safe requirement.

'Hullo!' Love called as cheerfully as he could. 'Hope I'm not disturbing you?'

'Who the hell are you?'

A Chinese wearing jeans and rubber-soled shoes came round the side of the lantern, paused when he saw Love.

They recognised each other instantly. He was the fourth man who had fled after attacking Harry Ling on the Esplanade in Cairns. He shouted an urgent command. Love heard a squeak of rubber soles on the metal floor. A second Chinese, a stranger, raced up, pistol in his hand.

'Kill him!' ordered the first man in English. 'Now!'

As his companion raised the pistol to fire, a piercing shriek filled the narrow space. This was so unexpected, so loud, hugely amplified by the curving wall that, for a fraction of a second, both men paused.

In that instant, Love jumped.

He seized the gunman's wrist, twisted it to the left with all his strength, then to the right. The pistol fired twice into the ceiling. Love hit him hard in the stomach, brought his right knee into the man's face as his head came down.

Love grabbed the pistol as he collapsed, aimed it at his companion, pressed the trigger.

The hammer clicked harmlessly. The pistol had either not been fully loaded, or it had jammed. The two men stood facing each other warily, each waiting for the other to move first. From above their heads came the faint whine of an electric motor starting, then a metallic crunch as geared wheels meshed and turned.

Slowly, the curtains began to move to one side, uncovering the giant lens. Now the sun blazed into the confined space with the magnified incandescence of a million candlepower, the concentrated heat of an inferno.

It shone straight into the face of Love's opponent. He cried out at the sudden, excruciating and totally unexpected pain, instinctively flung up one hand across his eyes to shield them from the glare. Love jumped, tipped the man up and over his right shoulder. He fell heavily, cracking his ribs on the guard rail, slithered to the floor.

'*Run!*' Love bellowed to Camille.

She came round from behind the lantern. The curtains went on turning. Love had to stop them before they again shrouded the lens. On tip-toe, he reached up to a metal box on the wall above his head, gripped the lever marked 'Over-ride control'.

Years of disuse had locked this in one position. Love could not move it. He smashed at it desperately, using the pistol as a hammer. The fourth blow loosened the lever sufficiently for him to force it over to the 'Stop' position. The curtains stopped obediently. Sunlight flooded through the lens with a fearful and unbearable brightness.

Love grabbed Camille by the hand, ran down the stairs. Parkington came out of the lower room as they passed.

'You sound in good voice,' he told Camille approvingly. 'So I thought I'd help by putting a bit of light on the scene.'

'Thanks!' Love shouted back. 'Let's get out *now* – while they're sunbathing!'

CHAPTER TWELVE

*THE PRESENT: HOG ISLAND AND
CAIRNS COAST, NORTH QUEENSLAND*

As they left the dimness of the downstairs room, noonday
heat struck them like a hammer blow. Suddenly, Parkington
sagged weakly against the wall, feeling the warmth in the
stones through the palms of his hands, as though he could
draw strength from it. He was feeling reaction from his
wound.

'I can't go on,' he said flatly. 'I can't. No good pretend-
ing I can.'

'You have to,' Love told him. 'It's just down to the beach
and into the boat – and we're away.'

'I can't make it,' Parkington protested. 'Leave me here.'

'Don't be a bloody fool. You *must* come.'

Love gripped Parkington's good arm, Camille pushed from
behind. Together, they tried to propel him through the thick
green prickly scrub towards the beach. Their feet slipped in
the soft floury sand as they struggled to drag him along,
now half conscious, head lolling like the head of a punctured
sawdust doll. Above them, the palms rattled dry fronds with
the clatter of dead men's bones. They reached the edge of the
scrub and collapsed in an untidy heap, facing the sand and
the sea.

'Look, Doctor,' Parkington said weakly, 'I simply can't
make it to that boat. It's too far out.'

'We'll pull you,' Love assured him. 'We'll hold you up.'

'No,' Parkington repeated. 'Leave me. I'll be all right.'

'Not if those guys in the lighthouse get out, you won't.'

'I'll take the risk. I'll crawl to the far side of the island and hole up there. They'll think we've all gone.'

'They may not. What then?'

'Then that's my bad luck,' said Parkington stoically. 'But before that you'll be back to pick me up – I hope. I'll rest for a bit, get my strength back and be raring to go.'

There seemed no point in arguing; Parkington's mind was made up, and every minute they remained, their danger increased. The men in the lighthouse could easily have a radio-telephone. Already, reinforcements might be on their way.

'For the last time, you're sure you won't come?' Love asked Parkington.

'Certain. You both go, while you can. Like, *now*!'

Love raised his head cautiously and scanned the beach. The sea had never seemed so seductive. High above its shimmering surface, against a cerulean sky, a few thin white clouds drifted lazily, like shredded cotton-wool. In the distance, just visible on the mainland, the spine of mountains stood out blue as an electric spark, unreal as the painted back-cloth of a theatre stage.

To the right lay the fishing boat, spars carrying the nets still poking out at angles on either side. The faint brash sounds of a transistor radio reached him as the wind changed.

'Hullo, there. Radio Cairns here. On the hour, every hour, bringing you news, views and interviews. First, the weather. Great as usual. Temperature, forty. Bathing, good. But watch out for box jellyfish. Some are drifting inshore. Maybe they want to hear the music we're going to play right after this. Now . . .' The voice droned on inconsequentially.

There was a time to go and a time to stay: this was a time to go. Love turned to Camille.

'When you're ready,' he told her quietly.

She nodded.

They both stood up, walked slowly down to the beach, deliberately trying not to hurry in case anyone aboard the fishing boat saw them. Speed in such heat was at the best, unusual, and at the worst, could be suspicious.

The sea felt warm up to their ankles, slightly colder on their knees, their thighs. They started to swim slowly, gently. Love turned over, swam for a few yards on his back as he scanned the beach. It was still empty and there was no sign of Parkington. He must have gone back through the scrub, around the base of the lighthouse. He hoped he found a safe hideaway; it could be hours before they returned for him.

They reached the boat, swam round to the far side to keep the hull between them and the beach. Then they climbed aboard, and sat dripping on the hot plastic cushions. Love took the key from under the driving seat, started the engine. The two exhausts burbled, reminding him of his Cord. A few bubbles blew from the stern, and a faint blue haze of exhaust drifted over the shining sea.

He reeled in the anchor, crouched down behind the wheel. Then he eased the hand throttle forward gently. The boom of the exhausts increased purposefully. Slowly, the boat turned in a wide arc, carving a white curve of wake from the water. Then they were off. As speed increased, they gave each other the thumbs up. At last they were on the winning side.

Love experienced a sense of relief, almost of anticlimax. Their escape had been so easy that a tiny doubt worried him, nagging like a small stone in his shoe, eating into his confidence. Had it been *too* easy? But what could go wrong now? Nothing, he assured himself. He glanced behind him. Through the faint haze of exhaust smoke, he watched the fishing boat until distance shrank it to the size of a floating cork. When even this finally disappeared, he eased back the throttle.

The bows of their boat dipped in the water and their wake surged past them. As they slowed, he could see, a long way ahead, the six cargo hulks lying in line, and to the left, the faint rim of mainland beach. As he turned towards this he noticed, also to their left and perhaps half a mile away, a stationary motor yacht rolling slightly on the swell. The crew or passengers were probably fishing, or had dropped anchor to enjoy a swim. As Love drew nearer, someone in white uniform began to wave at them from her bows.

'That's my father's yacht,' said Camille excitedly. 'Head towards her.. He'll be on board.'

Love swung the wheel over towards the yacht. The crewman in the bows saw them change direction and waved more vigorously.

'Mr Robinson aboard?' Love called, as he drew alongside, throttling back his engine.

'No, sport. And just as well he's not. We're on our way to pick him up. He's out in one of those old freighters. But we've got a problem.'

'What sort of problem?' asked Love.

'Bloody motor. Blown a gasket.'

'Can't she run, get you back into port?'

'No. It's a head gasket. She's spitting out oil, water, shark shit everywhere. Can you come alongside and give one of our boys a lift back to Port Douglas? He can pick up a gasket from the factor, and come on out in another boat. Then we'll have the motor running in an hour.'

'Sure,' Love agreed.

As he manoeuvred up against the soaring polished white hull of the yacht, two Chinese crewmen steadied his boat with boathooks. A third came down the gangway to climb in.

'Thanks, sport,' he said to Love as he jumped aboard. He nodded up to the others, as though to tell them to cast off. Love bent over the wheel, pushed the throttle forward, ready to head for the shore.

'Hi! Wait a minute!' shouted the man suddenly. 'Look out!'

He pointed up in the air. Love throttled back, glanced up. At that moment, the man hit him on the back of his head with a spanner.

As Love fell, the man brought up the edge of his hand against Love's throat. He collapsed across the wheel. The speedboat rocked dizzily for a moment under the sudden movement.

'Get the bastard out,' the crewman ordered shortly. 'And the girl.'

The only sounds now were the hum of the boat's idling engine, the burble of her exhaust. The man bent over the ignition, switched it off, pocketed the key. Another member of the crew, smart in white duck, came down towards them. Together they picked up Love, carried him aboard the yacht and laid him down on the deck.

Then the crewman looked at Camille more closely and his attitude changed subtly.

'Sorry, Miss Robinson,' he said with mock deference. 'Didn't recognise you.'

'What do you think you're doing?' asked Camille, angry and bewildered. 'Are you mad? This doctor has just saved my life. And this is my father's yacht.'

'It was,' the crewman corrected her. 'But he's not using it any more.'

'You mean you've stolen it?'

'Taken it, shall we say, Sheila. Borrowed it. Now sit in the back there and make no trouble. We've got a lot of horny fellows aboard who'd love to shut you up if you don't. And as for this doctor bloke, he'll get a taste of the same medicine again if he moves.'

'You're not my father's regular crew. I've never seen any of you before.'

'Right. But you will see a lot of us in future. Now shut up. Not another word. We've got work to do.'

Camille sat down reluctantly on a deckchair, totally unable to believe this could be happening. The crew poled Love's boat to the stern of the yacht, made her fast.

'We don't want to have to claim insurance on it, now do we?' explained the man who had jumped down into the speedboat. 'We'll take it back, say we found it floating, the *Marie Celeste* of the Coral Sea.'

Someone called down from the bridge.

'Ready to go?'

'When you are, skipper.'

The muted slam of powerful engines turning over, a slight trembling in the great hull, and the yacht began to move out to sea. The crewman who had hit Love swung a plastic bucket on the end of a rope over the side, brought it up full, emptied the contents in Love's face.

Love shook the water away, sat up slowly, feeling his head. He was still dazed, did not immediately realise what had happened. Then he remembered about the blown gasket.

'Your engines sound fine to me,' he said.

'Sure, they're fine. It's you who has the problem.'

'Me? Who the hell are you?' asked Love, confidence returning as he sized up the situation.

'I'll ask the questions,' said a voice behind them.

They both turned. A man in white duck, wearing white yachting shoes, smoking a Turkish cigarette in a tortoiseshell holder, stood looking down at Love.

'Let me introduce myself,' he said. 'My name is Lo. Richard Lo. You should have stayed with your patients, Dr Love, not got out of your league.'

'What are you talking about?'

'You and your friend, Mr Parkington. You hire a little motor boat and, like two schoolboys on a prank, as you'd call it in England, you sail out to Hog Island.

'You both get into the lighthouse, fool around there with some amateur fisticuffs. Then you have to leave him behind, and you come on with the girl here, like a hero in a film – so you think. We let you go through all this because we were waiting here to pick you up. And instead of us having to come to get you, you came out to us. Saved us a lot of trouble.'

'I don't know what you're talking about,' said Love stoutly, but beginning to feel that he knew exactly what they were talking about, and not liking what he knew.

'Then I'll spell it out, sport,' Lo continued. 'You walked right into a trap. My men in the lighthouse did not mean any harm to Camille. I just wanted her out of the way for a time, to persuade her father to come round to our way of

thinking. But we want you and Parkington out of the way –
for ever.

'We can pick him up whenever we want. He can't get off
the island on his own. We'll just call and collect him when
we're good and ready. And as for you, Dr Love, we're ready
for you now. And you're going for a swim. A long, cool
swim, to clear your head after all your exertions.'

He called an order up to the bridge.

'Cut both engines.'

Instantly, the engines slowed, died. The yacht's wash
swelled up behind her stern. She shuddered slightly, then
began to roll gently with the running tide.

'Get up, Doctor. Take a look over the side.'

Love stood up, flexed his muscles. He was perpendicular
at least, which must be better than being horizontal. He had
not lost everything yet; it just seemed that he had. He walked
slowly to the side of the deck, leaned thankfully on the warm
wooden rail.

Water slapped the hull. For a moment, it looked as inviting
as any other part of the Coral Sea. Then he saw the box
jellyfish, the killers. Not one, not two, but dozens. They
swam so close together, stretching for a distance of several
yards, that they appeared like a thick opaque carpet. Moving
just beneath the surface, their tentacles trembled in the clear
water. Love regarded the sight without enthusiasm. If he was
thrown in, he could probably avoid one jellyfish, perhaps two,
but never the number he saw just feet away from him.

'Have a good look, sport. For that's where you're going
swimming,' said Lo. 'Say goodbye before you say hello.'

Other sailors now came out on deck, grinning in anticipa-
tion. One opened two bolts on the rail, slid a section to one
side. The jellyfish swarmed beneath the opening, bumping
into each other. It would be impossible to miss them. Love
felt he was looking at his executioners.

'You're going to walk the plank,' a crewman announced.

'You'll have to make me,' Love retorted, facing them, his
back against the rail.

'Willingly.'

The man rushed angrily at him. Love dodged to the right, swung his attacker up and then sideways, using the man's own weight and impetus to throw him. He dropped heavily on the deck. For a moment, he lay there, winded, then slowly crawled to his hands and knees.

A second man now squared up to Love, but Lo put out a hand to restrain him.

'I have a far better way,' he said gently. He turned to another Chinese.

'Get a can of gas,' he ordered him. The man ran down a companionway, returned carrying a full jerrycan. In the heat, some of the petrol it contained had vaporised, and hissed like an angry serpent as he snapped open the lid.

The crewman who had hit Love aboard the speedboat now untied the bucket he had dipped into the sea, filled this with petrol. He came towards Love, grinning.

'Don't feel like a swim, then, Doc?' he asked him. 'Maybe you'll be glad to – to cool off.'

As he spoke, he flung the bucket of petrol at Love. Two gallons hit him in the face and streamed down his body, drenching him. He gasped in pain and shock as the spirit stung his eyes, momentarily blinding him. He choked with petrol in his mouth, his nostrils.

He spat it out, desperate to breathe fresh air. His whole body reeked of fuel. It began to evaporate in the heat, leaving his skin tight and dry.

'He's still not walking!' someone called jeeringly. 'Warm the bastard up!'

Love forced himself to open his eyes. He could not focus them properly, but through a mist of pain and petrol he made out another Chinese holding a blow-lamp. A tongue of blue flame a yard long leapt from its nozzle as he adjusted the jet.

The man directed the flame on the deck, where spirit had swilled across the varnished planks. This petrol took fire with a great gout of flame and a sudden erupting roar. Flames began to travel hungrily across the deck towards Love. He could see the varnish blister and bubble beneath its burning tide. Involuntarily, he took a step backwards, away from the heat and the fire – a step nearer to the gap in the rail.

'Keep walking, Doc!'

He turned – and saw his danger. He was now only feet away from the edge of the deck. A second bucket of petrol hit him, dowsing him. If the fire came within a foot of his soaking clothes, nothing could save him. He would be burned alive, roasted within seconds to a living cinder. The flame leapt with a hungry crackle from one streaming patch of petrol to another. He knew he had to dive – or die.

Love took a running jump, a deep breath, and dived right into the swimming, swarming mass of jellyfish. He felt slimy bodies stroke his, flesh on flesh, and then he was beneath them, down in the cool welcome darkness of the deep.

He opened his eyes. Salt water stung them furiously after the petrol. He felt as though his eyeballs had been sand-papered, but he forced himself to try and make out the shape of the yacht above him and his motor boat behind. It was imperative he did so, that he did not come up beneath their hulls. He swam under the yacht and surfaced cautiously on her far side. He raised his face from the sea and thankfully filled his lungs with air. He breathed slowly, steadily, trying to calm his racing, raging heart. Jellyfish were everywhere, swimming around him, brushing against him.

Their long tentacles, spread out like the spokes of quivering wheels, had the loathsomely spongy touch of a drowned child's fingers. Then he saw that the jellyfish were beginning to move away from him. Soon, they were yards away. They had made contact, skin to skin, but the petrol in which his body was soaked had made him unclean to them, a pariah. He was as unwelcome in their company as they were in his. His gamble had worked. He had survived. The petrol that could so easily have killed him had in fact saved his life.

From the other side of the yacht's deck, he heard a man shout.

'That's got rid of the bastard, then! Not a sight of him anywhere.'

'Reckon he's dead already. Never heard of anyone survive a couple of jellyfish stings. And there were scores, maybe hundreds, there.'

'Start up the engines.'

Love recognised Mr Lo's voice.

As the captain fed in power, the yacht surged forward. Love dived to avoid being hit by the speedboat behind her. He let her hull pass over him and then surfaced cautiously, and hung on to one of the two handles at her stern.

These were designed to help skiers climb out of the water, and were too high up for him to grip easily. Also, he realised that his head and shoulders might be visible to anyone aboard the yacht who chanced to look out over the stern.

The sea water felt surprisingly chilly. The petrol had purged the natural oils from his skin. But being pulled through the ocean at speed cleared Love's brain, and he managed to raise himself high enough to reach up with one hand over the rear of the speedboat's decking. His fingers searched desperately for the thin rope coiled there to anchor the boat aft. He found it, tugged frantically until the rope floated lazily down into the sea near him.

While hanging on with his right hand, Love wound the end of this rope around his waist with his left, tied a double knot and then thankfully, on the point of exhaustion, let go of the ski handle.

The rope gave his body a tremendous jerk as it took up the slack. He gasped for breath, choking as sea water was forced up his nostrils, down his throat. Finally, he managed to grip the rope with both hands and so keep his head just out of the water. And then he hung on grimly, while the yacht's huge wash surged past him, a yard high on either side.

Love had no means of measuring time or distance. He had therefore no idea how long he hung on like this, being pulled at speed, one moment totally submerged, the next, struggling to keep his face above the waves so that he could breathe.

Sometimes, he wondered if he was even conscious. He would open his eyes wearily, painfully, and see ocean and sun and a deep blue sky streaked with thin clouds. And then, when he closed them, it seemed he still saw exactly the same things.

Love only realised they were actually coming in to shore when the yacht slowed and, on one side, he made out the long finger of the wooden jetty with its roof, and small boats anchored nearby. The yacht stopped. The motor boat nudged her stern and bobbed about as the yacht's engines died.

Love tried to untie the rope around his waist but the salt water had shrunk the knot too tightly. He struggled weakly, finally gripped the rope in his teeth and tore it free with the strength of despair.

Love swam towards the jetty and surfaced underneath it. He climbed on one of the cross-pieces, thick with mussels and other shellfish, and streaming green beards of weed, and lay back thankfully, eyes closed, weak with exhaustion.

He must have dozed in this position, half in, half out of the water, for he shook himself awake as he was on the point of falling back into the sea. He saw the yacht not many feet away, and a small tender taking Mr Lo and several crew and Camille across to the steps on the jetty, only yards from him. He waited until they climbed these steps, gave them five minutes by Parkington's watch to make sure they had all left the jetty. Then he swam round, climbed up the steps himself.

He had not realised the strain of being towed for so long behind the boat. In the heat of the sun, with his flesh shrivelled and dried by petrol, and then soaked by salt water, he felt dizzy and faint. For a moment he leaned on the rail. His whole body felt raw, his shoulder muscles ached, and he squelched sea water with every step he took. He went into a bar and sat down. A waitress approached him.

'Good on you,' she said approvingly. 'Been swimming in your clothes?'

'Yes,' he admitted. 'Not something I recommend.'

'No? I used to do that wearing jeans. They shrink on you. Makes them look sexy.'

'The last thing I feel or look,' said Love. 'But I could work on it. Meanwhile, have you a double rum and a black coffee?'

'If you've got the money, we've got anything, sport,' the waitress assured him cheerfully, leaning low over the table to show off her breasts to their best advantage.

Love drank the coffee and rum gratefully. The mixture seemed to have no effect whatever on him, so he ordered the same again. Gradually, he felt life return; and with life came new hope. He paid with several sodden dollar bills.

'I'd better dry these out and then iron them,' the waitress said.

'Do that. I feel someone's just done that to me,' Love told her.

He stood up, walked through the restaurant, past a long corridor of boutiques, into the car park. Outside, in the heat, the reaction of rum and weariness produced a feeling of profound melancholy. He had escaped with his life, agreed, but on every other count he had failed totally.

Robinson had appealed for his help across the world, and he had failed him. He should never have allowed Robinson to leave Cairns alone. Now he had disappeared, and judging by the violence Love had experienced so far, he could already be dead.

Parkington he had abandoned wounded on a tiny island from which there could be no escape from his enemies. As Lo had said, they could collect him whenever they wished. Perhaps they had already done so. Camille he had rescued briefly and then, by his own stupidity, delivered her promptly into the hands of the men who had originally taken her captive.

Reviewing this sorry debit balance, Love felt it would have been far better for all these people if he had never become involved with their lives and their problems. Clearly, things could hardly have been worse.

The only course of any honour left to him that offered any hope of even marginal success was to go to Police Headquarters in Cairns and tell them what he knew and what he believed. It would be better to contact the Australian security officer he had met with Parkington, but he neither knew his name, nor any address where to find him. The police might dismiss him as an idiot Pom suffering from too much sun. In his present mood, Love thought they might not be far wrong.

He paused for a moment, looking for a taxi, and then saw Robinson's Cord standing majestically above all the other cars in the park. Love could have wished for a less conspicuous, less easily recognisable vehicle, but at least it was here, and no taxi was in sight. He climbed in behind the wheel.

Love did not have an ignition key, but he guessed there would be a length of wire kept in the dashboard cubbyhole for such an emergency. There was in every old car he had ever driven, and it would only be a moment's work to short the switch.

As he searched, he heard footsteps approach the car, and hoped that some stranger would not pause and inform him gravely, as though they had just made an important discovery: 'They don't make them like this any more'.

To Love's irritation, a man leaned on the door, pushing his head and shoulders into the cockpit. Then Love took no notice of his head and shoulders. What concerned him was the Smith & Wesson .38 Mr Lo was holding an inch away from his chest.

'Well, well, sport,' Mr Lo said easily. 'You make life too hard for yourself. My friends told me you were down at the bottom of the sea, playing nooky with Neptune. But I thought you might not be – and I was right. You're not going anywhere in this funny old car. You're coming with us. A last mystery tour.

'Now get out, or I'll shoot you out, put the gun in your hand, and say you killed yourself. Move your bloody arse.'

Love climbed out, stood by the Cord, feeling the warmth

253

of its hot metal through the thin damp cotton of his clothes. Recapture in this way must surely be the last humiliation, his ultimate failure.

Lo jerked his head towards the jetty. Several of the crew from Robinson's yacht were standing there, arms folded, watching them. He saw a speedboat moored on the jetty's far side, engine running.

'Get in,' ordered Lo.

Love felt too depressed to speak. He climbed down the steps into the long cabin, sat down on a bench seat. A Chinese sat on either side of him, two others stood in the cockpit. Lo lit a cigar, tossed the match into the water.

'Where is Camille?' Love asked him.

'Being taken care of.'

'Why this obsession to separate Robinson from his daughter?'

'Step-daughter, actually, although he thinks of her as his daughter, even introduces her as that. He had a son, but he died young and very recently. He lacked your good fortune, Doctor. But now even that has run out. So, since you ask a question, I can answer it. Robinson stole money that belonged to others. As a direct result, lives were lost, face was lost, and all seemed lost. But then we discovered where he was living, who he really was. To persuade him to give back this money to its proper owners, we have to lean on him.'

As the boat's bows hit bigger waves off shore, the hull jumped and slapped down in a great flurry of spray. Windscreen wipers cleared the glass screen so that soon Love could make out the six old cargo ships ahead.

The speedboat turned round on their far side. From sea-level, their hulls seemed vertical black cliffs, streaked with rust. A few sea birds squawked from a broken deck rail. The boat came in against one hull, moving very slowly now, and paused under the fading name, *Kansas Rose*.

A Chinese leaned over the rail, threw down a rope; a crewman made it fast. The engine died. A rope ladder with wooden rungs dangled only a few feet away. Lo indicated it.

'Up there,' he told Love shortly. 'Then we'll discover whether you swim as well when you dive from a greater height.'

Love began to climb, instinctively keeping his knuckles away from abrasive rust on the hull's ancient plates. It was easy to get blood poisoning with a cut from such metal. He should worry, he thought wryly. Blood poisoning could only be important to someone with life ahead. Somehow, this thought cheered him; he was not beaten yet. Sir Thomas Browne had once mournfully declared: 'Man is a Noble Animal, splendid in ashes and pompous in the grave.' But he was a lot more noble while alive – and that nobility Love intended to preserve.

He came up on deck, stood looking into one of the holds. Far beneath him, he could see pumping engines and a portable generator working, and in the well of the ship, bright lights burned through a blue haze of exhaust smoke. Two canvas hose pipes, each thick as a man's thigh, were draped over one side of the hold, spewing out into the sea a constant stream of water from the bilge. Love was no sailor, but it was clear that the old hull must be taking in an immense amount of sea-water.

A dozen Chinese wearing shorts and canvas shoes were sweating down in the bowels of the ship. They held shovels and hard-bristled brooms, clearing a thick black sediment of charred wood from the base plates of the hull. Huge links of rusting rudder chains stuck up from a filthy frothy lake of sea-water, rust and oil.

Other Chinese, wearing blue-lensed welding goggles, were working with electric arcs, cutting the floor into strips. Love saw an unexpectedly bright glitter of metal, and realised with astonishment he was not looking at a mass of useless scrap iron being carved into manageable lengths. He was looking at a fortune.

Gold had melted in the heat of that explosion years ago,

and then solidified. And having been concealed in the base of a scrap iron ship for a decade, this golden floor was now being cut into slabs to be removed. Love was looking at a floating Fort Knox in the Coral Sea.

On one side the Chinese had already piled lengths of gold they had cut out, jagged-edged, like blocks of unpolished brass. The men were working on what remained. As Love watched and wondered, he heard a sudden dull boom from the far end of the hold; then a second, a third nearer to him.

Several blue plastic tanks, each shaped like a giant sausage, forty feet long and ten feet thick, had burst in the heat of a welding torch wielded too close to them. They were buoyancy tanks pumped full of air under pressure to help keep the leaky vessel afloat on the long voyage from India to Australia. Without their aid, and because she was constantly taking in water, the *Kansas Rose* would probably have sunk – and her hidden golden fortune with her.

Then, beyond the shredded plastic, he saw Robinson. Not as he had last seen him, glass of whisky in his hand, but with his wrists bound in front of him, his face streaked with blood. He had clearly been beaten up. But how could he be here? Love wondered dazedly.

For a moment, Love wondered whether he was suffering from some rare tropical illness, and imagining all this. Would he wake up soon and find it had only been a nightmare? He leaned back wearily against the rail, and closed his eyes to try and gather his thoughts.

A blow on the side of his head nearly knocked him to the deck.

Love staggered, opened his eyes. A man he had never seen before was standing, grinning at him. Then Love realised that while he did not recognise his face, he remembered the black-lensed glasses. The man had no hands, only a steel claw at the end of each arm. These were the crude type of artificial limbs Love had often studied in photographs in medical journals, describing the backwardness of Russian surgery. And Love knew then where and when and how they had met before – in Mr Stevenson's house in Cairns.

'You know me all right,' said the man. 'But not by name. I was Maximilian Serov. Now I'm Mr Singer, if it matters. I should have killed you then, for you're a friend of Rodinsky, or Robinson. And that means you are my enemy.'

He held up his metal hands.

'Look what he did to me – and left me for dead. So expect no mercy, you English bastard, none at all.'

As Serov spoke, he was moving forward slowly, carefully, as a cat moves on a mouse, savouring the prelude to the kill as much as the death.

Serov struck suddenly. Love dodged the ferocious blow to his face, but the hard steel edge of Serov's artificial hand scored his cheek to the bone. This man was a killer. Love had escaped from him before. But how could he conceivably escape now?

'Take it easy,' said Lo warningly to Serov. 'We have plenty of time to deal with the doctor – our way.'

Serov took a step back. His grotesque hands swung by his sides like the elongated arms of a demented ape. Love watched him warily, his head still ringing and throbbing from the blows.

Another buoyancy tank burst with a boom like a distant gun, and now the hull dipped slightly. A great gout of sea water suddenly spouted up like a geyser into the faces of two Chinese with welding torches in the bottom of the hold.

They staggered back, gasping for breath, and fell into the oily water. Their torches lay uselessly on their sides, long blue flames melting the solid gold. One of the torches had come too close to the rusting metal plates beneath the gold. The red heat had weakened metal already corroded, so that water had forced a hole through the wafer-thin plates.

The ship began to list seriously. As she did so, pressure on other base plates increased. The sheer weight of the *Kansas Rose* increased every second as more and more sea-water flooded in through new gaping jagged-edged holes. This weight of water forced the vessel deeper – and then even more water gushed in with much greater force.

Instantly, Lo realised the danger. If the ship dipped much further, she could sink and the gold would go down with her.

He had at the most possibly ten minutes before this would happen. He shouted down into the hold.

'Hurry up with the cutting! Leave your shovels. Everyone use a torch, and get all the gold up here, and into the boat alongside.'

The hold was instantly ablaze with the orange-edged flames of cutters, and the brilliant, eye-aching blue blaze of electric thermal lances. Someone opened the throttles of the petrol engines powering the generators to increase the current – and so the power of the arcs. The roar of their exhausts increased, echoing back from the sides of the ship. The entire hull began to resonate and boom like a gigantic gong.

A heavy cable led from each generator through the insulated handles of the lances, and on to the metal rod at its cutting end. A second cable from each generator was clamped to the ship's hull. The operator would touch a metal plate with the end of the arcing rod, and a spark would blaze from this direct electric short circuit. He then drew the rod back for a few inches while the spark grew, crackling and flickering, across the gap – fierce enough to slice through metal sheet as easily as a hot knife could cut a pound of butter.

The smell of boiling sea-water and red-hot rusting iron mingled with choking exhaust fumes. A heavy sulphurous fog filled the vast space, dimming the brightness of floodlights and the blaze of the cutters.

As Love watched, feeling, in a strange, unreal way, almost detached from events, he felt the buckle of his watch strap bite into his wrist. He had been pressing hard against the ship's rail. But with his mind on the scene beneath him, he had only just noticed his weight was forcing the strap into his flesh. He eased the strap. Lo saw him move, looked at him sharply.

'Don't try anything,' he warned instantly.

'Just getting rid of my watch,' Love explained easily. 'A swim in the sea proves there's nothing waterproof about it. The strap has shrunk, and a time-piece that doesn't tell time is useless.'

He undid the strap casually, held the watch out for Lo to inspect. Lo shrugged his shoulders irritably. He had more on his mind than a waterlogged watch on the wrist of a doomed man.

Love tossed the watch away into the hold as something of no value whatever. It hit a stanchion, and the glass splintered. For a moment, Love thought MacGillivray's gadget had failed, that the sea-water must have ruined it.

Then, just as he remembered the explosive charge's two-second delay, the entire hold erupted in a brilliant blaze of orange light.

A bellow like imprisoned thunder echoed and re-echoed through the hollow ship. Cries of alarm, shouts of terror arose from the depths of the vessel, above the constant roar of the arcing cutters and welding torches. Lo rushed towards Love.

'Get him!' he yelled furiously.

Love dodged to one side and Serov came running across the deck.

'Leave him to me!' he shouted, his voice clotted with fury. Love could see naked hatred glow in Serov's eyes like red-hot coals. He had escaped those deadly hands once. To escape them now would be far more difficult. But not to escape meant instant, certain death.

Chinese were swarming up the ladder next to him. They thought the ship was breaking up. One gripped an electric lance between his teeth to leave both hands free to grip the metal rungs. The lance's long power cable stretched down into the hold to the pounding generator. The man jumped over the rim of the hold. As he took the lance from his mouth, Love ripped it from his grasp. The Chinese shouted in rage and surprise, lost his balance, tripped backwards and fell down into the hold.

Love jammed the end of the cutting rod against the metal of the deck to complete a circuit. For a moment, scales of rust prevented it making an electric contact. He rammed the rod to and fro desperately, like a madman with a rake. Now the sharp end of the lance scored scabs of rust – and the rod burst into sudden furious blue light. Love held a deadly weapon in his hand.

The man with the steel hands realised this and came towards Love very slowly. Love whipped the red-hot end of the lance across his face, to the left and right and back again. The electric arc died as it lost contact. Love then drove the rod across the deck again to make it spark.

Serov paused – and suddenly his face caught fire. What Love had imagined to be flesh and blood was only a pliable plastic mask, the colour of human skin. The heat from the thermal lance had melted this. As Love watched, the plastic surged into fierce flame, burning, blistering, bubbling.

Serov screamed in pain as the mask burned away. Beneath it all traces of a human face had vanished. Instead, Love was looking at a raw mass of singed sinew and muscle. Eyes lacked lids. Serov's mouth was without lips. He had no nose. His nostrils were only two small phlegm-spattered holes in a mass of mutilation and disfigurement.

Serov put out one hand to grip the metal rail to steady himself in his giant agony before leaping at Love, determined to pound him to pulp with his steel fists, to ruin his face as his had been destroyed; to hit and hit again without mercy until he had purged his venom.

Love saw his danger – and swung the arc away from the deck. Its glowing tip touched Serov's metal hand as he gripped the ship's rail. A blue electric spark a foot across blazed with ferocious intensity, as metal fused with metal.

Serov screamed in sudden horror and realisation of his predicament. He tore frantically at his metal hand, but the hand could not move. He was welded to the rail. He and the sinking ship were one, fused together, man to metal.

Now other Chinese came on deck from the hold, shinning up steel and bamboo ladders.

'Kill him!' Lo bellowed to them in despair, all the time backing away from Love's swinging lance.

But these Chinese had left their own lances and oxy-acetylene cutters behind them, and none had the stomach to attack a man armed with such a deadly weapon. Down in the belly of the hold, flames from their abandoned lances roared with frantic fury, carving grooves a foot wide across a lake of rapidly melting gold.

Several Chinese, braver than the others, came at Love with lumps of wood, crowbars, a knife as weapons. And in that moment, when Love realised that, despite his own electric lance, he could still be overpowered by sheer weight of numbers, he saw behind them other Chinese faces suddenly appear over the side of the ship. Twenty young men, wielding chains and clubs and swords, vaulted the rail with the litheness of professional fighters, and landed on deck.

Lo also saw them, and realised who they were and why they were here. These newcomers would offer him no parley, no mercy. He started to run to reach the ladder that led down to Robinson's boat. Love put out his right foot as he passed by, tripped him.

For a second, Lo stood poised, mouth open in anguished surprise and disbelief. He raised both hands almost in supplication, as though appealing to heaven for help. Then he lost his balance and fell.

Love peered down over the edge of the hold. Lo lay where he had fallen, face down in a lake of flowing, glowing liquid gold. For a moment, Lo's body heaved convulsively in a last desperate paroxysm, and then all movement ceased. Lo's hands and his face were welded into the glittering, solidifying metal. In death he and the gold he had sought so assiduously were finally united, indivisibly. As with Serov, man and metal were one.

As Love stared at this astonishing sight, he recalled the dying words of Harold Lasseter, who had spent years outside Alice Springs searching for a reef of gold he never found: 'I am paying the penalty with my life. May it be a lesson to others.'

The water level inside the *Kansas Rose* was now rising rapidly. So much water was pouring in through holes in the thin plates that, within seconds, the sea totally shrouded Lo's body.

The steadily rising water reached the gas torches and the electric arcs the Chinese labourers had left behind. Petrol engines puttered to a spluttering standstill. Generators stopped. One by one, torches and the arcs died, and all was darkness down below, in savage contrast to the blazing sun above.

'That'll cool them off,' Love heard a familiar voice say. He turned. Parkington was standing by his side. His hand was tightly bandaged with a strip of shirt, but he had colour again in his cheeks; his natural jauntiness, missing when Love left him on Hog Island, had returned.

'Thought you might need a bit of help,' he explained casually.

'How did you get here?' Love asked in amazement. 'I thought you were too badly hit to move.'

'I'll tell you how when we're safely away from this ship. But at the moment, we're all bad insurance risks, and that's not something I want to be. She's going down any minute. But when we get home, do me a favour. Tell Colonel MacGillivray I have lived up to his new motto, which I now will adopt as mine.'

'What's that?'

'Late – but in earnest. With some friends.'

The Chinese, who had poured over the side of the *Kansas Rose* in such welcome numbers, were now climbing down her hull again on ropes thrown up with grappling irons to grip the rim of the deck. Love looked over the rail. The prawn fishing boat he had last seen off Hog Island had been driven hard up against the *Kansas Rose*, a wall of motor tyres keeping metal from rasping on metal.

'We didn't want to announce our arrival,' Parkington explained, climbing down the rope ladder. 'So we came in silently – and under sail.'

Love followed him. Others helped Robinson down. They went into the captain's cabin of the prawn boat. This looked unexpectedly homely: shining white paint and polished brasswork, chintzy seat covers.

'How *did* you get here?' Love asked Parkington for the second time.

'I had something to do with that,' said a voice behind him. Love turned. John Ling was standing in the doorway, a glass of rum in his hand.

'For medical purposes only, Doctor,' he said solicitously, and grinned. He looked like a benign and benevolent Buddha. 'My personal prescription. To be taken as often as may be required. Neat.'

Love drank gratefully.

'Mr Parkington appealed to me,' Ling went on. 'And, as I told you when we met in my house, one good turn deserves another. So this seemed my opportunity to pay back a debt of honour.

'I thought we should deal with these Triad fellows *and* Mr Lo at the same time. This seemed prudent – and has proved totally successful. Mr Lo liked gold, sure enough, and he would do anything to get it. But I don't think he ever wanted it *quite* so close to him.'

'Before you and I went out to the lighthouse,' Parkington explained, 'my Australian contacts persuaded Mr Ling and his friends to take a day's fishing off Hog Island. Lucky for them – they've made quite a catch.'

As Parkington was speaking, the fishing vessel surged away from the line of black hulks. Looking through the nearest port-hole, Love saw the reason why. The *Kansas Rose* was beginning to sink, bows first. Chains holding her to the other ships held fast for a moment. Then links snapped under the tremendous weight of a hull filled with sea-water. She went down with a rush. A great spout of water welled up like a geyser and subsided. The wide circle of foam was littered with floating spars and other debris.

Later, much later it seemed, but in fact only hours as time was counted, if half a lifetime in experience, Love sat with Parkington and Robinson in his hotel room overlooking the Bay. Birds were landing on the calm water, paddling up and down in line, just as on the evening when he arrived. Were they the same birds? he wondered. Was he the same man? Outwardly, maybe he was; but inwardly, no. Memories of Lo, trapped face down, entombed in gold, of Serov welded to the iron ship whose cargo had first ruined his life and now had claimed it, were not easily erased.

Parkington's matter-of-fact voice brought him back to the present.

'I thought it best for all concerned if we met here,' he explained. 'Neutral ground. Without prejudice, as the lawyers like to say before they stick you thick with writs as St Sebastian was stuck with arrows.

'If we met in the Midland Widows' office, for example, or in the police station, or Australian security's local HQ, there could be a lot of awkward questions to answer and maybe a hell of a lot of prejudice. Are you with me?'

As Robinson nodded agreement, there was a discreet knock on the door. The Australian security officer came in, nodded cheerfully to them. Behind him walked a woman in her late thirties. Her hair was damp.

'Miss da Souza,' he explained. 'I think you were expecting her, Mr Parkington? As I told you, we sent a patrol boat out to look for her. A very strong swimmer, and an even better diver,' he added admiringly. 'I took her back to her hotel to change, and here she is.'

'Great work. No need for you to stay any longer. We'll

264

take over from here. I'll thank you properly for all you've done when we meet tomorrow. Right?'

'Right.' The Australian waved a casual goodbye, left the room.

Victoria da Souza smiled nervously at the three men. Love offered her a chair. She sat down thankfully.

'First time we met, you were Miss Dukes,' said Love. 'Last time, Annabel Crawford.'

'And the time in between, we didn't even speak. I was behind you – and hit you over the head in Mr Stevenson's house. I felt very bad after that.'

'So did I,' replied Love.

'It was a spontaneous thing. I had a key to the house. I'd come to meet someone else. And then I saw you. And if you recognised me – that would be that.'

'I see,' said Love, but he didn't. 'So who was – is – Mr Stevenson?'

'I'd better explain,' said Victoria da Souza. Her voice sounded flat, deflated, as though she had been running up a long hill, and then found that what she had imagined was its top was actually only a false peak.

'From the beginning, if you please,' Parkington prompted her.

'From the beginning,' she agreed, and paused.

'I lived in Bombay and had a dull job, a dull life, and very little future. Then I found I was pregnant by my fiancé John Winters. I thought he suspected this and was deliberately keeping out of my way. He didn't really want to marry me – and he'd be even less keen if he knew for certain I was expecting a baby. I was desperate to see him. I went to his house – and found him dead in his garage next to a box full of dollar bills.

'I could do nothing for him, but that money – millions of dollars – could do a lot for me. I had no idea where it came from, but I knew where it was going to – into my bank account. I took it, and as I did so, I saw another man watching me through a window.'

She turned to Robinson.

'You,' she said. 'I didn't know who you were then. I didn't know your name. I'd never even seen you before. But I'd know you if I saw you again – and I guessed you'd recognise me.

'I went to England, had an abortion and decided to live quietly until I felt that any hue and cry over the missing money had died down. To my surprise, I never saw any reference to this loss in any newspaper, but I was still wary of living as my wealth could have entitled me to live. I employed a housekeeper, Miss Dukes, and put it about that I never went out, that most of what we needed came down from London, and Miss Dukes bought any local things for me. Actually, I did that myself, but everyone thought that the lady in dark glasses and so on was her, not me.

'And then one day – there was Mr Robinson *in my living room.*'

'What do you mean?' asked Love sharply.

'What I say. I was watching a programme on TV about entrepreneurs in Australia, immigrants who had made fortunes from nothing. There he was, smiling out of the screen. As I watched, I felt somehow that, since *I* now knew where *he* was, he must know where I was. Absurd, of course. But then many fears are absurd – when they don't affect you. And I felt that this could affect my whole life. He alone knew I had stolen a fortune.

'I employed a woman private detective in Australia to find out everything she could about him. I didn't trust her to fax me, or telephone in case you found out, Mr Robinson. So she sent me her reports by mail.

'She lodged in Cairns. Stevenson was her landlord. Then she warned me that the Triads wanted that money and so were after Robinson *and* me. They got on her trail, so she backed off smartly.

'I had a pre-arranged code with her that if she ever had to drop her enquiries suddenly, she would simply write and say Annabel Crawford had died.'

266

'That was her name?'

'No. She suggested it. I think it was her mother's maiden name.'

Victoria da Souza turned to Love.

'I had to drop any further enquiries, but when I heard you were going to visit Mr Robinson here, I thought I could still stir up things a bit if he heard *you* were making enquiries on my behalf. I was frightened, so I wanted to frighten him. The best – and only defence I had – was to attack. Or so I thought.'

'And what were you doing in Stevenson's house?'

'Trying to trace my detective. If I could find her, I hoped she would tell me more, face to face, when she was afraid to put it down on paper.'

'And the money, you still have that – or most of it?' Parkington asked her.

'Some. But not most. Miss Dukes turned out to be rather more than the harmless spinster I imagined, glad – even grateful – for a job that offered a home as well as a wage. She found out that I'd acquired my money in a doubtful way, and also about the Triads. She blackmailed me. Threatened to tell the police and the Triads what I'd done, who I really was. I paid her a lot of money not to. Maybe she still told them – which could have resulted in a visit by a Mr Kent.'

'What did she do with the money?' Love asked her.

'I have no idea. Maybe she just liked to have it, gave her a feeling of power, independence.

'When she had a heart attack, and was obviously unlikely to recover, I thought that would be a way of escape for me out of the shadows. *I* would die and *she* would live. Now, it seems the bill is being presented for settlement. Everything has gone wrong. Am I right, Doctor?'

'Yes and no,' Love replied. Like the Mad Queen in *Through the Looking Glass*, he felt he had run very fast just to keep up with himself. But maybe even this was more than Victoria da Souza had achieved? Did anyone come out of these events with even the smallest shreds of honour? He turned to Robinson.

'You have lost your ship and your gold,' he said.

'"When a ship sinks, gold weighs down its possessor,"' said Parkington sententiously. 'And that's not from Sir Thomas Browne. It's Petronius.'

'Nonetheless, in my case, all is not lost,' Robinson replied. 'Life to my mind is like a game of tennis. You lose a set. You win a set. And here I have lost *and* won. As I told you, Mr Parkington, I took the precaution of insuring the ships – and whatever they contained – with your company, the Midland Widows. I had no knowledge then that one could contain gold – only the possibility, the faint hope, that it might.'

'But, Mr Robinson, as a policy holder, I am sure you would not wish my company to dispense money on any spurious claim?'

'Of course not, Mr Parkington. But you saw for yourself that the ship sank – with its cargo.'

'I did. We all did. The ship sank, yes. That is a legitimate claim. But the gold, no. The gold was not yours in the first instance. It was, shall we say, acquired by you. Some might put it more strongly and say it was stolen by you. The Midland Widows' lawyers, for instance. That could be the start of actions that could run for years – and doubtless would, since you could not possibly win, and would have to pay horrendous legal costs.'

For a moment the two men stared at each other. Parkington smiled; Robinson did not. Love broke the silence.

'You are like two wrestlers,' he said. 'Each has an armlock on the other. I have a proposal to break this deadlock.'

He turned to Robinson.

'What would you say your companies are worth today in US dollars?'

'Twenty million possibly, knock-down price. More if it's not a forced sale,' he replied at once.

'And what would you take for the gold? Now – in cash? If, in fact, it was yours to sell?'

'It's impossible to say how much is there. But for the sake of argument, I would suggest, it is probably worth a few million dollars.'

'And how much have you left from your original money?' Love asked Victoria.

'Perhaps a half. No more. Miss Dukes was very greedy.'

'If this matter goes to law, no-one wins, except the lawyers. As Parkington says, they'll scent huge fees and the longer they can drag the case out, the more they'll make. And you will all attract a lot of very bad publicity all the time. The Midland Widows because it will appear they don't want to pay out, you two because you took what wasn't yours in the first place. So whether you won the case, Mr Robinson, which I would think impossible, you could still do time.'

'What is your proposal then, Doctor?' Robinson asked him.

'This. You don't claim for the gold, which isn't yours anyway. The Midland Widows have already paid its original value to the ship's owners, so this would even out that transaction – and possibly give them a profit. Even though some of the bullion is missing, what's left will have increased in value.

'You pay all salvage costs – and also any difference between what the gold fetches now – and its original value.

'It is impossible to pay back the dollars to the Chinese who contributed to it forcibly. The Triads have no more right to it than you – but you and Miss da Souza actually have it. And here possession seems to me to be ten points of the law. So we forget all about that. What do you all say?'

'I think I could get my people to agree to that,' said Parkington slowly. 'On condition there's no publicity, of course.'

'Do you agree?' Love asked Robinson and Victoria.

They looked at each other and nodded.

'But what's in this for you?' Parkington asked Love.

'My Cord. I promised it to you,' said Robinson quickly. 'I'll have it flown to England.'

The bedside telephone rang before Love could reply. He picked up the receiver.

'Is that Dr Love?' Camille asked.

'The same. Where are you?'

'On the jetty. Your friend Parkington kindly arranged a reception committee with his colleagues in Australian security. They dealt very quickly with Mr Lo's men. I am told they should not have any accommodation problems for the next few years. They will be guests of the state.'

'And you're safe?'

'Totally. And waiting to see you. To remind you of a promise you made.'

'A promise?'

So much had happened so quickly that Love could not remember.

'You said you would teach me to drive. Remember?'

'Of course I'll teach you anything. Willingly. On one condition.'

'What's that?'

'You have your first lesson now.'

'I'm on my way.'

Love replaced the receiver. For a moment, the room was very quiet. A sudden sound behind Love made him turn. Parkington had collapsed in his chair.

'What's the matter with him?' asked Robinson anxiously. He had all the distaste of the very rich for any evidence in others of illness or injury. He feared it might somehow brush off on him.

Love crossed the room, felt Parkington's pulse.

'He's all right,' he said. 'Just reaction from the shot in his hand. Nothing here we can't cure quickly.'

'Of course,' said Robinson, relieved. 'I had forgotten you're a doctor.'

'So had I,' said Love with feeling.

In all the events of greed, lies, violence and murder, he had overlooked the fact that he should be concerned with saving life, not taking it. From now on, he would remember.

Outside, the birds in the trees around the hotel lawn began their evening song. For the first time since his arrival Down Under, Love felt like joining in.